Becoming Billie

– A Novel

Laurie Allyn , Carrie E. Pierce

Morgan Pierce Media & Publishing

Published in the United States by Morgan Pierce Media & Publishing
www.MorganPierceMediaPublishing.com

ISBN 979-8-9919514-0-1

Ebook ISBN 79-8-9919514-1-8

Library of Congress Control Number: 2025932405

Contents

Preface

Dear Reader,

Laurie Allyn was an amazing spirit, a beautiful woman-inside and out-and an incredible jazz singer that understood and delivered a lyric on par with Frank Sinatra and Tony Bennett. She was also my mom and very best friend. She took her last breath in my arms, while looking me straight in the eye, leaving this earthly plane at exactly seven AM PT on the morning of February 11th, 2022.

The day before her death, as she lay slowly hemorrhaging from the Multiple Myeloma that consumed her, we held hands at the In-Patient Hospice facility and watched the sun sink low over the snow-covered grounds outside. (Side note: There is no dark, no cold like that of a winter's sunset when you know it will be the last one you will ever experience with your most cherished one.)

In that moment, I asked Mom what she was thinking. Her answer surprised me. Looking at me with her seafoam-colored eyes, now weary and filled with pain, she answered; "I know this will sound vain, but I hope as a writer, you will take my story 'Becoming Billie' and turn it into the book I always hoped it would be."

You see, Mom had written a serialized story years earlier, that had run in installments in a women's magazine over the course of many months. Written while in her late seventies, she'd poured herself into its creation, having drawn from some of her personal mafia-related encounters while singing in the Chicago jazz clubs of the mid-nineteen fifties. Because the story was published in a women's magazine, it had been 'sanitized' for that readership, leaving it quite an entertaining and captivating read, but much less hard-hitting and raw than the subject matter truly deserved.

Mom had carefully crafted her characters, and it saddened her they were languishing, with an important story to tell, while all around us, the world was growing darker, and sex trafficking was on the rise.

I immediately promised Mom I would do as she requested, and did so for two primary reasons: the first being, the story is a good one with an important message, and the second being, I knew -as did she- that by making this deathbed promise, this obligation would serve to keep me alive at a time when I most wanted to die.

It's taken me two long years since her passing to fulfill my promise, and what you now hold in your hands is, more or less, my memorial to her.

I carefully reviewed and pulled from her notes and stayed as true to her original storyline as possible, but in order to keep it fresh and current, given all that's unfolding with Epstein Island and the P Diddy scandal, had to create some new characters and challenges, in order to get it all where it needed to end up in keeping with her final scenes.

I am deeply grateful to Sandra Morgan of Morgan Pierce Media & Publishing for her willingness to publish Mom's manuscript in its true presentation and entirety.

Mom lived an astounding life and endured many traumas, tragedies and heartbreaks along the way, but her love of life and her passion never once faltered or faded. Not an easy feat, and to this day, I marvel at that.

She also faced fears, pushed past limits and bucked the system at a time when 'nice girls' didn't do that sort of thing. For more on that, you will find a memorial tribute to Mom at the very end of this book, complete with some of her modeling and singing photos from back in the day.

It's important to me that you understand the backstory of this book, its legacy of love, and how and why it came to be.

Thank you for your time. Mom and I hope you enjoy her story... now novel, and we appreciate you.

Sincerely,
Carrie E. Pierce

Chapter One

Augustus 'Gus' Walker and his daughter Theresa had attended an early Mass, lit a candle, and now stood together in the rainy silence of the cemetery, looking down at a small headstone. The carved angel's head serenely bent over the inscription: 'Mary Elizabeth Barnick Walker -Beloved Wife and Mother- Gone to be with Jesus'.

The rain was chilling, but still they lingered, each reflecting on the two years that had passed since Mary died. They'd been agonizingly painful, deeply empty years - devoid of light or any semblance of joy and Gus was still numb from the biting loss. And when he wasn't numb, he had just enough left in him to make it to his next breath. Over and over and over again, despite not wanting to. Much passed unsaid between father and daughter, but Gus knew Theresa felt Mary's loss every bit as much as he did, yet together, they found a way to carry on—an incredible feat in and of itself.

Theresa gently took her father's hand and said in a soft voice, "Come on, Dad. We'd better get you home for a nap and some dinner before your shift tonight. There's pot roast, carrots, and potatoes in the crockpot. You need to eat."

With that, she touched her father's arm, looking at him with equal parts love and concern. Gus nodded, his eyes still closed in heavy thought, his mind processing the hollowness within. Despite the cold rain, he was grateful for its presence. He hoped Theresa hadn't noticed his tears.

***

At that very same moment, five miles across the city, an ambulance was pulling up to Madison General Hospital. The medics jumped out of the vehicle and quickly wheeled the body of a battered young woman through the automatic sliding doors. No identification accompanied her. Wearing only one shoe, her beaded cocktail dress soiled and ripped from shoulder to waist; she painted a picture of happy times gone horribly wrong.

The ER triage process hurriedly began inside a curtained cubicle. Her face was a bloody, beaten pulp; eyes swollen shut, nose broken, lip split, and a large chunk of her strawberry blonde hair ripped from the left side of her scalp, just above the ear. There was bruising around her throat and wrists, front teeth missing—and with every breath, a sick, rattly wheeze filled the small room. Attending physicians and nurses scurried back and forth, and orders were semi-shouted in authoritative tones. Bright lights flooded the cubicle, and tubes and syringes were prepped with skilled but rushed hands.

Dr. Filmore stood in the midst of the orchestrated chaos, carefully looking over the nameless woman's injuries. Shining a small flashlight into her eyes and observing a slight pupil response, he peered into his patient's mouth. Taking his gloved hand, he grasped the tip of the young woman's tongue, moving it gingerly from side to side. A piece of something caught his attention. Taking a sterilized tweezer from the tray by the side of the gurney, he reached down along the woman's lower gumline, retrieving the soft, pliable, cream-colored object. Holding it up to the light, he carefully examined his find. It appeared to be some sort of flower petal. He looked at it curiously for a moment and then passed it over to the nurse. Taking the specimen, she then placed it in a small container, sealed it tightly, and wrote on the label. Dr. Filmore returned his attention to his patient. Staring up at the ceiling, he stood motionless, brow furrowed, listening to the wheezes and rattles filling the room. Taking his flashlight and shining it into the woman's mouth once more, his voice suddenly filled the cubicle. "Oh My God - roll her over on her side-- quick! She's choking on her front teeth!"

***

Back home and seated at his kitchen table, Gus swallowed the last bite of pot roast and potato and washed it down with a sip of coffee from his mug. The combined taste was comforting. He'd managed to sleep a bit after returning from the cemetery, and Theresa's dinner had helped revive him somewhat. Taking his coat and keys from the hook by the backdoor, he kissed his daughter on the cheek. "Thank you." He said and shot his only child a loving wink.

"Be careful, Dad. The weather's lousy out there. I'll see you in the morning. Have a good shift."

With that, he pulled his collar close up around his neck and headed out into the driving rain. Business As Usual -five nights a week- for the past year. He was tired of his job but grateful for it all the same. The work was mostly boring, but at times, he felt he made a bit of a difference, and that still mattered to him.

The rain was tapering off as Gus eased into his spot in the hospital employees' parking lot. The wiper blades kept time to the tune on the radio: *'It's like reaching for the Sun. It's like reaching for the Moon. It's like reaching for the Stars- Reaching for you...'* Gus sighed as he reached over and clicked off the radio, letting the words wash over him, a poignant reminder of just how much he desperately missed his wife of forty years.

Two years hadn't dented the loneliness. If anything, now that the shock of Mary's death was wearing off, it was becoming worse. It was difficult to keep it all bottled up inside, but he didn't want to burden Theresa any more than he already had. She had enough on her plate. She'd given up her career and life in the city to move home, first to take care of Mary after the awful cancer diagnosis came - and now to take care of him in his grief. Theresa never complained about moving back to the house and town she'd grown up in, yet Gus wondered how much she missed her independence and freedom.

Each of them had made major changes when Mary quite unexpectedly went into kidney failure and was diagnosed with Stage Four Multiple Myeloma. Gus had never even heard of the disease that would quickly take his beloved wife. The images of the weekly chemo treatments and three-day-per-week visits to the dialysis ward still haunted him. Mary had fought like a champion, and for a while, it looked like the treatments were working. And then the awful day came; Mary awoke pale and sweating. Racing her to the hospital, Gus refused to leave her side, holding her hand the entire time they sat in the ER waiting for test results. The news wasn't good. Mary was slowly hemorrhaging, and there was nothing that could be done. Myeloma had won. Two days later, she was gone, dying in Gus's arms at an In-Patient Hospice facility he didn't even know existed prior to Mary's rushed admittance.

Taking a deep breath and checking for his badge, he let his mind briefly wander back to the distant past. After his years in the Army, it seemed only natural to enter law enforcement. With Mary's steadfast support, Gus had worked his way up through the ranks of the NYPD, rising to Detective First Grade. He'd found the work intriguing and had been instrumental in bringing several cold cases to justice. But he took early retirement when Mary became ill, choosing to be with her throughout those final, agonizing days, and he'd never looked back. He still had buddies on the force, just about to retire, and at times, they'd check in on him. This made him glad- and also irritated and embarrassed—a strange and confusing mix of emotions.

Gus switched off the ignition, squeezed the crucifix on Mary's rosary he carried in his pocket (a ritual he repeated before every shift), and stepped out onto the wet pavement, carefully avoiding the puddles. His heavy, black Rothcos did their job, keeping his feet good and dry. They'd served him well, seen him through much- just like Mary's rosary. The automatic doors slid open noiselessly, and the bright fluorescents shook him back to reality. He walked into the ER and immediately became 'Gus Walker, Chief of Security, Madison General Hospital'. The Charge Nurse looked up from behind her desk. "Evening, Gus! Still raining out there?"

"Hi, Rhonda," Gus replied. "Not so much, but it was a real frog-strangler drivin' in."

Rhonda smiled. "Stop by the breakroom—I think the coffee's still warm, and there's cake left over from Pat's Birthday... chocolate and rich! That oughta warm you up!"

"Thanks- but not tonight...I'm off my feed." Gus winced a bit and raised a hand to his stomach. The contents of a half-empty Wild Turkey bottle stashed under his bed was the actual culprit, and although Gus had never once gone to any job 'under the influence,' the influence had taken another route of interference now, bordering on an ulcer. He knew he needed to lay off, but there seemed no real reason to care now.

"Ok then. More for me!" Rhonda chuckled. "Oh. By the way, Gus, we have a new 'visitor' in ICU tonight. Came in earlier today in a really bad way. They think it's drug-related, and she's really busted up. A Jane Doe. You'll find her on your rounds." Gus nodded and started down the hallway.

First Floor. Always quiet. Just the Admittance Desk, the darkened gift shop -closed for the night- and the empty cafeteria. Custodians were mopping the floors and vacuuming the Billing office. Gus waved at the two cleaning women. They smiled and waved back, though no one spoke over the loud whir of the vacuum cleaner. Gus checked the main front doors and then took the stairs to the second floor. No one was at the desk. Down the hall, he looked into a room where a young patient was still awake, playing a game on his iPad. The boy didn't look up.

Gus rounded the corridor and heard agitated voices. Passing the other darkened rooms, he came upon a young nurse struggling to quiet an older man who was belligerent. "What's going on here?" Gus asked in an authoritative voice.

"Oh, Mr. Walker," the nurse exclaimed, "I'm so glad you're here! Mr. Ward's insisting on going home, but that's just not possible!"

Gus guided the frail Alzheimer's patient back to bed. His uniformed presence put a comforting light on the situation, and soon, the old man was asleep again. Gus stayed a few more minutes to make certain all was well and then proceeded on his rounds. He checked the doors to the operating theaters and then moved on to ICU. Most of the occupied rooms were dark but for one. This room was lit by the light at the head of the bed. It was difficult to distinguish much about the form lying motionless under the blankets.

A nurse joined Gus in the doorway. "It's always so sad- this hovering between life and death." She sighed. "This one in particular."

Gus paused a moment and looked into the room, squinting a bit to get a clearer view in the dim light. "This the Jane Doe?" He asked in a low voice.

The nurse nodded and continued. "You'd think as sedated as she is, she wouldn't be able to make a sound. Funny thing, though, she is! Not the usual moaning we sometimes hear... it's like... well... like she's humming a tune!"

Gus shot the nurse a questioning glance. "Are you sure it's not the radio at the desk? He asked.

"Well, I do have it on VERY softly," came her answer, "but I swear the humming is coming from HER- and it's the same tune over and over!"

Gus drew in a long breath and exhaled. For a fleeting moment, he thought of Mary and how much they had loved jazz. It had kept her alive during the worst and made her pain less. He swallowed hard and replied, "Well, they do say it soothes the savage breast..." The nurse smiled, nodded, and shrugged her shoulders before turning and walking back down the hall toward her desk, paperwork, and radio. Gus turned and continued on his rounds, looking back just once at the thin, battered body lying in the bed. Raindrops splattered across the windowpanes, and the night wore on....

***

A stray cat hastily retreated from the porch as Gus approached the back door, another shift completed. Making a mental note to put out a dish of scraps -and hang the birdfeeder out of reach- he entered the kitchen just as the last drop of coffee splashed unceremoniously into the pot. "I was beginning to wonder if you'd started your day early!" Theresa jokingly chided, grabbing her coffee and sliding onto one of the kitchen chairs.

"Not a chance." Gus smiled tiredly.

Theresa continued, pouring a cup of coffee for her father and handing it to him. "Planning to visit the guys in the city today?"

Gus took a long sip before answering. The coffee was rich and strong and felt like a transfusion as he swallowed. "Haven't decided yet..." he evaded. "What're your plans?"

Theresa replied, "The makeup Mrs. Simmons ordered came in. I'll drop her products off to her and then do the grocery shopping. Want anything special from the store, Dad?"

Gus sat in silence for a moment, staring out the window above the kitchen sink. He felt the sour churning in his stomach and sighed. "A bottle of Mylanta... Extra Strength... and a carton of Parliament Blues." This last item, he threw in matter-of-factly. He immediately sensed Theresa stiffen, and he knew what was coming.

"Dad, you said you were quitting!" There was a mix of frustration, anger, disapproval, and sadness in her voice.

Drawing his lips tight, Gus sat, his hands wrapped around his coffee cup, nodding his head in defeated agreement. "I know, Sweetheart. Now's not the time... Now's just not the time...." With that, Gus raised his eyes to look at his daughter. He could see she was angry- but surrendered to the situation. Theresa stared back at her father for a moment, raised her eyebrows, and fidgeted in her chair. Gus already knew everything she was about to say, and she was right about it all.

Like every good soldier, he'd picked up the smoking habit during his time in the Army. Once he met Mary and they decided to build a life together, he'd quit and hadn't picked up a cigarette throughout their entire married life. Even during his most disturbing cases on the force, he'd not smoked despite being surrounded by it on the job. Once Mary died, however, he let himself fall prey to the habit as a way to soothe his jangled nerves. Smoking also served to pass the time. He did, however, limit himself to just half a pack a day. Even at that, he could feel himself losing his grip.

Gus Walker was sliding deeper into the muddy pit of Late Middle Age, and it was starting to take hold fast. He'd packed on twenty pounds since Mary died—most of it grief and alcohol-induced. In the last year, his hair had turned a dull, slate gray, and there was a bit of strange pallor to his skin. His brown eyes had lost their sheen, and it was becoming more and more evident with each new morning he was developing erectile dysfunction. This was the least of his worries. He hardly recognized himself when he looked in the mirror, and it all just seemed hopeless and not worth the effort. His life had become a sad round of working the night shift at the hospital and then sitting at home on the weekends, waiting to do it all over again the following week. Although he was well-liked and respected at the hospital, it just wasn't enough. He missed his old life, and he missed who and what he used to be. The tedium was relentless.

And then, there were the monthly get-togethers with his old cop buddies still working the streets. He'd grown to hate these- not because he didn't like the guys, but because he no longer felt he belonged. Most of his NYPD Detective buddies were now coming up on retirement, but they were still very much active and engaged. They kept themselves sharp and reasonably in shape, and, except for a few divorces, none of them had gone through the loss he had. As he'd learned from the Hospice Grief Counselor who came to call after Mary's funeral, grief is isolating but can be especially so when you find yourself surrounded by people who have yet to experience it. Gus had spent the last two years learning this Truth firsthand- repeatedly. Sure, as Detectives, they'd all seen death -gruesome death- but at the end of the day, it was always someone else's burden to bear. Not so for Gus- and

Theresa. Gus's coworkers at the precinct had been genuinely caring and supportive when Mary passed, and they went to great lengths to keep Gus and Theresa in the fold. Still though....

Swallowing the last of his coffee, Gus slid his chair away from the table. Reaching for his jacket, he pulled several bills from one of the pockets and slid them over to Theresa. "This ought to cover it. Thanks, Honey." He said in a low voice. Theresa drew in a breath, shook her head, and reached for the crumpled money, rolling her eyes as she did so. Gus just rested his hand on her shoulder, giving it a loving squeeze, as he made his way into his bedroom for some much-needed sleep.

CHAPTER TWO

Easing his car into the parking lot of Herb's Restaurant and Delicatessen, Gus drew a breath as he listened to the traffic breeze by on I-78. He'd had a solid five hours and was ready for a good meal. Midway through that sleep, he'd remembered it was the second Wednesday of the month, and that meant lunch in Hillside with his old friend Brad Bandeshaw. Cutting his nap short, Gus had just enough time to shower, put on his work uniform, and drive to their regular meeting place. He was annoyed and not in the mood to visit - but relieved he hadn't forgotten and left Brad hanging.

Walking into the establishment, Gus waved off the hostess and made his way over to their usual booth, where Brad already sat drinking coffee. Shaking his friend's hand, Gus made his apologies for being late.

"Not at all!" Came Brad's quick but sincere reply. "The time to sit and process did me good."

Brad's blue eyes crinkled into a grin, but Gus detected another emotion lurking there just under the surface. He couldn't quite define it.

The two men sat across from each other, staring at menus. After a few minutes, the waitress came over and took their orders. Brad ordered the turkey burger and a side salad. Gus went with the meatloaf special. He was looking forward to the mashed potatoes and gravy easing his still-churning stomach. They made small talk while they waited for their food. This was the part that always made Gus fidget.

Brad Bandeshaw was a good friend - and a damn fine Detective. He and Gus had known each other and worked together on the force for a solid fifteen years. Brad was sharp, three years away from retirement, and -by appearances- had life pretty well pulled together: kids grown and gone, grandchildren, and still happily married to his 'original' wife. Gus held up his end of the conversation pretty well, smiling at the latest pictures of the family and listening with half-hearted interest to the plans for the upcoming Bandeshaw Family Reunion, all the while half screaming, half crying on the inside, just wanting to go home. *Christ,* Gus heard himself thinking, *why did I even come?!??*

Just as his eyes began to glaze over, their meals arrived. Gus slapped two pats of butter onto the mound of mashed potatoes and watched them melt in a stream of yellow, which then rather unceremoniously oozed into the brown gravy. Brad took a bite of his food, chewing slowly as he turned his gaze out the large window overlooking the parking lot. Gus took a few bites of his lunch and observed his friend. No one spoke. Finally, after a few moments, Gus cleared his throat. Brad shook his head and laughed a soft, embarrassed laugh.

"Sorry, Buddy." He replied.

"Got something on your mind?" Gus asked.

Brad took another bite of his turkey burger, set it back on the plate, wiped his hands on his paper napkin, and sat for another minute. Finally, he spoke. "Working a really troubling case. And... I think Lorraine's cheating...."

Gus took a hefty swig of coffee, setting his coffee cup back on the saucer with a clink. He drew a breath before responding. "I'm sorry, Brad. Anything I can do?"

Brad's blue eyes looked at Gus, and, for a fleeting moment, Gus saw a pitiful, pained expression shoot across them. Brad nodded a look of appreciation at his longtime friend. "Tell you what." He answered with a forced chuckle, "Since I'm not entirely sure about the latter, you can help me with the former. Let's talk shop!"

Gus took another sip of coffee and nodded his agreement. "Tell me what you got." He answered, relieved not to have to hear the sordid details of Brad's marital woes.

"Well…" came Brad's reply. "We're in the middle of something bad, Augustus- and for the life of me, I don't know what to think."

Gus looked at his friend and noted a controlled alarm. Brad continued, "In the last four weeks, I've been called to three ritual killings. All the same MO, but nothing matches any of our Usuals."

"Go on." Gus said, looking at his friend with interest.

"Gus… the vics…three young women beaten to death—and I mean BEATEN. The full lead pipe massage. All wearing beaded cocktail dresses – and - and crazy as it sounds…each one found with a gardenia shoved down their throat."

Gus reached for his coffee cup, not because he wanted a sip but because doing so would afford him a much-needed moment of distraction. Finally, he responded. "A gardenia? You mean like the flower??"

"That's exactly what I mean," Brad responded. "The flower. A gardenia- shoved almost all the way down their throats."

Gus could feel his mind perking and his pulse increasing. Trying to act calm and only mildly interested, he continued questioning his friend. "So, what'd'ya think?"

Brad's face grimaced into a look of deep concern. "Gus, I've come at this from all angles, and I can't get a solid lead. Not one solid lead. None of the Hood Rats are talking, nothing happening in any of the usual street courts. The streets have gone silent, yet these bodies are piling up. No one's seeing anything - or at least nothing they want to cop to. This has Serial written all over it, but none of our past files show any type of freaky flower thing. I don't get the gardenia. And why are all these women wearing evening garb? Are they being nabbed from parties? No ID on any of 'em. I can't make any connection. Different races, different ages."

"Sexual assault?" Gus questioned, holding his voice steady.

Brad replied in a half-whisper. Gus could see his friend growing agitated with concern. "Nothing immediate. No signs of forcible rape or evidence of recent ejaculate, but there's evidence of light ligature marks on their wrists and ankles - but not like you'd expect."

"Meaning what?" Gus responded.

"It's like... well, Gus... it's like these women have been tied up but not forcefully enough to cause lasting burns, scrapes, or scars. But Christ, Augustus - why care about NOT leaving marks if you're just gonna beat them to death?"

"Why indeed? " Came Gus's terse reply. He then added, in a businesslike tone, "What about the Tox screens?"

His mind was already back in Madison, and he wanted his body to be there, too. Just as fast as he could get it there. Brad drew a breath and replied, "Just the usual party crap: weed, E, and some prescription opioids."

Gus nodded acknowledgment, his eyes distant, deep in thought. Brad then added, shaking his head, "If the press gets wind of this, it's gonna be panic. Any more bodies show up, we won't be able to spin it." Gus nodded his agreement.

Letting Brad tell him all he could figure, Gus then politely feigned interest as Brad divulged his concerns about Lorraine's possible infidelities. Finally, after another forty-five minutes, Gus found himself walking swiftly back to his car, mind whirring. Getting in and starting the engine, he quickly lit a cigarette and took a hefty drag. Exhaling, he began to think more clearly. "Christ!" He muttered under his breath and rubbed his forehead.

Wedging the lit cigarette firmly between his lips, Gus threw the car into reverse and backed out of the parking space, heading toward the on-ramp and home. There was a distinct chance the Jane Doe lying comatose in Madison General was totally unrelated to the three victims Brad had on his hands in the city. Could be total coincidence - but Gus didn't believe in coincidence. And if not, Madison General Hospital had something truly big -and truly evil- on their hands, and they had no idea.

As Gus merged onto the I-78, his mind raced. He didn't notice the man that followed Brad out of the restaurant and to his car. He didn't hear the silenced shot that neatly took Brad's life or see his friend slump dead over the steering wheel, shot behind the ear. And he didn't notice the car tailing him as he accelerated toward home.

Due to heavy traffic and a fender bender blocking three lanes, the trip back to Madison had taken longer than usual. Pulling into his space in the hospital employees' parking lot, Gus glanced at his watch in irritation—just five minutes to spare before his shift began. Giving Mary's crucifix a quick squeeze, Gus slammed the car door and walked briskly toward the hospital ER entrance. As he walked, his cell phone began to ring. "Christ!" He muttered under his breath, fishing the phone out of his pocket and glancing at the incoming number. 646 area code and not a number he recognized. *Must be a robocall*. He thought, stuffing the phone back in his pocket without answering.

Gus made his way down the hall and reported for duty at the front desk. Sylvia was the Charge Nurse on duty. Pleasantries were exchanged, and a moment of small talk concluded. Clearing his throat and trying to sound unconcerned, Gus asked, "Anything I need to know, Sylvia?"

The nurse glanced at her notes and replied casually, "No - just an ordinary day, Gus. Nothing out of the regular!"

Gus nodded, cleared his throat, and tried again. "How 'bout that sad case that came in the other day? Young woman in ICU, badly beaten?"

Sylvia nodded her head in recognition and replied, "Ah, yes. Sad case. Not much progress yet. Still comatose, so I don't think there'll be much trouble for you there, Gus." With that, Sylvia smiled and turned to answer the phone.

"Thanks, Sylv..." Gus feigned a smile.

Turning down the hall, Gus began his usual rounds. As he did so, his cell phone rang again. Glancing at the screen, he once again noted the number of the incoming call. 646 area code. "Damn scammers!" He muttered under his breath and stuffed the unanswered phone back in his pants pocket.

He continued on his rounds, and although things appeared normal, Gus had an uneasy feeling in the pit of his stomach, and it was growing. Passing by the Billing office, the usual waves were exchanged with the cleaning crew. Front doors secured, Gift Shop closed and dark, cafeteria empty but still smelling of institutional lasagna, brownies and beef soup. All as it should be.

Making his way down the long corridor toward the stairs on the second floor, Gus's cell phone rang again. "Son of a Bitch!" He muttered under his breath. Yanking the phone out of his pocket again and preparing to just switch it off, he noticed the incoming number. It was Theresa's. Stepping into an empty room, Gus answered. "Hi, Hon. I'm at work. What's up?"

There was a momentary silence on the other end. "Hello??" Gus responded again.

"Dad? Dad??" Gus could hear fear and deep emotion in his daughter's voice.

"Sweetheart, what is it?" Gus questioned with concern.

"Dad, I just got a call from Lorraine Bandeshaw. Did you see Brad today?"

"Yeah, Honey. Had lunch with him at Herb's like usual. What'd he do now?!" Gus asked with a laugh. An unnerving silence was Theresa's reply, and the slight smile on Gus's face quickly faded. "Theresa, WHAT?!" Gus demanded.

"Dad, Brad's dead. Shot to death in his car...in that restaurant's parking lot!"

For a moment, the room swayed, and Gus felt his knees go soft underneath him. Making his way to a chair, he drew a breath and sank into a seated position. "When?" He heard himself ask.

"They found him about an hour ago," Theresa answered. "Lorraine's been calling you, Dad."

"What's her number?" Gus asked.

"646..." Theresa began to answer.

"Aww, SHIT!" Gus grimaced.

As he did, he gazed downward, and his blurred thoughts suddenly became crystal clear. He'd met Brad for lunch wearing his hospital Security Guard uniform—something he never did. Gus had suspected their visit would keep him late, and there would be no time to stop by home to change before his shift. If Brad's killer was trying to silence Brad because of the case he'd been working, then that meant there was a possibility they'd seen Gus talking with him over lunch. And an even stronger possibility he'd just led them to the only one of their victims still alive.

Gus's mind was cranking a mile a minute now - and his next thought made his stomach sink even lower. If they knew about Gus -where Gus lived and worked- they knew about Theresa. Gus's hands began to shake slightly, and he fought to contain his fear. Keeping his voice even and calm, he spoke matter-of-factly. "Theresa, listen to me, Sweetheart. I need you to listen to me. Call Noreen next door and tell her you need to borrow her car. Slip over to her house using the back door. It'll be dark in twenty minutes. Wear a cap, and don't linger. Get here to the hospital as fast as you can and make sure you aren't followed."

"But Dad!!" Theresa stammered.

"Honey, do what I tell you! We don't have time for this! Get to Noreen's. Leave the lights on in the house, but get the hell outta there, NOW! I'll be at the ER entrance waiting for you in thirty minutes. BE HERE!" With that, Gus disconnected the call.

He sat, running his hands through his hair and taking several deep breaths, attempting to clear his head. After a few moments, he rose to his feet, exited the vacant room, and made his way quickly but calmly to the second floor, ICU, and the highly vulnerable Jane Doe, hanging there between Life and Death. When Gus reached the room, he paused in the hallway and glanced around. Nurses and Doctors conferred at the desk, and no one bothered to note his presence. Slipping into Jane Doe's room, Gus walked quietly to the bedside and stood for a moment. Casting his eyes over the comatose figure, he scanned her injuries. His jaw tightened. The facial swelling showed signs of lessening somewhat, but other than that, the young woman lay still and lifeless, her bruises deepening in color over her pale skin. Gus gazed at the sad sight and found himself thinking of her family - perhaps frantic at her disappearance. *This is someone's daughter...* was all that crossed his mind - and heart.

Glancing at his watch and worriedly anticipating Theresa's arrival, Gus turned to make his way downstairs to their designated meeting place. As he did so, a strange, disembodied sound came from the figure lying motionless under the covers. It was humming. And it was a tune Gus recognized.

Chapter Three

Twenty minutes later, Gus stood outside by the doors to the ER entrance, exactly where he'd told Theresa he would meet her. Each minute passed like an hour, and with each, Gus's apprehension grew. While his eyes scanned the entrance to the hospital parking lot, his mind flashed through his lunch meeting with Brad, playing each picture in detail- frame by frame. Try as he might, Gus couldn't get any definitive detail to solidify in his mind's eye... no recollection of anyone sitting near their booth as they talked and ate... nothing untoward or out of the ordinary.

Gus stood in the misty darkness, the sound of raindrops plopping on wet pavement, his eyes squinting for signs of an approaching car. Suddenly, and without fanfare, there it was: a clearly formed mental image of a dirty red car, changing lanes, falling back, and finally blowing past him as he'd exited the freeway and entered the Madison city limits. It shocked him he'd not noticed it at the time. Too much on his mind....

Gus fidgeted and forced his mind to pull the image into sharper focus, all the while muttering under his breath. "Theresa, come on. Come on, Sweetheart- GET HERE!"

Closing his eyes, he honed the mental image, using every ounce of his training. He could recall the image of a man behind the wheel... dingy brown hair, nondescript, nothing hanging from the rearview mirror. Gus strained, pulling the image more clearly into focus. Cheap leatherlike jacket... last two letters of the Empire Gold license plate: 'FR'... a farm vehicle.

"Makes no sense..." Gus muttered as his eyes caught sight of headlights entering the parking lot.

Focusing intently, Gus squinted again, holding his breath. The car moved closer. Breathing a sigh of relief, Gus watched as Noreen's bright blue Ford Escort pulled into a parking spot. Seconds later, Theresa emerged and made her way to her waiting father.

"Dad..." she began to speak.

Taking his hands and placing them firmly on Theresa's shoulders, Gus dominated. "Honey, there's no time. Listen to me very carefully. Trust me. You've got to trust me! There's a badly beaten woman upstairs in ICU. The one I told you about, remember?"

Theresa kept silent, locking eyes with her father. She simply nodded her head 'Yes'.

Gus continued, his voice level, calm and barely above a whisper. "She's in grave danger, Theresa... and so are we."

Gus looked at his daughter. She noted fear in his eyes.

"Dad... does this have anything to do with Brad getting killed...?"

Gus swallowed hard. "It has everything to do with it, Sweetheart." He replied.

Theresa's eyes glistened with tears, and she fought to compose herself.

"Breathe and listen, Sweetheart." Gus continued. "I'm going to walk you into the hospital and up to the desk in ICU."

Glancing at his watch, Gus added, "Rhonda should be on duty now. You both know each other. I need you to act like Business as Usual and follow my lead. Lives depend on this, Theresa. I know you can do it. Take a second to collect yourself, but we gotta move. We're sitting ducks out here."

Theresa pulled at her cap and took a couple deep breaths, wiping the tears from her eyes. She felt her heart racing, and her palms begin to sweat.

"OK?" Gus prodded.

Nodding and stamping her feet to calm herself, she responded with resolve, "OK."

Taking Theresa by the elbow, Gus led her to the automatic sliding doors of the ER. The second the doors opened, Gus lifted his shoulders back and laughed a loud, long laugh- a broad smile beaming across his face. Theresa looked at him questioningly.

"Oh, Sweetheart! That's a good one! I'll have to remember that punchline!"

Gus glanced at Theresa, urging her to laugh along with him. She did- at first unconvincingly, then getting her bearings as she went.

Finally, making their way toward the desk in ICU, Gus sidled up to the Nurse's Station. Theresa stood beside him, removing her cap and letting her hair fall loose around her shoulders.

"Howdy, Rhonda!" Gus said to the nurse behind the desk.

"Hiya, Gus. How's your shift so far?" Rhonda asked him pleasantly.

"No complaints!" Gus lied with a laugh. He then continued, "Rhonda, you know my daughter, Theresa, right?"

"Why sure I do!" The nurse replied, smiling at Theresa.

Theresa smiled back. "So good to see you again, Rhonda!" She said as nonchalantly as possible.

Gus slapped a hand on Theresa's shoulder, giving her a little playful wiggle as he spoke. "They thought it might be good for our Jane Doe to have someone to sit and chat with her a bit... You know, maybe help get her brain tracking some. Theresa volunteered, and here she is- reporting for duty!"

Rhonda looked confused, and her forehead furrowed. There was a moment of awkward silence. Finally, she picked up the chart and thumbed through it. "Funny, but I wasn't informed..."

She looked at the pair and stood for a moment before continuing, "Well, I'm sure it's fine and can only help. Poor thing has been all alone in there since being brought in, with only her weird humming to keep her company. You go on in, Theresa, and let me know if you need anything!"

Gus and Theresa smiled in unison, turned, and made their way toward Jane Doe's room, breathing a deep sigh of relief as they went.

"Man, that was close!" Theresa whispered as they entered the small room.

Gus shot her a look of agreement but said nothing. Reaching up to remove the scarf from around her neck, Theresa caught her first glimpse of the battered woman lying motionless in bed.

"Oh My God!" She gasped and staggered backward a couple steps.

"I know Honey..." Gus replied.

"Dad, what's going on??!" She whispered, terror in her voice.

"Steady, Theresa..." Gus whispered back and then continued, "Sweetheart, I don't know. But what I do know isn't good. This is body number four that's turned up like this in just the last month. Three in Manhattan, all beaten to death. All with gardenias stuffed down their throats."

Theresa looked up at her father, her eyes wide with shock and horror, her hand subconsciously reaching up to her throat. "Dad...?"

"Brad was on the case. Theresa, whoever is doing this, did him- after they saw me having lunch with him at the diner today."

Gus's voice dropped low and became monotone. "Honey. I wore my uniform to meet Brad today..."

"BUT DAD!" Theresa exclaimed in horror.

"I know," Gus whispered. "I shouldn't have. Don't know what I was thinking. I guess the grief has made me rusty... I've been followed here. I've led them right to us... all...."

The color drained from Theresa's face, and she instinctively slapped her hand over her mouth to stifle the audible gasp that escaped her. She locked eyes with Gus, who immediately read her questioning look.

"They're in the wind, Honey. I have no leads. Neither did Brad, but there are anomalies, and they're disturbing."

Theresa lurched toward the chair in the corner of the room, wrestling to remove her coat, spilling the contents of her purse on the floor with a clatter.

Gus looked down at the woman lying in bed. "Sweetheart," he spoke to Theresa while keeping his eyes on the bedridden figure, "I don't know who I can trust yet- but all our lives depend on the next few hours. This woman here is the only living vic. They'll be coming for her. I need your head in the game."

With that, Gus cut his gaze back to his daughter. Stuffing the scattered items back into her purse, she nodded her understanding and agreement.

Glancing toward the door in an effort to ensure no one was watching, Gus walked quickly over to his daughter. Thrusting his work pager into her hand, he next reached down and quickly hiked up the pantleg of his uniform. Removing a snub-nose revolver from his ankle holster, he passed it discreetly to Theresa.

"You're a crack shot, Girl." He stated matter-of-factly. "Now's not the time to forget that. Keep this under your coat and stay at the ready."

With that, Gus started toward the hallway.

"Dad, where are you going?!!?" Theresa whispered, her voice filled with fear.

"I have to go to the third-floor Administrator's office to see the boss. Anything happens, use that pager and I'll be here quick. I'm just one floor up."

Theresa nodded, obviously unnerved.

"Honey, head in the game. I won't be long."

With that, Gus walked out of the room, closing the door behind him.

Theresa sat rigid, feeling completely and utterly alone. The whirring and chiming of the hospital equipment was the only sound in the room. Nervously fidgeting in her chair, she finally stood and walked to the window. Rain pattered against the glass as she watched the darkness outside deepen. The world seemed strangely disconnected, as though moving in slow motion. Time stood still, and she found herself longing to be anyone else- anywhere else. Casting her gaze on the figure lying in bed, Theresa found herself staring. She detected strange stirrings inside herself, and she didn't like them. An unidentifiable anger began growing, its presence taking her by surprise. Her mind flashed to her youth and the endless stream of sad sacks and Down and Outers that had paraded through her family home, invited by her well-meaning parents, consuming the family resources and leading to difficulties, not of her making. A hard expression crossed Theresa's face, and she walked over to the woman lying helpless.

"So here we go again..." She heard herself whisper. "The only thing different this time is your appearance...another hard luck case about to turn our lives upside down."

Theresa pursed her lips, crossed her arms across her chest, sighed, and continued, "Listen, my entire life growing up was one endless stream of junkies and hookers trying to get clean, with my folks trying to help. Dad and I just don't have what it takes for this anymore...especially now that Mom's gone. It's just too much, OK?? I mean, I hope you get better, but this is your mess- not ours. NOT OURS!"

The last bit, Theresa all but hissed, and she was immediately ashamed of herself. What happened next only made her feel worse.

With no warning, Jane Doe's eyes fluttered open. Deep blue and glassy, they started at the ceiling, a look of abject horror reflected in them. Suddenly, an almost imperceptible humming began.

"Oh, Dear Lord, what've I done!!" Theresa gasped as she simultaneously paged her father and ran for the nurse.

Chapter Four

In the interim, Gus had taken the back stairs to reach Mark Anderson's office. He'd hoped he'd made the right decision, not calling ahead. As Hospital Administrator, Gus's friend and employer, Mark had presented himself as a loyal ally. But now, it fell to Gus to put the relationship to the test. Mark was well-versed in matters of Life and Death- but getting him to fully grasp the scope of this particular issue wasn't going to be easy. Gus had a dicey feeling. And rightly so. He wasn't surprised by Mark's reaction as he outlined the facts of the grim and outlandish situation.

There, in the privacy of Mark's office, Gus quickly laid out his best case- and worst fears. The woman in Room 260, marked for assassination by unknown killers, was helpless prey. 'They' were coming for her -but exactly who, how, and when- was anybody's guess. Time was not on their side. In the flurry of conversation that ensued, Mark interrupted Gus, stating the obvious. "Shouldn't we be calling the Police, Gus?!! I mean hell- this is preposterous!" Mark was agitated, incredulous, and combative—a side Gus had never seen.

Matching Mark's agitation, Gus raised his voice to a loud, insistent whisper, banging his hand on the desk as he spoke. "Mark, I know it's been a long day, and you want to go home, but for chrissake, you've got to trust me! We've got to buy time and distance. There's too much not adding up- and you guys... you guys are in way over your heads with this!!"

Gus and Mark locked eyes. "Just what the fuck does that mean?!!" Mark shot back, an indignant look flashed across his face, taking Gus by surprise. "What does that mean??"

Gus repeated. "It means, Mark..." Gus replied, growing strangely calm, "You have other patients in this facility. Vulnerable patients- not to mention your staff. As long as Jane Doe's here, they're all at risk! Big risk. Every single one of them. Are you telling me you're willing to trust their safety to me and two other tired, overworked rent-a-cops? We don't know what we're up against, Mark. Mafia? Serial killer? Satanists? All I do know for sure is this is the only one of four women that's survived. How'd she end up here? Why Madison General? The others died in the city. I've got a murdered cop on my hands... one of my oldest, dearest friends, and he was afraid, Mark. He took a bullet in the brain, for godsakes! We're up to our asses here. What's there to lose? She's basically written off as a vagrant at this point. The second she starts to recover, you're gonna pitch her over to a county nursing facility anyway, so why not just convince the staff of our plan? I need time, Mark! SHE needs time!!"

Mark sighed heavily with exasperation and slammed a file down hard on his desk. Swiveling his chair toward the window, he turned his back to Gus. It seemed an eternity before he turned back, looked at Gus, and reached for the phone. There was a look in his eye and a set to his jaw, Gus observed but couldn't quite identify. It gave Gus a curious, unsettled feeling.

"Miss Grayson, please call Dr. Stafford and inform him that his patient in Room 260 is being sent to private facilities. We're transferring her from care ASAP. He's to provide case notes, protocol, and suggested follow-up stat." There was a pause, and Mark continued, "Yes. That's correct." Hanging up the phone, Mark's eyes narrowed and there was anger in his voice. "Gus, my neck is on the block here..."

Gus only nodded. "I'll need a leave of absence, Boss." Was all he replied. Mark waved a hand in agreement. It was at that moment Gus's pager went off. "I gotta go!" He mumbled and made his way quickly back to Theresa.

Gus flew down the stairs, collecting himself as he reached the second floor. Walking as calmly as he could, he made his way to Room 260 as though nothing was amiss. Pushing open the door, he found a pale and flustered Theresa at the window and a nurse and doctor standing over Jane Doe. "Oh- excuse me..." Gus said professionally. "I just received a page to this room."

The nurse looked up, and Gus and Theresa's eyes met briefly. "Well...yes. That's right, I suppose." The nurse replied. "Big change of plans with this one, it seems. She's opened her eyes, and we're getting strong pupil response. Looks like she's slowly coming around. New orders for her, too. Transferring out, it looks like. We've just been informed. We can use your help with that, Gus."

"Sure thing," Gus answered, nodding his head toward the door as he eyed Theresa. "Come on, Hon." He spoke nonchalantly. "Let's get out of here and leave these good people to their work!"

Theresa quickly and silently followed her father out of the room and down the hall, taking his cue as he opened the door to an empty office. Locking it behind them and turning on a desk lamp, Gus pulled Theresa closer and in a hushed and hurried voice, told her of the plan. She stared back at him, eyes wide.

At a loss, Theresa stood numb, stammering for words. With trembling hands, she smoothed the front of her coat and fumbled nervously with the purse strap hanging over her right shoulder. Terror was building inside her, and Gus stood watching it happen.

Looking into his daughter's eyes, his forehead furrowed. "I'm sorry, Sweetheart. This is the only way. It's all I can think of to try and save our skin." Fighting tears, Theresa looked back at Gus and simply nodded her understanding. "Come on, Girl. Head up. Here we go."

With Theresa following close behind, Gus made his way to the first floor. Walking into the break room, just as he'd hoped, Gus found Curtis Rikerson, second in command on the hospital security team, clocking in.

Keeping his voice low and calm, Gus patted his coworker on the shoulder. Curtis turned to greet Gus. "Curt, got an unforeseen family issue I'm going to need to deal with. Will be gone for a few days. Mark's already cleared me for leave, so you're in charge. Sorry to put you in a bind with short notice, but it couldn't be helped."

Curtis looked at Gus- and then at Theresa. An expression of kind concern swept over his face. "Sure. Sure thing, Gus." The younger man replied. "I'm hopin' it'll be OK for you... both. Don't worry about anything here. Got it covered!"

"Thanks, Curt. I appreciate it." Gus replied, shaking the man's hand.

Curtis gave a little affirmative wink in Gus's direction and then shyly nodded his head toward Theresa, turning to begin his shift as he did so.

"Well, we'll soon find out if this hair-brained scheme's gonna work..." Gus pursed his lips, raised his eyebrows, and drew a breath, looking at Theresa as he spoke. Together, they began the long walk toward the basement morgue.

At precisely 9 PM, a black-topped, silver hearse respectfully approached the morgue entrance. A tall, thin young man exited the driver's side, tugged on his cap, and whispered to Gus as he made his way to the back of the car, "Hiya Gus. Do we look funereal enough??"

"I can almost smell the lilies..." Gus shot back in a hushed voice. "Now hop to and work your magic, Arlo. We don't have all night."

The young man's face grew serious, and he nodded, continuing with his solemn preparations.

Five minutes later, on the other side of the hospital, a private ambulance service pulled their blue and white ambulance to a stop by the ER doors. The hospital drive and entrance were extremely well-lit, standing out in stark contrast against the deep darkness of the rainy night. 'Woodhaven Convalescent Home' was emblazoned on the side of the vehicle in an elegant, large, gold scroll for all the world to see. The crew scurried to the back, opened the doors, and stood in attendance as one of the crew went inside.

At that moment, a gurney carrying a draped body was wheeled off the elevator and approached the waiting hearse. After carefully sliding the tender cargo into the back and closing the door with a ceremonial thud, Arlo shot a wink at Gus, briefly tugged at his oversized cap, and slid back behind the wheel. The hearse and its motley driver were then joined by a woman discreetly carrying a medical bag. Together, they made their way slowly back down the circular drive, disappearing into the darkness. A couple moments later, the Woodhaven Convalescent Home's vehicle and crew followed, taking extra care not to jostle its payload: a gurney full of sheets shaped to resemble the body of a petite woman.

Gus tensely scanned the surroundings as he and Theresa stood concealed in the shadows. No one spoke. Gus's eyes and ears strained. The seconds passed like an eternity, and just as Theresa was about to whisper, Gus shot his hand up, silencing her. There, off in the distance, at the far end of the hospital parking lot, a car slipped out of its parking space, lights off, tailing the ambulance.

As it made its exit, the headlights from a passing car illuminated it. Gus made out a flash of dirty red. Making note, he whispered to Theresa, "They've taken the bait! Quick- let's get to the truck!"

Mark Anderson stood silent for a moment, watching from his office window as the kabuki theater played out in the parking lot below. Taking a large swig of scotch and setting down his glass, he then reached for the phone; his jaw tightened, and he winced involuntarily as he dialed and tensely waited for an answer.

Chapter Five

Four hours and a few strategic detours later, Gus and Theresa drove past the Andover exits, onto an isolated and well-worn backroad that then ended at a place called 'DeAngelo's Truck Farm'. En route, Gus had spent more time staring in the rearview mirror than he did at the road ahead. Theresa had no idea where they were, but she was relieved to be arriving safely somewhere... anywhere. Pulling the pickup up close to the dilapidated farmhouse, Gus tapped the horn two times.

A rosy-cheeked, elderly woman quickly came out of the house and made her way from the porch to the truck. Smiling broadly, she grabbed Gus and gave him a hearty hug. Theresa looked on with a feeling of bewilderment as Gus hugged the woman back and said with warmth in his voice, "Good to see you again, Ange. Thanks for this."

The woman nodded. Turning her attention to Theresa, she extended a calloused hand and spoke with care and concern, "You must be Theresa. I'm Angie. Angie DeAngelo. This must be a scary time for you, Child. Come in and take a load off!"

With that, Gus followed as Angie led the way. Halfway up the rickety steps, he turned and bid Theresa to follow. She did, mind racing as she looked at her father with a questioning expression.

Following Angie through the door, Theresa stopped short. The inside of the house was nothing like the outside. Warm, cozy, neat, and tidy, the kitchen was lined with shelves holding home-canned vegetables, jams, and jellies. Houseplants lined the windowsills- and all were thriving. The smell of fresh ground coffee filled the air, and a fire crackled in the wood stove. Three people sat in the den, playing dominoes. One of them looked vaguely familiar. Theresa squinted and couldn't believe her eyes. It was Arlo. The driver of the hearse. "You all must be tired out and starved to boot!" Angie's voice broke the awkward silence. Slicing freshly baked bread with a large, serrated knife, she continued, "Best I got right now is bread and cheese! You two want bacon? I got bacon! I can fry some up real quick."

Gus smiled. "No, Ange. Bread and cheese will be just great. Thank you."

The woman looked at Gus and smiled. "Nothing's a bother for you, Augustus." Theresa noted the woman blushed slightly. Gus just winked and smiled.

Theresa then turned her gaze back to Arlo and the two others sitting at the table with him. The man was tall, gangly and had a thick shock of unruly brown hair she hadn't noted earlier. He looked all of twenty-five, but there was a confidence and a bit of swagger to him. As she took in the scene, Gus walked over to the group and engaged them. It was obvious they knew -and respected- each other, although one of them held back and appeared much more reserved. This caught Theresa's interest.

As his daughter watched, Gus reached out a hand to Arlo and greeted him much more warmly than he had at the hospital morgue. "Any trouble?" He asked.

"Nope. Clean as a whistle!" Arlo responded. "Went down just like you planned, Gus."

"No one tailed you?" Gus questioned again, probing for more detail.

"Nope. Nobody made us. Those bastards took the bait hard. They're probably mad as hornets by now! Must've been a real shock to find out they'd spent an hour tailing SHEETS!" Arlo chuckled, and Gus just nodded and smiled, but as he did, there was a nagging feeling in the pit of his stomach.

"Where's the ride?" Gus then asked.

"Stashed in the old barn out back, along with Jessie's wheels!" Arlo replied, turning his attention back to the domino game.

Shaking off his concern, Gus next turned his attention to the thin, blonde woman sitting to Arlo's left. She seemed much more formal in tone and demeanor and didn't seem terribly at ease. "You must be Nurse Silvers," Gus stated, extending his hand.

"Yessir." Came the somewhat chilly response. The woman accepted Gus's handshake as she spoke. Theresa then recognized her as the woman with the medical bag.

"How's our patient?" Gus asked with a tone of urgency.

"Stable, Sir." Nurse Silvers replied with a studied tone in her voice. "She's resting now but is definitely coming around. Shouldn't be long now. I'm following the care plan exactly as written."

Gus nodded again. Taking a breath, he then looked the nurse directly in the eye, speaking in a sincere and serious tone. "You're brave- and we appreciate your help and expertise." Nurse Silvers didn't hold Gus's gaze, cutting her eyes away as she nodded her acknowledgment of the compliment and then said nothing else. Gus's and Angie's eyes met briefly, and Theresa watched as a strange expression shot between them.

Gus then turned his focus to the figure sitting to his left. Theresa watched as his demeanor shifted. She wasn't sure what it was she was seeing, but it left her feeling flustered and off kilter.

The woman Gus was now addressing was attractive in an unassuming way, approximately fifty-five years old, brunette, brown eyes, pleasant- and with an air of quiet strength and assurance about her. As Theresa stood watching, she heard her father speak. "Jessie. Really good to see you again." His voice was kind, with just a hint of intimacy to it. Theresa noted a current of mutual respect and familiarity pass between the two. She watched Jessie shake her father's hand, noting a look of affection in the woman's eyes as their hands met. Theresa also noted her father lingered just a moment too long before releasing his grasp. And then, just like that, the connection was broken, and Gus moved on.

"Ange," Gus spoke, addressing Angie as she stood plating up bread and cheese and pouring coffee. "Jessie and I will be heading back to the city. Got a couple important meetings there- and a stale crime scene to visit. We'll be back soon, but in the meantime, Arlo will keep you, Theresa, Nurse Silvers, and our patient safe and sound. Anything any of you need when we get back? Nurse Silvers?"

Angie nodded her agreement and understanding. Nurse Silvers shook her head 'No'. Theresa gasped.

"One thing I do ask, Augustus..." Angie replied as a quick afterthought. "You get a couple hours shuteye first." She spoke in a caring but authoritative manner. "No one followed you here. It's a clean getaway. This thing heats up like you think it will; this may be your last chance for some rest. Better take it while you can get it. I'll throw together some food to keep you going for the trip back. You two shouldn't be stopping anywhere along the way, ya know." Gus knew Angie was right and made no argument. Nodding his agreement, he and Jessie glanced at each other. Gus then turned his attention to his daughter. He could see she was distressed-and somewhat angry.

Upon finishing their meager dinner, Gus took Theresa aside as she settled into the guest room that had been designated for her. Taking her hand, he caught her gaze squarely, his voice cracking with emotion a bit as he spoke. "Your Mom would be so proud of you for your brave trust right now. I certainly am."

Theresa squirmed, but tears came to her eyes. She hugged her father. "Be safe. I love you, Dad." Was all she could muster.

"Theresa," Gus continued, "there's a lot about me you don't know..." Theresa turned her back to Gus, plumping pillows and pulling down the bedcovers for distraction. "I loved your mom..." Gus said wistfully.

"I know." Theresa responded.

Gus drew a breath. "Arlo flunked out of the Academy two years ago. Damn good guy. Too cagey for his own good but I've worked with him before. Trust him." Theresa nodded again. Gus continued, "Angie was a longtime informant of mine before she got out of the city and made it here upstate. I've known her for years and she's Good People. She's always had my back."

Theresa nodded again, but this time added with a hint of challenge, "What about the other one??"

Gus looked past his daughter, off into the distance, and continued, "I don't know this Nurse Silvers, but she comes highly recommended by Mark at the hospital. Anything our Jane Doe needs by way of care, she'll provide...and I suspect there will be a lot needed in the days and weeks to come." He turned to leave but stopped himself as he reached the door. Turning back to Theresa, he took her gently by the shoulders. "Jessie is a fine woman. One of the most highly regarded Bounty Hunters in the country. We've worked together many times." Theresa swallowed and raised her eyes to meet her father's gaze. "I loved your mom," Gus repeated. "And I love you. Goodnight, Sweetheart. If we're not back in two days, Arlo and Angie will know what to do. Stick close to them- and the house." With that, Gus kissed his daughter on the forehead and returned to the den.

The fire in the wood stove was dying down and cast the faint glow of embers. Everyone else had turned in for a few hours of much-needed rest. Reclining on the couch, Gus pulled a coverlet from the back of the sofa and placed it over himself, waiting for brief sleep to come.

As he did, his mind and heart wandered back to a not-too-distant memory...

a night too long,

a case too gruesome,

a historic New York City blizzard,

and what wasn't but might've been....

Chapter Six

Jessie's Mustang GT purred down the highway. She and Gus had traveled the first many miles in silence, neither speaking. It was five AM and still dark, though a faint change of color already challenged the horizon. Gus's mind whirred, and he knew Jessie's was doing the same. Finally, he spoke. "Coffee, Jess? Angie's packed a thermos and cups..."

"Sure, Gus. I could use some."

"Still taking it black?" He questioned.

Jessie allowed a faint smile to cross her lips. "Still." Came her reply, and it was all she said.

As Gus handed her a cup, she guided the car onto the freeway, bound for Manhattan. Traffic was still light, yet she kept her eye instinctively on the rearview mirror.

"Anybody tailing us?" Gus asked.

"No. No one." Came her answer.

They drove in silence for a few moments more, taking occasional sips. Finally, Jessie addressed the obvious. "I was very sorry about Mary, Gus. I'm sad for your loss... and Theresa's. I've thought of you... both."

Gus stared straight ahead and, after a moment, replied. "Thanks, Jess. It's been... well, it's been. The flowers you sent were lovely." Jessie nodded her acknowledgment.

Another mile passed before she spoke again. This time, there was an air of professionalism in her voice. "You want to hit the scene first- or Pete's?"

Looking down, Gus glanced at his watch. "Let's hit the scene first. The day will be full on by the time we get there. Give ol' Pete a chance to rise and shine before we overpower him." Jessie nodded with a slight chuckle.

About three hours later, they eased to a stop in always-bustling K-town. Traffic was already heavy in the Korean sector -both car and foot- and a light mist fell. Stepping out of the car, Gus stretched, pulled the collar of his coat up snug around his neck, raised a match to his cigarette, and took a long drag. His chest felt heavy, and his lungs burned. Mixed with the drizzle, the tobacco tasted musty and stale. Taking one more forced drag, he tossed the cigarette on the sidewalk, stomping it out with the heel of his boot. As he looked up, Jessie met his gaze. "Bad Habits..." He muttered self-consciously, casting his gaze down the street behind Jessie.

Jessie turned and followed suit. "That it up there?" She asked, pointing to an alleyway halfway up the block off Sixth Avenue.

Gus squinted. "Yeah. Has to be." He replied. "Fits the description Brad gave me that day over lunch. Let's go see what we can find."

As they walked, Gus replayed that last day with Brad at the diner. During their entire conversation, there were only two concrete pieces of information Brad had revealed about the case he'd been working. The first; the address of the alley where Jane Doe had been found. The second; the name of Brad's new partner who'd been working the case with him. Gus had noted both as a matter of routine. As Jessie and Gus made their way into the dingy alley, they surveyed the scene. The stench from the dumpsters hung heavy in the damp air, and the smell of urine burned their nostrils as it reconstituted in the drizzle. Off in the distance, dogs barked, and car horns blared. "Not a pretty place to cash in..." Jessie murmured. Gus agreed.

They began slowly canvassing the area. Two bums stretched out unconscious on pieces of cardboard stuffed under a building overhang, sleeping off whatever had been their poison of choice the night before. As Gus rifled through one of the open dumpsters, Jessie stood surveying the layout of the buildings overlooking the alleyway. As she did, a drunk staggered toward her, slurring slightly. "Hey, Lady... I'm awful thirsty. Buy me a bottle!?!" Losing his balance, he reached out and grabbed Jessie's arm to steady himself.

Gus instinctively ran to her aid. "Hey! Hands off!" He commanded. Jessie freed herself from the man's grip and shot a look at Gus. He checked himself.

At that moment, the man looked at Gus, his eyes growing wide. "Mr. Gus! That you??!?"

Gus stared for a moment at the worn and dirty face and then recognized the man. "Hey, Sam! Yes, it's me. Longtime No See, My Friend! How have you been?"

Sam brushed self-consciously at his threadbare coat and, casting his eyes down at the pavement, answered, "Things aren't like they was back in the day, Mr. Gus..." The old man then added, " Sorry about grabbin' your lady friend. I kinda lost my footing."

Gus smiled and nodded. Reaching out, he patted the man's arm, motioning to Jessie as he did so. "Sam, meet Jessie. Jessie, this is Sam. One of my most reliable informants." This part, he whispered in a low voice.

Jessie reached out and shook Sam's hand. "Nice to meet you, Sam." She said graciously.

"Pleasure's mine, Ma'am," Sam replied with a twinkle.

Gus leaned in and spoke, looking Sam straight in the eye. "Sam, we need your help. Anything of interest happen here the last few days?"

The disheveled man looked around nervously, wiping at a bit of spit forming at the corner of his mouth. Gus noted Sam's trembling hands. "Same price, My Friend?" He asked.

Sam's eyes widened, and he took a moment to nod. "For you, the same, Gus." Came the timid reply. Gus pulled a folded bill from his wallet and slipped it into Sam's cold, calloused hand. The money was quickly stuffed into what was left of Sam's coat pocket. Sam stood nodding at nothing in particular for a moment, staring off into space with eyes that looked afraid. Finally, he spoke, grimacing somewhat. "This here's the place you want— right over here, Mr. Gus. She was in an awful way. I musta got here right after they did it, but I didn't touch nuthin', I swear!"

Gus and Jessie followed Sam's gaze, coming to rest on a pile of overturned crates and bins in the back corner of the alley. Walking over, Gus rifled through the debris with the toe of his boot. Standing back, Sam watched in silence, looking intently at Jessie. After a few moments, Gus found what he was looking for, and given the weather, and bustling activity, it was a miracle. Squatting, he reached down and touched the wet ground with his fingertip. Lifting it to his nose, he sniffed. Blood. He then stood and slowly paced back and forth over the scene as Jessie watched.

"What're ya lookin' for, Mr. Gus?" Sam asked in a hushed voice.

"Mistakes," Gus answered, not raising his eyes from the debris scattered about.

"Sam," Jessie spoke to the old man, looking squarely at him, "is there anything about that night you can recall? Anything out of the ordinary... not usual?"

As Gus continued to carefully sift through piles of trash and debris, Sam stood motionless, straining to pull fragments of memory from his already fragmented mind. Jessie pulled another bill out of her coat pocket and handed it over to Sam. He grabbed at it haltingly, a look of embarrassment passing over his face. Jessie just smiled at him.

"Red car..." Sam said matter-of-factly, wiping at more spittle. "Dirty... three men... they talked funny."

"Talked funny?" Jessie repeated. "Like how, Sam?" She gently prodded, being careful not to pressure the man.

Sam stood grasping for words he didn't know to describe a language he'd never heard. "Don't know." He finally answered. "Foreign stuff."

Jessie nodded. "Foreign, like how?"

"You know... FOREIGN. Not like the usual here. Like not American... or Ayrab...or Asian-like." Came Sam's response.

"Oh. OK, Sam. Anything else for us?"

The frail man stood thinking a moment more. Jessie could see his shakes were increasing in intensity. Looking her in the eye, he then added slowly, a sound of incredulity in his voice, "Just one more thing maybe... a fella, like... like you, Mr. Gus... he was workin' the scene with a bunch of other cops, and while he thought no one was lookin', I saw him kickin' stuff under the dumpster- and hidin' some stuff in his pocket like."

Jessie's forehead furrowed, and she cast a glance in Gus's direction. Sam wiped his mouth with his filthy sleeve. "Sam needs his 'breakfast,' Gus. I think he's been enough help to us today." With that, she winked at Sam.

Gus walked over and patted Sam on the shoulder. "Indeed, he has. Gus spoke kindly. "Just one quick thing, Sam. You sure about that fella you just mentioned? You saying he was a Dick? And you saw him tamper with evidence??"

"Yessir. No doubt. I know what I saw." Sam answered adamantly.

Gus glanced at Jessie; a look of concern shot between them. "Where was this man when you saw him?"

Sam wrapped his arms tight around his trembling, reed-thin body. "Right over there where you was, Mr. Gus. Right over there..." He pointed with a shaking hand and let out a small moan.

Gus turned his attention back to Sam. "What color hair, you recall?"

"None!" Sam sputtered. "None?" Gus repeated. 'You mean he was bald?"

"Like a cueball!" Sam laughed, and a toothless grin lit his face momentarily, making him appear almost childlike.

Gus stood a moment longer, exhaled, and nodded. "It's been good to see you again, My Friend. You take good care of yourself now and thank you for all your help."

With that, he shook the man's hand, and he and Jessie watched as Sam made his way unsteadily out of the alley and down the street toward the nearest Liquor Store.

"Find anything useful?" Jessie asked once they were alone.

"Blood," Gus replied. "And a goodly amount. Stand watch for a minute, Jess."

As she did, Gus made his way back to the dumpster he'd just checked. Following Sam's lead, he bent down low onto his knees. The urine-tainted rainwater soaked through his pants and coated his hands as he leaned low for a better look. Sure enough, there, under the wheeled dumpster, something caught his eye. Reaching far underneath the large metal container, almost out of his reach, he strained to retrieve a soggy, brown object. Making his way back to Jessie, he held out his hand. She looked at the decaying object for a moment and then at Gus inquisitively.

"Half a smashed gardenia..." Came his reply.

CHAPTER SEVEN

Like the heaviness of the cigarette smoke swirling in the room, the atmosphere of the inner office at Acme Bail Bonds was stifling. After a few minutes silence, Gus turned to Pete. "I know we're both thinking the same thing."

Pete met Gus's gaze and then shot a look in Jessie's direction. He grew agitated but contained himself. "You're asking me for the moon, Gus. This kind of thing's not kosher. It just isn't done!" Gus nodded, let out a heavy sigh, and walked over to the window. Placing his finger between two slats, he parted the venetian blinds and stared at the wet street below. He hated dead ends, and this was one he simply couldn't -and wouldn't- accept.

Collecting himself, Gus turned and walked back over to the chairs in front of Pete's desk, joining Jessie, who sat silent, a look of determination and concern on her face. Gus glanced at her and then turned his focus back to Pete. He spoke calmly, and his voice didn't waver. "Pete, Brad took a cap in the head chasin' this case. He was way in - and afraid. That means just one thing: he was surrounded on the job and knew it. Couple this with what my source told Jess and me this morning, and we're talkin' dirty cops on this, man. How else is it possible there are no leads? ZERO! ZERO leads and dead women piling up out there! This is a Blind, Pete - and Nick's ass is on the line, not to mention his life."

Pete's expression hardened, and he winced at Gus's words. Finally, he rose and walked to the window, standing motionless. Outside, the rain was letting up, but gray clouds hung low over the city. Pete turned and spoke. "I love my nephew, Gus. You know that. It would kill Cecile if anything ever happened to her boy."

"You don't help now," Gus replied, "That's a given."

Jessie watched as Pete walked back over to his chair and sank into it. He looked totally overwhelmed, deeply uncomfortable, and fearful. Finally, after another long moment, Pete raised his eyes and spoke. "Nick had only been partnered with Brad six months for chrissakes. That's not a long time, Gus! They were still learning each other's patterns. You're telling me he was in on this investigation and is now alone, surrounded by dirties??"

Gus shot back, "Six months is long enough to build the bond, Pete. You know that. Very strong possibility they'll be coming for him - and he has to know it by now. His only hope is to meet with us and play ball."

Pete leaned down, opening his lower right-side desk drawer. Matter-of-factly, he pulled out a bottle of bourbon and three water glasses, one still containing residue from the last usage. Placing them in a row on his desk, he poured the amber liquid equally into each. He caught Gus's eye and held a glass out toward him. Gus waved him off. Next, Pete lifted one toward Jessie.

"Little early for me...but what the hell." She smiled and retrieved the glass from Pete's hand. "Salut!" She said as she lifted the drink to her lips and drew in a long sip.

Pete smiled a fleeting smile in return, but Jessie noted it was quick and insincere. He killed his bourbon in one large gulp, wincing a bit as the liquid burned its way down his throat.

"Pete, you get what I'm saying." Gus pressed again. "In all the years I've known you, I've never seen you take a drink before noon! Here's the Takeaway: we're already All In- every single one of us. That Jane Doe we've got stashed is the only known survivor. And they know it! It looks like they know me. And if that's the case, they know A LOT of things. We have to level this playing field - and fast!"

Jessie swallowed down the last of her drink and set the glass on Pete's desktop. Rubbing the silver-gray stubble on his chin, Pete asked in a hushed voice filled with surrender, "What's the plan, Gus?"

Gus reached for the rumpled pack in his left breast pocket and pulled out his last cigarette. It was bent, but he lit it anyway. Drawing a deep drag, he fished a piece of tobacco from off the tip of his tongue as he thought. Pete and Jessie watched him stand and pace the floor. They could see Gus's wheels turning. Finally, he spoke. "Call Nick and tell him to meet you at Washington Square Park ASAP. By the fountain. You take your car. Jessie and I will follow. Don't get into details with him on the phone, Pete. Just tell him you have to see him about an important matter. NO DETAILS. We've got one shot at this and can't fuck it up. And too, there's a big chance they've got him tapped." Pete nodded in agreement as he reached for the phone.

Gus again took his seat next to Jessie and watched as the call was placed. He observed small beads of sweat forming on Pete's forehead and upper lip as he talked with his nephew. Despite the sweat and jangled nerves, Pete held his own, cool as a cucumber. Disconnecting the call, Pete lifted his eyes to Gus. There was a strange, veiled look in them. "He'll make it in an hour," Pete stated, then paused. Slowly continuing, he added, "He's working a fresh one at the moment...some drunk's been found filleted in an alley off Sixth..."

Pete looked at Gus. Gus looked at Jessie.

Jessie cut her eyes and looked down at the dingy, burnt orange carpet. "Sam..." She whispered.

Gus and Pete then replied in unison and with absolute, icy certainty, "SAM."

"DAMMIT!!!" Gus hissed as he banged his fist on Pete's desk.

Pete hissed in response, "These Fuckers are half a step behind us, Gus. JUST HALF A STEP! You better damn well know what you're doing, or we're all dead! GOD HELP US!"

***

Exactly one hour later, Gus and Jessie sat side by side on a still-damp park bench in Washington Square, their backs to two men sitting on the other side of the same bench. The weather had cleared somewhat, but off in the distance, more rain threatened. Not many people were active in the area at that moment, a very rare, welcomed, and much-needed lucky break. Gus turned to face Jessie as though he was speaking to her but instead spoke low and in a grim tone to the young man sitting opposite him. "Thanks for coming, Nick."

Keeping his eyes staring straight ahead, the young man responded, "There are a million places I'd rather be, Mr. Walker, but after the scene I just worked, I gotta do this, come hell or high water— and I'm afraid it'll be both."

"Tell me about the scene in the alley." Gus requested. "And don't skip anything."

Nick continued, staring straight ahead while responding. His color drained a bit as he spoke. "A grisly scene, Sir. One of the worst I've worked. The poor bastard's guts were hanging out like a gutted fish." Gus winced, and Jessie raised her hand to her forehead, covering her eyes and massaging her temples as she listened to the accounting. "This wasn't just a roll job. This was deliberate - every bit of it. Like they were sending a message. The vic's throat was slit. Half his tongue missing too."

"Anything else?" Pete broke in, prodding his nephew.

"Yeah." The young Detective replied matter-of-factly. "They left their calling card..."

"Gardenia...?" Gus half asked, half stated.

"Yessir." Came Nick's monotone reply.

Pete cast an intense gaze directly at his nephew, speaking in a voice that was an equal mix of determination and terror. "Nick, we're in deep - all of us. You know Gus was Brad's longtime partner on the force. You can trust him. WE can trust him...." He added decisively. "And, you know Jessie's reputation. Top notch. She's solid. We're dead if we don't act, Son. And most likely, you'll be next." With this, Nick stared into his uncle's eyes, swallowed hard, and nodded in knowing agreement.

"So what do you think?" Gus asked, adjusting his position on the park bench, turning to more squarely face Jessie.

Nick drew a slow, deep breath and then replied, "There are Mob marks all over this, Sir -but which Mob, I can't tell- and yes, we have dirties involved. Not sure how high up, but law is in on it, too, no doubt.

"Anything else?" Gus questioned again.

"The streets aren't talking, Sir. That leads me to believe we're looking at a lot of tentacles - and they run deep."

"Any neighborhoods in particular gone silent on you?" Gus again pressed.

Nick thought a moment and then answered, "Haven't had time to run patterns, Mr. Walker..."

"Get to it- FAST! And keep your eyes peeled for our mysterious, bald spook!" Gus shot back. "He crosses your path; you better get small quick." With that, he rubbed his hand over his face and through his hair and then stood, staring off in the distance at nothing in particular, speaking as he did so. "Thanks, Nick. Stay connected, and for chrissake, watch your six." Gus then reached down, lightly tapping Jessie on the shoulder. She rose, and they walked off together, not once looking back. A good fifteen minutes later, Pete and Nick exited the park just as the next round of rain began to pelt down around them.

***

Commuter traffic surged as Jessie merged the Mustang onto the feeder road parallelling the Interstate. Dusk was setting in, right along with the next round of inclement weather. It had been an exceedingly long day and she and Gus were deeply weary -on many levels- and they had many miles still to travel. They'd driven in silence the last few minutes since leaving the park, both reviewing the information Nick had provided and thinking of Sam. As they drove on, Gus finally spoke. "Our Jane Doe needs to get real small, real fast. And right now, she's not small enough."

Jessie nodded in agreement. "Whatcha thinking, Gus?" As she replied, Jessie cut her eyes sharply back to the rearview mirror. Gus noted a distinct change in her demeanor. "We've got company, Gus!!" She spoke, gripping the steering wheel instinctively.

Gus removed the seatbelt and twisted around in his seat, grabbing his Chief's Special from his shoulder holster. He placed the snub-nosed revolver in his lap and braced for what was to come. "They're not Friendlies, that's for certain..." He mumbled as Jessie pressed the accelerator and cut her eyes to the road in front of them, weaving in and out of traffic with precision. Seconds later, the unknown car came alongside them. The darkened windows concealed the occupants, and the dim light of dusk made it difficult to ascertain the exact color of the vehicle. Tires squealed, and the pursuing car veered into Jessie's left front bumper. Jessie jerked the wheel, compensated, and hit the brakes. The car shot past them, blew through a light, and merged onto the freeway, quickly consumed by the mass of traffic flowing by.

Punching the accelerator again and turning the wheel hard left, Jessie gunned the engine, heading back the way they'd come. Her hands trembled slightly as adrenal surged. After a moment, she calmed, pulling the car into the parking lot of a Denny's. "DAMMIT!" She exclaimed. "Second time this year I've been hit!" She looked at Gus, and he smiled slightly.

Suddenly, a different look swept his face. "I appreciate your help with this mess, Jessie. I'm afraid I've put you in real and deep danger." Jessie held Gus's gaze for a moment, and her eyes scanned his face, resting briefly on his lips. She then lifted her gaze back to his eyes a moment longer. Finally, staring straight ahead, both hands on the wheel, she replied, "I've known real danger, Gus. I'm not afraid. What comes next, Partner?"

Gus looked straight ahead through the windshield and drew a deep breath. "Well," came his reply, "looks like we've shaken our tail for the time being. Let's eat!"

Jessie nodded in agreement, reaching onto the backseat for her purse. "You won't have to twist my arm!" She answered enthusiastically.

When it was their time to be seated, Gus leaned in and spoke to the hostess in a low voice, "The booth in the far back, please."

Glancing over her shoulder, the young woman protested. "Sir, that table hasn't been bussed yet. How about this one instead?"

Jessie stepped in, slipping the woman a five-dollar bill. "Tell you what, loan me your rag and a tub, and I'll bus it myself!"

The woman looked confused and flustered. "Ummm..." came her stammering response.

Jessie winked and smiled. "It's a sentimental booth for us. Please. Anniversary and all..."

With that, the hostess's face lit up and she smiled an embarrassed yet knowing smile. "Oh well. For that, we can make an exception! Back booth it shall be! Follow me, please!" Gus looked at Jessie. She shot him a quick wink.

Finally seated side by side, their backs against the wall, Gus and Jessie surveyed their surroundings. No windows around them, right by the door to the kitchen and an easy exit if necessary. The patrons were all legitimate, actively eating their meals, and engaged in conversations. Nothing unusual. No one paid them any heed. The only attention Gus and Jessie garnered was from the fawning waitress standing at the ready to take their order. Looking over the menu and sipping hot coffee, they allowed their guard to drop somewhat. "Hmmm..." Jessie finally spoke. "I'm starving. I'm going for the sirloin plate!"

Gus sat a moment more, pretending to look at the menu. Instead, he glanced down at his midsection. "I'm thinking that loaded vegetable omelet looks good..."

Jessie cut a look over to her left, where Gus sat next to her. Her eyes were wide with bewilderment. "What the hell, Augustus??!? We haven't eaten in eighteen hours! An OMELET'S the best you can come up with? What gives?!?"

Gus glanced at Jessie, and a smile crossed his face. It was sincere and deep and bright. A kind of smile he hadn't smiled in a long time... a very long time. He chuckled, "That was close! Don't know what came over me!" Glancing at the waitress, he stated emphatically, "The T Bone for me, please! Medium Rare." The waitress scribbled on her order pad and scurried into the kitchen.

Jessie grinned and took a sip of her coffee. "Thank God." She laughed. "For a minute, I thought you'd been taken over by Pod People or gone all California on me!"

After a few minutes, the waitress brought their meals. Gus and Jessie sat side by side, eating in silence. Finally, Jessie spoke. "It's good to be working with you again, Gus. I've missed you."

A soft smile curved Gus's lips. Finally, he replied. "It's good to see you again, Jess. I've missed you too."

Jessie sat for a moment, stabbing at the broccoli spears on her plate. "I was out of line that night, Gus. I'm sorry. I never meant you or Mary any disrespect. I've wanted to tell you that for a very long time. Glad to have the chance to now."

Gus set his knife and fork down on the table and dabbed his mouth with his napkin. "No need to apologize, Jess. I was just as guilty. Truth be told, though, there's not actually much to be guilty about. Nothing was acted on. Most others in that spot wouldn't've stopped themselves. Speaks volumes as to our character, huh?"

Jessie smiled wistfully, and there was a faraway look in her eyes. Finally, she replied, "I suppose so. You're special to me, Augustus. Always have been, and that's never changed."

Gus glanced over at Jessie and caught her gaze. He smiled again and, inside, felt a warm sensation he'd all but forgotten he could feel. Just then, his cell phone rang.

Grabbing the phone from his shirt pocket, he glanced at the incoming number. "It's Pete." He announced. "Yeah, Pete. What's up?" Jessie watched as Gus focused intently. "How long ago? Spell it for me." Jessie grabbed an unused paper napkin from the table and then fished in her purse, retrieving a ballpoint pen, quickly sliding both over to Gus. "Ok, got it. Spell that one for me. Ok. Ok - got it." Jessie watched as Gus scrawled a woman's name, followed by another and then what looked to be the name of a nightclub. "You sure?" Gus pressed Pete over the phone. "OK then. I'll head there tonight. Jessie can drop me. She'll call you once I'm on my way. Thanks, Pete." Gus disconnected the call.

Jessie glanced over at him. "What's up?" She asked, slipping back into her professional demeanor.

"Nick called Pete a few minutes ago." Gus divulged. "An abandoned car's been impounded. Registration still in the glove compartment. Registered to one 'Lindy Abrams.'" A questioning look crossed Jessie's face. Gus continued. "About an hour ago, a BOLO was issued under that same name. Gal out of Chicago, last seen here briefly. Looks like maybe our Jane Doe's been made. I have to get to Chicago tonight. I'll need you to drop me at the airport."

Jessie sat a moment, taking in the information. Looking at Gus, she responded, "We better get going then."

Well fed, Jessie and Gus exited the restaurant and made their way back to the car. Casting a quick glance at her beloved car's crumpled fender, she pursed her lips in disgust. "Good thing it's only cosmetic!" She sighed.

Gus nodded and replied, "Sorry, Jess. I owe ya."

She smiled and tossed her purse onto the back seat. Upon leaving the parking lot, Jessie made the block three times. Finally certain no one was following them, she punched the accelerator, merging quickly, making for LaGuardia as fast as legally possible.

Pulling up to the American Airlines terminal, Gus collected himself. "I'll be gone a couple days at most. I'll have my phone on, and with me the entire time I'm shaking down these leads. You get back to the farm ASAP and check in with Pete while you're on the way. He's waiting for an update. Stay in touch with both of us while you're back at Angie's. And be careful, Jess. Give Theresa my love, too."

Jessie looked at Gus. "Safe flight. You be careful too, Augustus."

Gus nodded. Leaning over, he gently kissed Jessie on the cheek. Placing her hand on Gus's arm, she gave it a gentle squeeze. "Now Git!" Gus commanded. "We've got to keep moving!" Shooting a wink, Jessie's way, Gus exited the Mustang and made his way quickly into the terminal. Jessie watched as he disappeared into the crowd.

Locking the car doors and merging into traffic, she reached under her seat, pulling out her Glock 19. This she placed in the passenger seat. Next, reaching for her phone, she called in her update to Pete and began the long, lonely trip back to Andover - and Angie's farm.

Chapter Eight

Taking his seat by the window and buckling up for takeoff, Gus was eager for the almost three hours of uninterrupted silence that was to be his during the flight to Chicago. There was much information to digest, and he needed to debrief a bit before putting it all into his next plan of action. His thoughts were soon interrupted when a large woman plopped into the seat next to him. Placing her oversized purse in her lap, spilling herself -and her bag- over his armrest and into his plans.

"This is SO exciting!!" She babbled in amazement. "Can you believe that at seventy-six, I'm taking my first-ever plane trip??! Going to see my Great-Grandbaby! My daughter told me, 'If not now, Mom, when?' so I took her advice, and here I am! I told Harold -that's my husband- he would just have to fend for himself the next few days while I take this trip— 'my Bucket List' as my daughter Valerie calls it." Finally, the woman drew a breath but then quickly added, "Can you tell I'm a bit nervous?!" Gus nodded and managed a weak smile. He was exhausted and in no mood for conversation.

For the best part of the journey, the woman yammered on without a pause. Gus tried to smile in the appropriate places without being obvious he wasn't listening. Finally, unable to process the weighty thoughts whirling in his head, he unbuckled his seatbelt, excused himself under the guise of going to the restroom, and made his way down the aisle toward the back of the plane. Standing by the galley, he stretched and took a much-needed deep breath. The momentary silence felt like a balm to his ears - and his soul. He stared out into the inky darkness on the other side of the tiny window. "Last Call for coffee!" The flight attendant smiled. Gus nodded, and she handed him a cup. It tasted burned and was clearly the last dregs in the pot, but he was glad to have it. Blowing slightly to cool it, he turned and surveyed the cabin. Just the usual types catching the late flight to the Windy City. Taking another sip, Gus's attention came to rest on a man sitting midsection, three rows directly behind Gus's seat. Wearing a hat pulled low over his face, he sat oddly at attention while trying to look nonchalant. Gus recalled seeing the man dash into the plane just as the doors were about to close. Squinting hard, he tried to make out the man's features, but the hat served its purpose well. Handing the cup back to the attendant, Gus thanked her and then asked as an afterthought, "How long 'til we land?"

"Better head back to your seat, Sir." Came the reply. " Should be about another twenty minutes at most."

Starting slowly up the aisle, Gus approached his row and caught the eye of his talkative seatmate. She smiled and attempted to make herself smaller so he could squeeze past. For a brief second, he almost felt sorry for what he was about to do. Sidestepping his way into the row toward his seat, Gus suddenly grunted loudly and lurched forward onto the woman, catching the back of her seat rest in a feigned attempt to steady himself. The woman let out a stifled shriek as his weight pressed against her. Just as he'd hoped, the man in the hat instinctively raised his head at the commotion, affording Gus just enough time to make out the man's features before his head dipped low again.

⁂

Once on the ground at O'Hare, Gus found the information kiosk. Fanning through the brochures, he selected a Chicago city map and then turned his attention to the entertainment offerings. Spotting a narrow, green brochure matching the name of the club Pete had provided during the phone call at the diner, Gus plucked it from the rack. It read 'Tony's Grotto - Oldest and Best Jazz Club on the Swingin' Near North Side. Great Jazz Nightly!' He grabbed a couple of them for good measure and then turned his attention to finding affordable hotels somewhat near the club.

It was still very early in the morning as he took the shuttle to the heart of downtown and then a cab to the hotel he'd selected. The Camden had seen better days. With early check-in not until eleven-thirty AM, he had a long wait. Entering the Coffee Shop in the lobby, Gus took a seat at the counter. It was crowded with office workers on the way to work and late-night revelers reluctant to go home. The man behind the counter didn't bat an eye as Gus ordered a raw egg in a glass of half and half. He merely halfheartedly pointed to a sign posted on the wall behind the grill that warned of the risks of undercooked eggs. "Your peril! You get sick, Man, that's on you!" Gus nodded, and the man filled his order, placing the glass of milky goodness in front of him. Gus picked up his order and made his way to a booth in the back of the room, where he sat, back against the wall, sipping his cream and waiting for the time to pass. Finally, none too soon, he was able to claim his room key.

He didn't even notice the musty, mildew smell as he turned on the AC for white noise. Falling into bed, it would be four PM before he rolled over. Unwrapping the tiny bar of soap, Gus took a lukewarm shower and then, upon exiting the shower stall, switched the tap to hot, draping his rumpled shirt and pants over the shower rod for steaming. Slipping into the scratchy robe provided by the hotel, he sat on the bed and thumbed through the telephone directory, looking for the names Pete had obtained from Nick. First up: the name on the torn scrap of paper found in the impounded car. To his frustration, there was no 'Eleanora Fagan' listed in the Metro area or surrounding vicinities. He did, however, find a listing for a 'Lindy Abrams,' the name on the vehicle registration, the recently released BOLO back in the City, and, he hoped, the name of his mysterious Jane Doe.

Taking a breath, Gus dialed the number and waited while it rang. Five rings later, a breathless female voice answered, "Hullo!!"

Gus responded, "Yes, I'm calling to speak to Lindy."

There was a momentary, awkward pause on the other end. "Ummm... Lindy... Lindy isn't here right now. This is Samantha, her roommate. Can I help you?"

Sensing Samantha's discomfort, Gus took the bull by the horns. "Samantha, my name's Gus Walker. You don't know me, but I have some information about Lindy. Is there somewhere we could talk?" The next words would quickly indicate if his hunch was right. He didn't have to wait long.

The voice on the other end of the line quickly became distraught. "YOU CREEP! What have you done to her??!" Samantha half sobbed, half shrieked.

Gus held his cool and spoke in a reassuring voice, "Samantha, I'm a retired Detective from New York. I've seen Lindy, and she's in need of our help... there's been...an...accident."

"An ACCIDENT??!" Samantha gasped and stammered. "Look. I don't know you from Adam! There's only one place I'll agree to meet you, Mister. I'm a cocktail waitress at Tony's Grotto. If you want to come there tonight, I'll meet you on my break, but word to the wise, we're family down there. The bouncer's one tough SOB, too, and one sign from me, you'll be toast!"

"Fair enough," Gus replied, reaching for a cigarette. "I'll be there at ten."

***

Placing the knife and fork on his greasy plate, Gus paid the check and left a tip. The food and service had been adequate - but just barely. Catching the eye of the Cashier, he asked directions to the nearest drugstore. Walking out the door and heading down the street as directed, Gus turned up the collar on his jacket and walked against the wind. It was chilly and raw. After a few moments, he detected footsteps coming up behind him, keeping pace with his own. Slowing himself, Gus reached in his pocket and retrieved his rumpled pack of smokes. Purposely dropping them on the sidewalk, he stopped suddenly, stooping to pick them up. The figure behind him sped up and walked past - just under the glare of a streetlamp. It was a man wearing a hat, trying to look nonchalant but failing miserably. Gus recognized him immediately, the man from the airplane. Remaining crouched on the sidewalk, Gus listened as the sound of retreating footsteps faded down the street into the distance. Only then did he enter the drugstore.

Walking quickly to the counter and addressing the clerk, Gus requested a pack of cigarettes, some breath mints, and three rolls of antacids. Pulling out his wallet, Gus spoke in a hushed and hurried voice, "Say, Pal, there a backdoor to this place? I've got an irate girlfriend stalking me, and I need to make a fast exit."

A sly grin crossed the young man's face. "I feel your pain!" He chuckled, nodding toward a small hallway at the back of the store. "Through those doors, take a right at the pallet of Red Bulls. There's an alley on the other side of the back door... short trip to the street and the cab stand. She'll never know what happened to ya!"

"Thanks, Friend!" Gus lifted the left corner of his mouth in a forced grin, stuffing his change back in his wallet. "I'll do the same for you sometime."

Making his way into the alley, he kept his eyes peeled as he walked quickly to the street corner and hailed a cab. "Tony's Grotto-just off Rush Street." Gus instructed the driver as he settled in for the ride, glancing out the back window to see if he'd been followed.

"Gotcha covered!" The cabbie responded, cutting his eyes to the rearview mirror and sizing up his fare. "Up 'til just a few months ago, seems everybody I picked up wanted to go there. Now, not so much."

Gus nodded his head, not wanting conversation.

Undaunted, the driver continued, "If it's good, hot jazz you want, The Blue Moon's better. Fabulous trio there tonight!"

Popping an antacid in his mouth, Gus responded, "No Thanks. The Grotto will do fine." Turning his gaze out the window, he could feel the cabbie watching him. Finally, Gus spoke, "So what happened to change things?"

The driver smiled faintly, relieved to have a bit of conversation to fill the time. "Not really sure. Tony, the owner, always made the Grotto a home for good musicians. Used to be The Thing to play there. Story goes, Tony was a helluva jazz guitarist himself, back in the day. Played with all the greats in the fifties and sixties. That is, until they found him in an alley one night, shit kicked out of him, and his right hand all mangled up like hamburger."

This last comment caught Gus off guard and piqued his interest. "What the hell?" He questioned, curious for more details.

"Yep!" The cabbie continued. "Lost all his fingers on that hand. Never was able to play again. Don't go dippin' your pecker in a Made man's piece!"

Gus grunted his acknowledgment and raised his eyebrows at the imagery. The two fell back into silence as the car made its way toward the Near North Side. Streetlights rhythmically passed, and sirens sounded in the distance. Gus grimaced and reached for the open pack of antacids. Popping another round, he pressed himself into the balding velour seat cover. Finally, after five minutes of silence, the cab pulled to a stop outside a small hotel. Paying his fare, Gus threw in a sizable tip. "Thanks for the history lesson. Club inside here?"

The driver nodded and waved his hand toward the front door. "Sure thing. Down the stairs to the basement. It's named the Grotto for a reason. Have fun, Mister!"

With that, the car pulled away, leaving Gus standing alone on the curb in the biting wind, surveying the scene.

Chapter Nine

Opening the door, Gus stepped inside. Just as the cabbie had said, there were signs pointing the way to the downstairs club. The walls of the stairway leading to Tony's Grotto were covered with autographed photos and reviews of the artists that had performed there. Jazz fan that he was, Gus allowed himself a moment to linger and look. His gaze crossed over several, and then, without warning, Gus stopped dead in his tracks, eyes narrowing and pulse quickening. Smiling and full of life, there she was: his Jane Doe- staring out at him from a black-framed poster hanging midway on the Grotto's 'Wall of Fame'. Gus leaned in. 'Appearing Nightly: Lindy Abrams. The Grotto's Very Own Sultry Siren!' The words trumpeted as though announcing Sarah Vaughan herself. He'd never heard of her, but that meant little at this point. Her eyes were laughing, and her smile warm and inviting. There was no evidence of the trauma and terror Gus had seen in her back at the hospital. He found himself taken aback by her genuine loveliness. The find momentarily startled him. Finally collecting himself, he continued on, stopping at the landing and surveying the subterranean nightspot. Dark and smelling of booze, cigarette smoke, and stale popcorn, the club was a throwback to the late fifties. Next to the rarely used coat check counter, a dice girl sat at a small table, shaking dice in a cup and rolling them out aimlessly. Not many patrons- but it was still relatively early. The bartender stood cutting limes behind a long, wooden bar, the shelves behind him jampacked with booze bottles, all reflected in the floor-to-ceiling mirrored wall. Above the bar, in a huge gold gilt frame, hung a picture of a naked woman reclining on a rock at the beach. It was a masterpiece of breasts and bad taste. There were aquatic murals on one side of the room, fishing nets, plastic seaweed and crustaceans, and glass floats- every Grotto cliche known to man. Curved booths sat mostly empty, their cracked, red leather seats less than inviting, despite the candles glowing on the tabletops. More small tables were gathered around the bandstand, where a lone piano player sat playing softly- a tune Gus didn't recognize. The place smacked of Central Casting's take on the old Mafia, and it was clear to him only hardcore Jazz fans or deeply devoted friends of Tony patronized this archaic music haven. Taking a seat at the bar and catching the bartender's eye, Gus ordered Cutty, neat. As the man behind the bar poured, Gus asked, "Samantha around? She's expecting me."

The bartender raised an eyebrow and looked at Gus intently. "Yeah. She told me to watch for you. I'll let her know you're here." Came the terse response.

Picking up his drink, Gus had the distinct feeling several pairs of eyes were watching. He sat calmly and sipped.

Tony approached first. Stretching out his left hand in greeting, he walked toward Gus, maintaining eye contact. His right arm hung motionless by his side. Rising from the bar stool, Gus quickly glanced for the mangled stump of a hand the cabbie had told him about. Sure enough, there it was, devoid of fingers, completely useless, and somewhat resembling a fleshy hockey puck.

Tony made no notice of Gus's stolen glance. "Hey. How you doin'. I'm Tony Russo. I own this place." The voice was raspy from years of cheap cigars and too many Cubas Libres. He continued, "I understand you've seen my missing songbird..."

Gus looked Tony squarely in the face, and for a brief moment, the two men stood sizing up each other. Finally, Gus replied, "When Samantha joins us, we can all sit down and have a chat."

Tony's right eye twitched, and he lightly pounded his good hand on the bar. Gus couldn't gauge if he did so from agitation, anger, agreement- or an attempt to intimidate. Gus returned to his bar stool and his drink. In a matter of minutes, a woman approached. Tall, big-boned, a brassy blonde in her mid-thirties, her jaw was set. It was clear to Gus she wasn't the trusting type and had come by that trait the hard way. Setting her cocktail tray on the bar, she stated curtly, "You must be Gus Walker. I'm Samantha. We're all very anxious to hear what you know about Lindy." Tony motioned to one of the curved booths, but Gus ignored the suggestion and headed instead for a table in the darkest corner of the club. Reaching it before his companions, he selected the chair nearest the back wall, setting down his glass, marking his spot. The two reluctantly followed, glancing at each other as they walked.

Once settled, Gus revealed what he knew of the case involving Lindy, being careful to leave out the most disturbing and pertinent details. He then asked Tony and Samantha to fill in the backstory as to what took Lindy from the Grotto to New York City.

Drawing a deep breath, Samantha glanced uneasily at Tony. He nodded in her direction. Only then did she begin to speak. "What's it always take for a woman to turn her back on her day-to-day life - her friends - her dreams - and run away? A damn man! It's always a damn man!" Samantha spat out the words with a tone of disgust and barely contained rage. Gus sat silent as she continued. "I watched the night it happened and then had to hear about it constantly after the asshole broke her heart. One night, several months ago, Lindy had just finished going over a new arrangement of 'Stairway to the Stars'. She was great... it was our slow night -same night every week- so Tony hosts open mic night to bring in a fresh crowd. Lindy was in a good mood; in walks this guy, and he takes a table right up front by the bandstand. He has a couple drinks and listens to Lindy and her trio for a while. I waited on him. Nice enough guy, I guess, but he had that look that always spells trouble; a bit too pretty and pulled together. Smelled too good. Looked too good. WAS too good. Ya know??"

Gus nodded, sipped his scotch, and remained silent.

Samantha fidgeted in her chair, her fingers playing with the chain around her neck - a gold crucifix. Glancing briefly at Tony, she drew a breath and continued, "Anyway, very long, miserable, story short, his name was David Ailesworth. Helluva jazz guitarist. Had just arrived in town from somewhere down in Texas and was here to make a name for himself musically. Didn't take long... a real fast mover, that one. In no time, he'd convinced Lindy to fire her guys - all three of them! It quickly became the two of them - on stage and off. They were inseparable - and the crowds started flocking in to hear them!" Tony nodded, and Gus noticed a look of anger flash across the man's face as Samantha continued. "I hadn't seen Lindy this happy or inspired in years. At first, we thought it was great. They got rave reviews in print... interviews on TV... there was talk of recording contracts, bookings in larger venues, you name it. It was unfolding just like it did for Cinderella!" Samantha stopped a moment and looked sad.

Gus downed the last swallow in his glass. Casting a look at Tony, Gus fished in his pocket for his roll of antacids. Popping one in his mouth, he sucked on it while asking Tony, "What did you think about all this? The possibility of bigger things taking your prize 'songbird' away from your place?"

Tony grunted and took a swallow from his glass. "I hated that son of a bitch - but it did me good to see Lindy so happy. She's a good kid. I knew she needed -and deserved- a bigger break than I could give her - but damn straight, I was gonna milk it for all I could." Casting a sideways glance at Gus and raising an eyebrow, Tony added for good measure, "I ain't no fuckin' fool!"

Gus nodded, finding Tony's honesty refreshing. Looking back at Samantha, he crunched the antacid like a piece of candy. "Go on." He urged.

"You want another?" Samantha instinctively asked, eyeing Gus's empty glass.

"Nope. I'm good. Thanks." Gus replied and smiled somewhat. "What happened next?"

This time, Tony jumped in. "What happened?! I'll tell ya what happened! The fucker strung her and me along, and just when we were both good and hooked, he up and dumps her. Starts screwin' some prissy, high rent piece of ass out here 'on tour'!" With that, Tony raised his good hand and made half an air quote. Gus could see the blow still stung. Furrowing his brow, Gus tried to fit this new plot twist into his storyline.

Samantha looked at him and noting his facial expression, continued by way of clarification, "I'm sure you've heard of the great One Name Wonder herself: 'Francesca'! Gus wasn't up on pop culture but was vaguely familiar with the name. He nodded, and Samantha continued. "Bitch blew through here on tour, and, user that he was, David couldn't get to her fast enough. He practically walked over Lindy's back to get out of here. Broke her heart.

Gus sat for a moment processing all he'd heard. Finally, he spoke. "So, how did all this get Lindy to New York City?"

Tony banged his fist on the table and answered, obvious anger in his voice. "I'll tell ya how. The bastard up and left Lindy -and the club- with no warning! ZERO! Fucker just up and leaves! The crowds stop comin'- and I'm left with a heartbroken singer that can't sing! She even tries to off herself - TWICE! Christ, already." Gus watched Tony carefully during this outburst. Despite the 'tough guy' bravado, there was a genuine air of righteous indignation and true pity in his voice.

Samantha spoke again, "For weeks, Lindy couldn't eat or sleep. She started drinking - and Lindy DOESN'T drink. Then came the pills..."

"What kind?" Gus asked with interest.

"The usual... sleeping and pain - all prescription, but still..."

Gus nodded.

"I held her job open for her as long as I could but..." Tony said, bewildered. "She couldn't stand to be here anymore."

Looking at Tony, Samantha smiled a faint, loving smile. "That was big of you, Tony. We all know you took a big hit doing that." Samantha then looked at Gus. "Business went into the tank hard."

"Still in the crapper!" Tony hissed. "This went on for weeks."

Samantha returned to her story. "I never knew what I was gonna find when I went home after work; Lindy drunk? Lindy passed out and needing to be raced to the ER? Lindy sobbing and wanting to die? It was just too much. Something had to give! One night while I was on my break here, a customer told me about some Billie Holiday competition in New York City they'd heard about. They sang too and were going to enter."

Gus's interest piqued again. "A Billie Holiday competition?" He asked inquisitively. "What's that?"

"She was a jazz singer way back in the day. A real Great..." Tony chimed in.

Gus nodded. "Yeah. That I know. But what's with this competition?" He looked over at Samantha as he posed his question.

Tears were in her eyes, and she took a deep breath. "Some singing competition to find the next HER." She replied. "The top prize was supposed to be some big recording deal."

"Was supposed to be??" Gus questioned with emphasis.

"Yeah." Samantha answered as more tears came. "I talked Lindy into going there and entering. I just wanted to try to get her back into Life and Living again, ya know? Moving forward. She was so lost and miserable. She packed up and went the second they accepted her entry fee and application. I think she thought it would be a way to win David back. God only knows why she would've wanted him back, the pissant." Pausing for a moment, Samantha stared off into the distance. Suddenly, she began to sob. "It was only a matter of days after she got there we stopped hearing from her. She was supposed to call in every day, and for a few days, she did - like clockwork. Then we stopped hearing from her. There hasn't been a trace since!"

Tony reached out his one good hand and patted Samantha as she cried. "Girl, we've been all through this. Wasn't your fault." Wiping her tears, she nodded. Gus thought a moment and then spoke, a curious tone in his voice. "There has to be a cell phone..." Tony nodded and replied, "Rang for three days and we left a ton of voice messages. Damn thing finally quit connecting. We got nuthin', and she never returned our calls." This started Samantha's tears all over again. Looking up, Tony loudly snapped his fingers and raised his voice over the few patrons in the place, "Hey Paul, three brandies here!" The bartender nodded.

After a few short moments, a waitress brought the fresh round. Taking one of the snifters off the tray, he handed it gently to Samantha. "Drink this, and take the rest of the night off, Girl." Samantha patted his arm, nodded in appreciation, and raised the bulbous glass to her lips, taking a large sip to steady her nerves.

After calming a bit, she looked back at Gus. He spoke matter-of-factly, "I'm staying at the Camden... should be here one more day. If you can locate any information on this contest or where you sent Lindy's application and fee, I need to know." As he spoke, he scribbled his cell number on one of the cocktail napkins. "Anything else you can think of -whether you think it's anything or not- CALL ME." He looked at Tony and Samantha. They looked back at him and nodded. Gus questioned curiously, almost as an afterthought, "How did Lindy sound the last time you talked to her?"

Samantha thought a moment and then answered, a pained look on her face. "She sounded odd... kind of out of it - but afraid at the same time. She didn't really tell me anything, you know? It was just a tone in her voice...slow and strange."

Gus nodded, deep in thought. Downing his brandy in one big swallow, he wiped the corners of his mouth with his fingers. "Thanks for your time." With this, he rose from the table and began to walk toward the club entrance. Stopping and turning back to Tony and Samantha, he asked his final question. "Does the name 'Eleanora Fagan' mean anything to you?" Samantha shook her head 'No'.

Tony squinted his eyes for a moment and then answered, "Yeah, Man. That's Billie Holiday's real name. What the fuck you wanna know that for??!" Gus raised his eyebrows and nodded without answering. With this, he made his way out of the club and back up the stairs, leaving the darkened Grotto behind him. Back on the landing, he paused one last time, taking in every nuance of the poster featuring Lindy.

Two cab rides later, back at the hotel, he felt assured he hadn't been followed. Too late to check in at Angie's, Gus tossed his cell on the bedside table and crawled into bed. Three minutes after his head hit the pillow, he was out, believing things were starting to look up. He slept through the tone notifying him of incoming delayed voice messages and missed calls. There were several, and they were Urgent.

CHAPTER TEN

Gus woke at seven AM, very late by his usual routine. The events of the previous night had whirred through his brain, keeping him up well past two. Lying in bed, he reached for his pack of smokes on the bedside table, removing his cellphone from its charger as he did so. As he reached for his lighter, his phone notifications began to chime repeatedly. Surprised and curious, Gus took a drag, put on his reading glasses, and scrolled through his waiting voice messages. There were five, yet his phone hadn't rung in hours. "What the hell???!" He mumbled, queuing up the first call. The number was Pete's.

"Gus - Pete. We've got trouble, Man. BIG. Call me as soon as you get this!" Gus glanced at the timestamp. Eleven thirty PM, the night before. Queuing the next message, he glanced at the number. The call had come from Jessie just after midnight—no message left. Two more calls placed shortly after, one right after the other, and again, no messages. The fifth message then queued. It was also from Jessie. Gus accessed it and immediately, his worst fears were realized. This time, there was a message - and it was breathless and tense. Gus froze motionless, listening intently as he played it twice on speakerphone. "Gus - it's Jess. We're on the move.

They've found us! GO! GO!! Get to the car, quick!" Jessie was running and whispering commands as she spoke. Gus could hear fear and raw determination in her voice. The message continued, "Don't know where we're headed, but they're about one minute behind us. Will update as we can! Pray!" The message ended abruptly, but before it did, he heard Theresa's terrified voice cry out, "Oh My God! They're coming!!" Jumping up from the bed, Gus tamped out his cigarette in the ashtray and grabbed his clothes, heart and mind racing. How did he not hear his phone ringing? With shaking hands, he grabbed his cell and checked the settings. All were as they should be. He'd kept his phone charged, on and with him constantly since leaving Jessie at the airport... and then, it dawned on him. He'd spent two and a half hours in the Grotto with Samantha and Tony, the club located in the basement of the hotel. He must've had no reception the entire time he'd been there, and it had taken some time for his messages to be delivered once he'd left the club. Now dressed and running on pure adrenaline, Gus grabbed his jacket and quickly made his way to the elevator. Pressing the down arrow repeatedly, he waited for what seemed an eternity. The elevator didn't come. Glancing down the hallway, he ran to the stairwell and began the descent from the fifth floor, dialing Pete's number as he ran. There was no answer. Bounding quickly down the stairs, Gus next called Jessie. Also, no answer. Her phone rang three times, triggering a voicemail. Continuing to make his way down the stairs as fast as he could, Gus left a message after the beep. "Jess - just got your message. Was out of range and didn't know it. On my way! CALL ME!!"

Disconnecting, Gus reached the lobby. Stopping at the front desk, he rang the bell for service. The desk clerk came out of the office, surprised to see Gus standing there, breathing heavily.

"Good Morning, Mr. Walker! Are you checking out?"

Gus nodded 'Yes' and added, "I'm in a rush, please!"

The clerk nodded and reached for the room bill. As he did, he asked in a cheerful manner, "Did your friend find you OK?"

Gus glanced at the clerk with a questioning look. "My friend?" He asked curiously.

"That gentleman that's here to take you to your breakfast meeting. He went up the elevator to your room just a minute ago!"

"Oh... him...." Gus replied, shooting a glance at the elevator and around the hotel lobby. "Change of plans." He added, "Look, I'm running terribly late. How much do I owe you??" The clerk looked at the invoice and began his calculations. Glancing toward the elevator and again at the stairwell door, Gus fumbled for the cash in his pocket. Pulling out two crumpled one-hundred-dollar bills, he tossed them at the clerk, stating, "Keep the change," as he bolted toward the front door. With that, Gus sprinted down the block, hailing a cab as he ran. One minute later, the elevator of the Camden reached the lobby with a ceremonious 'ding'. The doors opened, and a man wearing a trench coat exited, making his way through the lobby, a hard look of disappointment and determination on his face. Reaching the exit, he lifted the hat he was carrying by his side and placed it on his head, pulling it down tightly. The unused .38 and silencer stuffed deep in his coat pocket were just itching to be used.

***

The day had passed in a panicked blur. Gus had made his way to O'Hare without being tailed. Once there, he'd had to wait for the flight to Elmira-Corning Regional. He felt like a sitting duck, and he didn't like it. Upon landing, Gus rented a car and made the drive to Andover; along the way, placing several unanswered calls to both Pete and Jessie. There was a deep gnawing in his gut, unlike the usual. By now, the sun was slipping low on the horizon, and the mid-March light was fading fast. Arriving at Angie's in the dark was not ideal, but he would have to take his chances. Gus pulled onto the country lane leading to the farm, guiding the car to a stop along the drainage ditch. Keeping the engine running, he glanced carefully around at his surroundings. Nothing out of the usual. Pulling his weapon from its holster, Gus checked it. Ready for action. He wished he felt the same. Although his security job felt suffocating, there were times it afforded him important perks. Now was one such time. Being able to carry while traveling almost made it worthwhile. Reaching into his jacket pocket, he pulled out his extra ammo. Just five rounds. Not much - but all he had. He'd intended to purchase more back in Chicago, but events hadn't allowed. He grimaced as he realized he'd have to make do. Gus sat in silence a moment more as the light around him dwindled and the car engine idled. Finally, drawing a deep breath, he uttered a heartfelt "Amen." Making the sign of the cross over himself as he ended his prayer. Throwing the car in gear, Gus drove the last two miles, not knowing what he'd find, as he rounded the bend to Angie's drive. The house was dark - no lights anywhere. Gravel crunched under the tires as Gus pulled the car to a stop. He surveyed the scene. There were no obvious cars on the property. Finally, reaching for the keys, he switched off the ignition and stepped into the eerie silence. Making his way toward the porch, he pulled his revolver and held it at the ready as he reached the front door. Swallowing hard and collecting his nerve, Gus reached down and slowly turned the knob. The door gave way with a muffled creak. No one greeted him, but he could immediately see the room had been ransacked, furniture overturned as though during a violent struggle.

Making his way through the chaotic mess, Gus stepped silently toward the back of the house and the kitchen, stopping briefly at each bedroom as he made his way. As he got to what had been Theresa's room, Gus winced, his eyes inadvertently filling with tears. The bedspread had been ripped from the bed, as though clawed off, and pillows were scattered across the room. A bedside lamp lay smashed on the floor, and a smear of blood had dripped down the wall next to it. Gus drew a breath and then continued on. Entering the kitchen, he found the scene equally disturbing; tables overturned, dishes shattered, coffee spilled and pooled on the floor... and then, he saw it. There, in the last rays of the fading light, Angie's lifeless body lay sprawled on the floor - battered and bloody. Gus groaned and made his way to her. Rolling the elderly woman onto her back, Gus smoothed her bloody hair and gently attempted to close her eyes. It was too late; rigor mortis had already set in. The lids wouldn't close, leaving Angie staring up at him in wide-eyed terror. Gus looked away, and as he did, something on the floor next to Angie's body caught his attention. Pulling out his cellphone, Gus used the light to see by. Bending low to the floor, he found three letters written in blood: U K R. He stared a moment and then reached down, taking hold of Angie's right hand. Sure enough, her index finger was coated in now-congealed brownish red. She'd used her own blood to leave this last cryptic clue for him. What it meant, Gus had no idea, but he made careful note of it. As he stood, his eye was pulled to a florist box sitting partially opened on the kitchen counter. The low light from his cell revealed the contents. Gus's jaw tightened. There, wilting and already decaying, sat four gardenias. Grabbing the lid, Gus checked the florist's name and address. The flowers had been delivered by courier from an Andover florist shop.

Turning his attention toward the back porch, Gus crossed the kitchen, exited the house, and made his way down the back stairs, heading toward the barn, where the hearse and Jessie's car had been hidden. Making his way slowly in the dark, Gus's foot soon hit upon something heavy. He stumbled, falling flat to the ground. The air temporarily knocked out of him; Gus struggled to breathe as he scrambled for the cellphone that had fallen from his hand. Quickly locating it, Gus activated it for light and turned to face the object he'd tripped over. The thin, wiry body of Arlo lay still and stiff in the weeds, shot in the chest and throat slit for good measure. Heart pounding, Gus scrambled to his feet and raced toward the barn, praying with all his might he'd find Jessie's car gone. As he neared the building, he breathed a sigh of relief. Jessie's Mustang was indeed missing. Glancing around the barn, Gus was jolted by the ringing of his phone. The ringtone pierced the silent darkness. Grabbing his cell and taking cover in the barn, he answered in a hoarse whisper. Gus stood, his jaw set and a look of incredulity in his eyes as he listened to the voice on the other end. It was Detective Nick Spinoza. The voice on the other end was monotone and simply stated, "Mr. Walker, this is Nick. Sir... Uncle Pete's dead." Gus drew a breath as he listened to the young man's accounting. Nick was filled with fear, but Gus detected an equal measure of resolve as the young Detective spoke.

"When, where, and how?" Gus heard himself ask, his many years of training kicking in, overriding his tangled emotions.

"Shot to death in his office, sometime overnight. No one saw or heard anything. They went looking for him when he missed a meeting this morning. Quite a mess."

"Any calling cards?" Gus pressed for details.

"Yessir." Came Nick's concise answer. Gus could tell from Nick's inflection he didn't need to ask for further details. Drawing another breath, Gus responded, "You on a burner, Nick?"

"Affirmative, Sir."

"Good." Gus replied and then continued, "Nick, listen closely. I'm at DeAngelo's Truck Farm, ten miles outside Andover. They've hit here too. I've lost my two best informants - both fatalities. Jessie, my daughter Theresa, a nurse and our vic are in the wind -no clue where they've gone- but these maniacs are about a minute behind them. I need you to call this hit in anonymously. Where do you want us to meet? We're next, you know."

There was a long silence, and then, finally, Nick spoke. "My uncle's office is crawling right now, and our bald 'friend' is heading the investigation. I got away by telling them I was needed at the hospital for acting-next-of-kin duties. They won't be looking for me until tomorrow, and if I call in, I can request an extra day..."

Nick paused to collect his thoughts, but Gus drove the point home: "The trick will be staying alive tonight! Nick, can you make your way to Scranton forthwith? Just as soon as you can." Nick mumbled his dazed agreement. Gus immediately took control. "Son, I know you're a skilled cop, but you're in this too deep. It's become too personal. I need you to listen and do what I tell you now."

Nick answered in a more collected tone, "Yessir."

Gus then continued, "Get to the nearest car rental and ditch your vehicle. Rent something nondescript and reliable. DO NOT touch base with your family. Repeat DO NOT. Meet me in Scranton just as soon as you can. I'll be at the Lamplighter Motel on Kane Street. Get there ASAP and keep your eyes peeled. You pick up a tail you can't shake, get your ass to the nearest squirrel cage and call me! For godsake do your damnedest to get as far out of the city as possible before seeking help. We don't know how deep this runs - and they're coming for us!" Gus disconnected from the call and made his way back to the kitchen. Feeling his way over to Angie's corpse, he again used the light of his cellphone to locate a dish towel. Taking it over to Angie's bloody message, he cast his eyes over the three letters, emblazoning them on his memory: U K R. He had no idea what it meant, but he knew he didn't want anyone else finding it. Taking the dish towel, Gus wiped at the coagulated blood, dabbing at it until it became a meaningless smear on the wooden floor. Reverently folding the blood-stained cloth, Gus again smoothed Angie's disheveled, matted hair. "Thank you, My Friend..." he whispered. "For this, and so very much more...." Touching a finger to his lips, he then placed the farewell kiss on Angie's forehead.

With that, Gus made his way back to the car, started the engine, and roared down the darkened road toward Scranton, the bloody rag lying on the seat next to him. As he merged onto the highway several minutes later, a line of cop cars roared past him, flying in the opposite direction, overheads blazing. Gus watched them blow past in the direction of Angie's farm. "Good Boy, Nick..." Gus muttered as he punched the accelerator and disappeared into the night.

CHAPTER ELEVEN

At precisely ten thirty PM, Gus pulled his car into the parking lot of the Lamplighter Motel. It hadn't changed much since his last visit and still sported the same seedy quality. The trip to Scranton had passed in a blur as the events of the past twenty-four hours raced through his mind while he drove. Gus's eyes burned, and he was now at the far side of exhaustion. His clothes were disheveled, he smelled of stale tobacco smoke and sweat, was hungry and greatly in need of a shower. The image of Angie's and Arlo's dead eyes haunted him every time he blinked.

Taking the key from the desk clerk, Gus made his way to his room, unlocked the door, and flipped on the light switch. The room that greeted him was modest - but clean. Closing and locking the door behind him, Gus walked over and sat down on the edge of the bed, collecting himself for a moment. He thought of Theresa, Jessie, Lindy, and Nurse Silvers. His mind then turned to Pete. It hadn't been a full week of this case consuming his life, and he'd already lost his three best informants - two of which he considered dear friends -his old partner- and now, perhaps, what remained of his own family. He was in deep, and there was only one way out unless he considered death a viable option. At this point, he wasn't even sure about his thoughts on that. Running his hands through his hair, it felt greasy, grimy, and filled with stench. Gus grimaced and stood, walking into the bathroom. Flipping on the light, he made his way to the shower and waited for the hot steamy water to build, removing his clothes while it did. Next, he unwrapped the cheap bar of soap and worked it into a hefty lather under the shower stream. The hot water felt lifegiving, and Gus groaned and did his best to suds away the awfulness of the past several hours. Only allowing himself a few moments, he then turned off the shower, stepped onto the threadbare bathmat, and dried himself with another threadbare towel. The exhaustion was crushing, but he had to keep moving.

A few minutes later, Gus stood once again fully dressed in his disheveled clothes, running a comb through his wet hair. Catching a glimpse of himself in the steamy mirror, he was surprised by the hollow, empty look in his eyes. He stood facing himself a moment longer, feeling the full weight of it all pressing in on him. "Dear Lord in Heaven... Save us. Save me..." he half-muttered, half-begged under his breath. It was one of the most heartfelt and humble prayers he'd prayed since Mary had died. And he meant it - with all his heart.

Despite his years on the force and knowing his instincts were some of the best in the business, Gus knew he was in over his head. The years away from the job had softened him a bit, and the loss of Mary had cast him adrift. He felt lost and simply not up to the task - but he was in it now and had managed to drag everyone he cared about into the abyss with him. It was going to take everything he had to get them all to the other side alive. "Head in the game, Pal..." He said out loud.

Just then, there was a muffled knock at the door, shaking Gus back to reality. Grabbing his gun, he made his way to the door and looked through the peephole, finding Nick standing in the hall. Quickly unlocking the door, Gus allowed Nick entrance, casting an instinctive glance down the hallway. The young detective was well-pulled together but worn-looking. "Any trouble?" Gus asked.

Nick shook his head 'No.' "No one tailed me." He answered.

Locking the door again, Gus glanced at Nick and motioned for him to sit. "Pizza, OK?" Gus asked.

Nick nodded. "Don't feel like eating but yeah...."

Gus nodded his agreement. "We've got to keep our strength up and grab what we can get while we can get it." He spoke, pulling a shabby phonebook out of the desk drawer and looking up the number to the pizza joint three blocks away. Using the room phone, Gus then placed the order: one large supreme pie, two large coffees, two bottles of water, and three orders of breadsticks. Turning his attention back to Nick, he found the young detective looking at him with eyebrows raised. "They'll deliver in thirty minutes." Gus stated and then added, the breadsticks are our emergency rations for the road." Nick shot a brief nod in Gus's direction. "I'm sorry about Pete," Gus added with feeling. "He was one in a million..."

The color drained from Nick's face, and tears came to his eyes. "Christ Almighty!" The young man sputtered. "Mr. Walker, what the hell is happening?? What the fuck are we into??! I mean shit!"

Gus observed Nick's hands begin to tremble. He drew a steadying breath and spoke. "Son, no doubt about it - we're in deep shit. DEEP SHIT." Nick turned and looked wide-eyed at Gus. "Best I can figure," Gus continued, "we're in the middle of the Mob and one of their 'enterprises'- but this isn't a Mob I know, and it's not shaking out like run-of-the-mill Vice."

Nick nodded, paced a bit, and then sat back down on the edge of the bed. He then spoke in a quiet, half-whisper, eyes staring straight ahead. "They found Uncle Pete slumped over his desk - shot once through his left temple. Must've never known what... who hit him."

Gus sat for a moment in silence and finally asked, "Did you call in the scene at DeAngelo's?"

"Yessir," Nick answered. "Just like you wanted. Stopped at a convenience store and phoned it in. They should be working the case now, I expect."

"Good." Gus replied, inwardly relieved to find Nick was truly trustworthy. And then, cutting his eyes to Nick, Gus added, "Call me Gus, son." Nick nodded and shot an appreciative smile Gus's way. The smile was brief and quickly faded. The two men sat in silence a few moments more. Suddenly, there was a knock at the door. Gus glanced at his watch. Weapons drawn, Gus and Nick both covered the door. "Yeah??" Gus grunted. "Who is it?"

"Anthony's Pizza Delivery!" A teenage voice croaked in response.

Gus looked through the peephole to find a pimply boy in his late teens standing in the hallway juggling a large pizza box and packed beverage holder. Keeping the chain in place, Gus cut his eyes at Nick as he slowly opened the door. Sizing up the visitor, Gus assessed the situation. "How much do I owe?" He asked through the partially opened door. Nick stood positioned on the other side out of sight. His face tense and rigid.

"Fifty-four bucks, Mister."

Pulling sixty from his wallet, Gus handed the money to the boy. "Leave the stuff in the hall." He directed gruffly. Eyeing his tip and finding it lacking, the boy rolled his eyes and did as instructed, turning and sauntering back the way he came, stuffing his earbuds back in place as he went. Once Gus was certain he'd gone, he slipped the chain from the door, grabbed the food, pulled it inside, and immediately locked the door behind him. Opening the box and handing Nick a slice of pie and a pile of napkins, he then served himself.

Gus chewed and watched Nick closely, his mind preoccupied. Finally, he spoke. "Why only four??"

Nick swallowed a half-chewed bite and looked quizzically at Gus. "Why only four what?" Came the questioning response.

Gus raised his eyebrows, surprised to know he'd actually spoken out loud. Looking at Nick, he again questioned. "Why only four gardenias in the box on the counter at Angie's... there were FIVE women!" Nick's forehead furrowed, and he struggled to follow Gus's line of thought. Gus nodded his head slowly and counted on his left hand, still holding a slice of pizza in his right. "Angie... Jessie... Theresa... Lindy - our vic... Nurse Silvers... FIVE women, FOUR gardenias. An oversight by the florist? An oversight by whoever called in the order? Not an oversight at all...?"

Nick's eyes squinted. "What're you gettin' at Gus?" The young detective asked, placing his pizza on a napkin and licking his fingers.

Gus could see the detective's mind was starting to whir. "How did these bastards find Angie's farm? How did they know where we'd go and who all would be there?" The two men sat in tense silence for a moment, deep concern growing.

"Fuck Man. There's a plant!" Nick all but spit as he uttered his realization.

"Precisely." Gus groaned. "Nurse Silvers has to be it...." Nick and Gus looked at each other. Gus stood and began to pace. If he was right, then Jessie, Theresa, and Lindy were dead meat. The enemy was in the car with them and knew their every move before they even made it. "Christ!" Gus exclaimed, a hint of controlled panic rising in his voice.

Nick stood and walked over to his briefcase. Pulling a manila folder from the zippered pouch, he opened it and cast his gaze at Gus. "Gus, I did a little digging yesterday. There's something else not right."

Gus glanced at Nick and, walking over to the file, took it from Nick's hand, looking questioningly as he did so. "What's this?" Gus asked as his eyes scanned the first page.

"Tox screens on the three vics Brad was working in the city. He told me they were all clean except for the usual party crap." Gus nodded, recalling the conversation he'd had with Brad that day at the diner. He'd asked him about the tox screens himself and recalled Brad's response: 'Just the usual party crap: weed, E, and some prescription opioids...' Looking at the file, Gus cut his eyes to Nick. "Whatcha got?"

Nick nodded with his chin toward the opened folder and answered, "Devil's Breath. Every single one of them."

"Scopolamine??" Gus clarified.

"Yes." Nick answered, his voice low.

Gus turned his gaze on Nick, and it was piercing. "When you say ALL of them - are you including the vic from Madison General, too?" He had a very bad feeling rising deep within him and held his breath, waiting for Nick's reply.

"Yessir. I called in a favor and got my hands on her file too."

Gus stood silent for a moment; his jaw clenched tight. "I met in detail with Mark Anderson at the hospital. He said nothing about this."

Gus and Nick looked at each other. "Yessir...." Nick finally responded.

"SHIT," Gus hissed. "SHIT SHIT SHIT!!!" Tossing the file on the bed, Gus turned to Nick, a look of fury on his face. "I've been played from the Get."

Nick cleared his throat. "Yessir. It certainly seems that way."

Chapter Twelve

Now agitated and enraged, Gus fought to keep his emotions and racing thoughts in check. Striding to the bed, he reached down, grabbed his cell, dialed, and waited. Nick sat silently watching. A moment passed, and Nick could hear a man's voice on the other end. It sounded sleepy and questioning. "Yeah..?" Gus cut his steely gaze straight at the wall in front of him and spoke in a low voice, "Jack. Gus."

The voice on the other end yawned and replied with surprise, "Gus! Man, you know what time it is? Great to hear from you, but I..."

Without hesitation or warning, Gus blurted out in a commanding tone, "SHARK."

Nick could hear the man on the other end immediately snap into action. "Gus, what the hell??!"

"You heard me." Gus answered and said again: "SHARK."

Nick's forehead furrowed as he watched and listened intently. The voice on the other end peppered questions: "You still the same size?"

"Nope. Better go up a size - or two..." Gus answered without emotion.

"What calibers you need?"

"Thirty-eights and Nines." Gus again replied and then motioned questioningly to Nick, who nodded his agreement. "And lots of them."

"Need rations?"

"Yes. Enough for two -but we have to move fast- so portable."

"Same place?"

"Yes." Nick heard the last bit before Gus unceremoniously disconnected. "Give me three. I'll be there."

Ending the call, Gus tossed the cell back on the bed and checked the time. Next, he breathed heavily and cast a hard look at Nick. "I'm gonna need you to forget that call, Son." Nick looked at Gus. Gus noted an uneasy expression cross the young man's face. "Well, hell..." Gus then spoke with a small grin of irony. "I'm getting you killed... I guess the least I can do is come clean..." Nick responded with a quick snort. It was as close to a chuckle as he could come, given the circumstances. Gus then continued. "A few years back, Brad and I worked a case that was an absolute SOB...the one that almost took me out...much like now..." He added by way of full disclosure. "Couldn't tell who we could trust and who we couldn't -and we had to get seriously small for a few days- seriously quick."

Nick listened closely. "That guy I just called..." Gus continued. "Retired FBI. Knows all the games and all the players - a Master Spook. He saved me and Brad, and we formed a helluva bond. We made a pact: he ever gets in trouble, he calls us... well... now ME..." Gus grimaced as he corrected himself. "I ever get in trouble - I call him, no questions asked."

"Except for the important ones!" Nick commented in amazement.

Gus nodded and then continued, "He'll bring us what we need - and can maybe help us get a handle on who -and what- we're up against."

"So, SHARK'S the word!" Nick said out loud.

Gus cut him a look and nodded, adding solemnly, "Now, forget it. For everyone's sake."

Sitting in silence, Nick looked around the room. "So, Brad hid out here when things got hot?"

"Yes." Gus answered matter-of-factly. No one spoke for a moment, and then Gus continued, "He'll be here by three thirty. Let's grab some shuteye. We need it." Nick nodded as Gus pulled a chair over to the door and placed the chair back under the knob, wiggling it for good measure. "Won't do a damn thing but make noise if they come for us - but that may make us or break us." Nick looked Gus in the eye, swallowed hard, and nodded, reclining on the floor by the wall and wedging a pillow under his head for a modicum of comfort. Gus sprawled out on the bed and, within moments, was snoring.

Jolted awake by a muffled knock at the door, Gus sat bolt upright, grabbing his gun and tossing a pillow in Nick's direction. Nick grabbed his weapon, rising quickly to his feet. The two men exchanged a glance as they approached the locked door. Looking through the peephole, Gus asked in a hoarse whisper, "Who loves spinach?"

"Popeye." The man on the other side whispered in response.

Slipping the chair away and removing the chain, Gus only partially opened the door. Nick watched with keen interest as a thin, older man in remarkable shape entered the room, several bags in tow. Gus immediately closed and locked the door behind him. The man tossed the bags onto the bed and turned to face Gus, who stood smiling, hand outstretched. "Good to see you, My Friend." Gus spoke in a warm and sincere voice.

"You too, Augustus, although I'd wish for better circumstances." With that, the man turned his gaze to Nick and waited.

"Nick Spinoza. Detective NYPD." Nick blurted out and reached to shake hands.

He could feel the mysterious visitor sizing him up as the man replied, "Jack. Let's leave it at that." Nick shook his head in acknowledgment of the boundary. Turning back to Gus, Jack cast a gaze over his friend. "Cripe, but they're making them younger and younger these days! You don't look so good, Pal."

Gus nodded his agreement, adding, "Don't feel so good these days either."

Jack folded his arms across his chest and chewed his lip. "Tell me." Came his reply. There was a tone of genuine caring in his voice.

Over the next hour, Gus told Jack about the case Brad had been working in the city and of his murder. He then shared everything he'd learned about Lindy, the Billie Holiday singing competition, Mark's betrayal, Nurse Silver's suspected involvement, the murders of Sam, Pete, Angie, and Arlo, the gardenia calling cards, the letters Angie had written in her blood as she lay dying, and his growing concerns for Jessie, Lindy, and Theresa. Jack remained motionless, only periodically nodding his head, listening intently as Gus talked. Nick watched the man carefully, noting his profound concentration.

When Gus finally finished speaking, a long silence passed. Finally, Jack spoke. "I was sad to hear about Mary, Gus. Deeply sad."

Gus turned a gaze toward his friend. "Thank you. Didn't know you knew."

A faint smile curved Jack's lips, and matching Gus's gaze, he merely nodded and replied, "I know everything."

Gus snorted his response and, with eyebrows raised, answered, "Pal, we're countin' on that..."

Jack's input was direct and came quickly. "You're ass deep in Dirties, My Friends - no doubt about it. God help you." Nick sat silent in the chair by the desk, carefully observing. He made no sound. Jack continued, cutting his eyes back to Gus. "I'm sure you already know; those gals of yours are good as dead, Augustus." Gus winced involuntarily. Crossing his arms across his chest by way of refusing acknowledgment, he tightened his jaw and held his gaze on the wall in front of him. "Everything you need's in those bags." Jack nodded his head toward the pile lying on the bed.

Gus nodded and merely whispered in a low voice raw with emotion, "Thanks, Pal."

Jack sat a moment more, deep in thought, and then, without warning, stood up, walked over to Nick, and stuck out his hand. Nick extended his own in what he thought was a farewell gesture. Jack shook Nick's hand vigorously and then said with a slight lilt in his voice, "Say 'Hi' to your 'Uncle Manny'!"

Nick looked flustered and confused and glanced at Gus for clarification. "Excuse me??!" The young detective sputtered.

Jack then cast a hard look at the man in front of him. "Boy, you ready to die young, or are you gonna play ball??" Nick again shot a questioning look Gus's way, only to find Gus standing with a slight smile and a look of relief on his face. Jack tried again, this time with a more commanding tone. "Say 'Hi' to your 'Uncle Manny'!" Flashing a look of total bewilderment, Nick slowly reached out and shook Jack's hand. Popping a stick of gum in his mouth, Jack then walked back to the edge of the bed and sat down again. "Best I can figure," he spoke solemnly, "You fellas are in the middle of a Mob job - but nothing like the usual. You're catching me with a couple weeks' downtime; nowhere to go and nuthin' to do. What say, I tag along on your little adventure?" Gus and Nick glanced at each other. Jack continued, looking squarely at Nick as he did so. "Listen closely, Detective. I'm sorry about your Uncle Pete - but hard as this sounds, he's given you a silver lining now that may just save your nuts." Nick's forehead furrowed and he looked questioningly as Jack continued. "Pete's death gets you out of that squirrel cage downtown and out of your usual routine. You have to know this: they're coming for you. You've got to find a way to stay alive - and the next forty-eight to seventy-two hours are gonna be the real trick." Nick nodded, and Jack again spoke. "Nick, get back to the city and get to the hospital where your Uncle Pete's body is being held. STAY THERE. And stay VISIBLE. I mean VISIBLE. Meet with the Coroner, meet with the morgue attendants, cry on a pretty nurse's shoulder, meet with the funeral home people— make them come to you there at the hospital. Call your Sarge and request your full family bereavement leave... and get this done before four o'clock this afternoon... you gotta pick up your 'Uncle Manny'. He'll be flying into LaGuardia to help with the funeral arrangements."

Nick raised his eyebrows and merely replied, "Yessir!"

Nick then shot a look at Gus and back at Jack, as Jack continued, "Good Italian families... so large... so close... death always brings us together." With that, Jack cut a questioning look at Nick. "I assume Pete was married?"

"No, Sir," Nick replied again.

"Makes that part a bit easier... What's your mom's name?"

"Cecile," Nick replied, the plot slowly coming together in his mind.

"Ah... Cecile..." Tossing a notepad and pen at Nick, Jack uttered his last command. "Jot down your immediate family tree for me, Nick, and then get a move on. Your ass better be at LaGuardia when I land. Do NOT leave me hangin' out to dry, Son. BE THERE, you hear me? I'll tell Gus my ETA once I have it -and Spinoza- I won't be looking like this the next time you see me. Be looking for a man with a paunch and thinning silver hair, wearing black slacks and a burgundy sweater. I'll be carrying a black travel duffel and pulling a matching suitcase. Capiche??" Nick quickly absorbed the details and nodded his agreement. Next, he scribbled his family details on the notepad and handed it back to Jack. Jack gave a slight smile to the young man as he took the information. "Detective, the minute I leave here, I'm going to phone in some protection for your family. You stay out of it and trust they will be scooped up and well hidden. You try to touch base with them, you'll get them killed, sure as fuck. I'll make sure you're notified on a need-to-know. We good?"

Nick nodded and shook Jack's hand, as he responded with a simple, quiet, yet deeply sincere, "Thank You, Sir."

Gus turned toward Jack and reached out his hand. "I second that, Jack. Thank You."

"Haven't done anything yet!" Jack grunted in response. He then turned and looked squarely at Gus. "This is one ugly pickle, Augustus. If those ladies are still alive, they won't be for long." Gus nodded his awareness of the fact. "That nurse has to be the plant." Jack continued. "You get a call from Jessie or Theresa; you need to get them free of her forthwith. No matter what it takes! If you don't - we're all dead in the water." Gus's gaze turned distant for a moment as Jack continued, "What were those three letters again??"

"UKR," Gus replied flatly.

"UKR..." Jack repeated, imprinting them upon his memory. Looking at his watch, Jack noted the time. Stretching himself, he walked over to Nick once more and patted the young man on his shoulder. "Nick, you aren't in this alone. You do what we tell you -how and when- you just might come out of this and live to be as old as your 'Uncle Manny.' Catch you later this afternoon." Folding the piece of paper with Nick's information and placing it neatly in his wallet, Jack then turned to Gus. There was a kindness and note of concern in his voice as he next spoke. "My old friend, don't start second-guessing yourself now. Your instincts are some of the finest I've ever worked with. They haven't left you... they're still in there - just buried under a shitpile of grief." Gus smiled an appreciative smile, his eyes wistful at the compliment. It had been a long time since he'd heard words of encouragement—a very long time. The last ones being from Mary before she fell prey to the cancer. "I've got work to do!" Jack said. "See you both in the City - and hopefully with more answers than questions."

With that, he slipped the chain off the door, pulled his ballcap low over his face, slipped out of the room, down the hall, and into the last low light of pre-dawn.

Chapter Thirteen

Gus jolted awake to the sound of his cellphone ringing. Still in a fog, he felt around the chenille bedspread, fumbling with his hand to locate it.

Light streamed in from the dingy motel room window. Squinting, Gus glanced at his watch—nine thirty AM. The time shocked him. The last he recalled, after dividing up the supplies Jack had brought, was that he had confirmed the new strategy with Nick. After Nick's departure, Gus had then sat on the edge of the bed to momentarily collect his thoughts before heading back to Andover to investigate the florist shop there.

That was three hours ago. He'd not counted on sheer exhaustion overtaking him. A momentary shiver shot up his spine as he realized how open and vulnerable this need for sleep had left him. The cellphone continued its incessant ringing. Finally, locating it under a rumpled pillow, Gus brought it to his ear without even glancing at it. Grunting a gruff 'Hello', he immediately bolted upright, his mind becoming laser focused. The voice on the other end was Jessie's.

"Gus? Gus? Are you there?!"

"Jess! I'm here! My God, where are you? Are you OK??" Gus's heart was pounding.

Jessie answered quickly, obvious stress in her voice. "Gus, they're on us! No matter what I do, we can't shake them! I've ditched the Mustang. We're in a rental. They're still on us. They know our every move before we even make it. I've only been able to buy us about a thirty-minute separation."

Gus's mind was whirring, and he heard himself blurt, "Jess - it's Silvers. She's a plant!"

"WHAT??!" Jessie shot back, incredulous.

"Can you talk safely?" Gus responded forcefully. "Where's Silvers now?"

There was a momentary hesitation, and then Jessie replied, "We're at a QuikStop somewhere in PA. She's in the restroom. Gus, what the..."

Seizing on the moment and with only seconds to spare, Gus spoke with urgency. "Are you, Theresa, and Lindy together now?"

"Yes." Jessie answered and then added quizzically, "Is Lindy our Jane Doe?"

"Affirmative," Gus replied.

"She's lying down on the backseat..." Jessie continued.

"Jess, listen carefully." Gus stood pacing the floor now as he spoke. "You and Theresa drive away, NOW! You've got to get away from Silvers immediately. Sure as shit, she's ratting you out right now. Whatever plans you've discussed in front of her, do NOT -repeat DO NOT- follow through with them!"

As Gus spoke, he heard the muffled sound of a car engine crank and then tires squeal. The next sound brought tears to his eyes.

"Dad??" It was Theresa's voice.

"Oh, Sweetheart!" Gus's voice wavered with emotion, and tears stung his eyes.

"Dad - I'm afraid."

Pressing his phone tight to his ear, by way of a hug, Gus replied, "I know, Sweetheart. Me too."

"What's happening, Dad? Who ARE these people??" Theresa continued, an equal measure of fear and anger rising in her voice.

Before Gus could reply, he heard Jessie's voice. "Hit speaker, Theresa. We've got a lot to cover before our signal drops!" He could hear Jessie was in command, despite her stress. They were on the move now. One second later, Gus was on speaker, and a quick conversation ensued. Jessie's voice chimed in again. "Gus, before we drop signal, what'd'ya know?"

Gus quickly and clearly told Jessie and Theresa about all he'd learned in Chicago, about Lindy, the bogus Billie Holiday singing competition, and then about what he'd found when he'd returned to Angie's farm. The news hit hard. As Theresa softly cried, Jessie sat silent for a moment and then answered in a sad, solemn tone, "I'm so terribly sorry to hear that..." She then added, "Augustus, are you OK?"

Gus swallowed hard and drew a breath. His answer was short, to the point, and sincere. "No." A sorrowful and worried expression crept across Jessie's face as she continued to drive. Not allowing for a response, Gus spoke again, matter-of-factly. "How's Lindy?"

"Slow coming around— but bless her. Gus, whatever she's been through, has been darkly awful. We may never get her back."

There was a momentary pause in the conversation, and then Jessie spoke again. "I don't get Nurse Silvers... Gus, she's been taking excellent care of her."

"Has she REALLY?" Gus questioned.

Jessie could hear the dubious inflection in his voice. Finally, she replied. "What are you thinking, Gus?"

Gus wasn't exactly sure himself but verbalized his forming hypothesis anyway. "Has Silvers given Lindy any injections?"

"Yes." Theresa chimed in this time. "Every four to six hours. For anxiety and pain control."

There was another pause, and Gus spoke again questioningly. "Is Silvers' medical bag in the car with you now?"

He could hear the muffled movement as Theresa removed her seatbelt and maneuvered to look at the back floorboard. Returning to her seated position, she answered in a composed voice, "Yes. Her purse is here, too!"

Jessie was next to chime in. "We left her flat at the QuikStop, Gus. She only had her phone with her when she went inside."

With that, Jessie grunted. "Shit. I just thought she was touching base with the hospital about Lindy's care - not phoning in our murders!"

A moment more passed, and Gus's voice again spoke over the phone. "Get a few more miles down the road, then ditch that car, Jess. Check Silvers' bags when you can and then call me back in..." Gus glanced at his watch. "Call me back in two hours."

"Roger That." Jessie replied and then added, "I'll be ditching this phone for safety, Gus. I left it alone with Silvers a couple times. Gonna get me - and Theresa - burners ASAP. So, answer no matter the number, please!"

"Copy that," Gus stated emphatically and then spoke again, his voice warm and filled with emotion. "You Girls stay strong. My heart -and prayers- are with you."

"I love you, Dad," Theresa said softly.

"Love you too, Sweetheart." Gus replied and then added, "Jess, watch yourself for me. I've pulled in Jack. He's working this with us now, as of this morning."

Theresa watched as a look of relief washed over Jessie's face. "Good. I'm glad. No time like the present!" She replied, only half-joking.

Gus spoke again as the conversation drew to a close. "Jess... I...need you safe."

"Roger That." She replied and then added, with warmth, "DITTO." Her tone of voice reached deep into Gus's heart. "We'll call in two!"

As Jessie reached to disconnect the call, Gus heard a low moan come from the backseat of the car, sending a wave of resolve through his exhausted body and troubled mind.

Chapter Fourteen

The call from Jessie and Theresa had energized Gus, and he found his mind clear and spirits somewhat lifted. It might have been the unplanned sleep, but he also found his instincts returning—sharp and keen once more. This, he welcomed, as he'd been knocked off his game, and it had really messed with his head. Not familiar territory for him.

After disconnecting, Gus had hurriedly collected his supplies, checked out of the Lamplighter, grabbed a cup of coffee in the lobby, and then, merging onto the highway, headed back to Andover. He consistently checked his rearview mirror, making certain he wasn't followed.

About an hour in, mind whirring, Gus clicked on the radio, searching through stations, looking for something to help settle him for the long drive ahead. Hitting upon a jazz station, he sighed and listened as Carmen McRae masterfully delivered the lyrics to 'So Many Stars.' Before he knew it, a wistfulness began to overtake him. His thoughts turned to Mary and then to life in general, the fleetingness and seeming futility of it all. He thought of Theresa and how close he was to losing her in this awful mess. And then, his thoughts settled on Jessie. Gus knew he was in love with her - and had been for a very long time. Much longer than he ever should've been - or could even bring himself to acknowledge. The truth was, he'd loved her from the moment he met her but had never allowed himself to act on his feelings, except for that one encounter when they both had almost stepped over the line. He had occasionally wondered what might've actually happened that night, knowing full well he would've stopped things before they reached the point of no return. Much to his chagrin, he just wasn't 'that kind of man', and having to live with the guilt every time he looked at Mary would've done him in, pure and simple. He knew, too, that crossing that line would've cheapened and eventually destroyed his friendship with Jessie. A price he simply was unwilling to pay. Despite all this, there was a great peace to being with Jessie... an ease he'd never known before, even with Mary. Despite Gus taking pains to limit his time with her, it was ever present - and there intensely in each and every interaction. As long as he was being honest, the fact was, he'd never trusted himself with Jessie after that night - and now...now he couldn't believe she'd even want anything to do with him. He'd become a shell of himself. Even if by some miracle Jessie did still feel attracted to him, Gus secretly feared 'push come to shove', he wouldn't be able to deliver. This truly depressed him. How in the hell had he let life grind him down as it had?

Gus continued on toward Andover, listening, thinking - and glancing perpetually in his rearview mirror. The case played through his mind as Billie Holiday's voice poured through the radio speakers. She was singing 'Some Other Spring,' a song he hadn't heard in years. He began to think of Billie's early life and listened intently as she sang: *Some other Spring, I'll try to love/Now I still cling to faded blossoms/Fresh when worn/Left crushed and torn/Like the love affair I mourn....*'

Gus thought of her early beginnings, working as an errand girl in a brothel. Suddenly, his mind stuck on that point. Billie

Holiday-Brothel-Prostitution-Mafia-Vice-Billie Holiday-Sex Trade...he wasn't sure where he was heading with the train of thought, but something sinister in feel and scope was starting to form.

As Billie held the last note and the song faded away, the station began to crackle, finally giving way to static. Reaching over, Gus switched off the radio and returned to his thoughts in silence.

Glancing at his watch, he had a little over an hour to go until he anticipated Jessie's and Theresa's next call. Cutting his eyes to the rearview mirror, things again checked out fine. He welcomed this general lack of excitement. The momentary lull was a true gift.

Gus's cellphone rang, jarring him back to reality and making him jump. He was surprised at how jangled his nerves were still. Reaching for his phone, he checked the number. It was Nick Spinoza. "Hey, Nick. What's up?" Gus answered.

Nick spoke quickly and in a hushed voice. "Gus, I've been doing some digging. There's a five-city Billie Holiday singing competition advertised in several rather dodgy, underground publications I've stumbled on."

Gus's eyebrows raised at this news. "What cities?"

Nick paused a moment and then read them off in the order they appeared in the ad: "Tampa Bay, NYC, Seattle, Houston, and LA."

"Interesting," Gus replied. "What do you make of it?" Gus waited while the young detective collected himself.

"Well, at first glance, Gus, these cities would make sense from an entertainment perspective - except for Seattle. That one's kind of an outlier, if you ask me. They're known more for Grunge than Jazz, and nothing much else by way of showbiz is happening there now. Even Tampa has a burgeoning film industry today, so that's somewhat understandable..."

"So?" Gus questioned.

"Well..." Nick spoke haltingly. "Gus, every one of these cities is a port town."

Gus's eyes widened. "Interesting pattern." He replied.

"Yessir. Isn't it just."

Gus continued driving. "So...you thinking international trafficking?"

"Affirmative." Came Nick's answer.

"That would make a helluvalot of sense!" Gus said, nodding his head subconsciously as he spoke. "Shoot me a pic of the ad, will ya, Nick? And a listing of the publications they appear in."

"Sure thing, Gus. ASAP."

"When are you heading out to pick up 'Uncle Manny'?" Gus asked, a slight smile crinkling his eyes.

"In a couple hours!" Nick answered. "Sure hope this works."

"It will," Gus reassured. "Jack's a Master. Watch and Learn. And keep your eyes peeled. This doesn't work; we're all dead."

"Yessir. Will do. Be careful too, Gus."

Gus disconnected from the call. He felt somewhat guilty for not telling Nick about Jessie, Theresa, and Lindy and their escape from Nurse Silvers, but until he knew more, this was one card he needed to keep close to the vest. This new detail from Nick was a major break, and Gus was eager to get on it.

Arriving in Andover, Gus was hit hard as he passed the exit that led to Angie's farm. There had been no real time to sit with the crushing losses and the horror that came with them. The world seemed completely different now, and it felt as though years had already passed. Gus knew he was going to need some serious help processing it all -if he came out the other side alive- and at this stage, that was a mighty big IF. Pulling into the parking lot of the downtown florist, Gus sat in the car and waited for Jessie's and Theresa's call. Exactly ten minutes later, right on time, his cellphone rang. It was a number he didn't recognize. Gus answered. "Yes?" After a second, Jessie's voice reached his ear. He breathed a sigh of relief. "Things OK?" He quickly asked.

"As good as can be." Jessie answered and then added, "We're driving new wheels, and both have fresh burners!"

"I noticed!" Gus responded. "Were you able to pull recon on Silvers' bags?"

"And How!" Jessie shot back. "Seems Nurse Silvers' last name ISN'T Silvers... and she's NOT a nurse!"

Gus tightened his jaw but kept himself in check. "No shit." He heard himself retort. "Who -and What- is she then?"

"Woman by the name of Jane Rudolph. A CNA at the Golden Acres Nursing Home in Madison."

Gus shook his head. He wanted to kill Mark Anderson and hoped he'd have the chance. "What else?" He sighed.

"Well, Dad," Theresa chimed in. "She's been pumping Lindy full of what appears to be heavy narcotics...morphine and some stuff called Toradol. We think that's why Lindy's not more coherent by now."

"Keeping her unconscious and quiet - until they can conveniently do away with her..." Gus interjected.

"It seems that way." Theresa replied and then continued, "And Dad, we found something else weird... at the very bottom of the medical bag, hidden in a velvet pouch, rolled up with a special syringe... some sort of clear fluid in an unmarked vial."

Gus heard himself immediately bark into the phone, "For godsakes, you Girls, steer clear of that vial! Don't even touch it!"

"What's up, Gus?!" Jessie fired back. "We're at a Need to Know, here!"

"Scopolamine, more than likely, Jess, but we have no way of knowing its potency. The kill shot."

"Christ!" Jessie muttered. Theresa looked at Jessie, her eyes questioning. "Not a trip you want to go on..." Jessie stated emphatically.

"Keep careful tabs on that vial, and when we can, we'll get it checked." Gus spoke and then immediately followed with, "What's your plan now?"

Jessie quickly answered, "For the time being, I think we've shaken our tail. You remember my brother's cabin, Gus? We're heading there. Should be far enough away to help us disappear until we can get Lindy back on her feet. Will grab some supplies on the way there. I think we can tend to her physical wounds easily enough, but at this point, I'm more worried about her psychological ones. She's been through it, Augustus."

Gus sat a moment and then responded, "Sounds like a solid plan. I'm chasing down a few leads now, but will head your way as soon as I can. Will call Jack and get him to enlist some reliable help for you."

Jessie acknowledged and then asked, "Where are you, Gus?"

"Back in Andover, Jess. At the florist shop that sent the gardenias to Angie's. Going to check out the info on that order to see what, if anything, I can shake loose." He then added, "I'd love to drop by the stationhouse here to see how they're working Angie's and Arlo's murders, but I don't dare..."

"No. No, you don't dare." Jessie replied. "Good Luck - and get to us soon, Augustus."

With that, the line went dead.

Gus sat a moment and collected himself. This reconnaissance mission with the florist would go one of two ways: Easy. Complicated. He hoped for the former but prepared himself for the latter. Walking to the entrance, Gus reached down, turned the knob and opened the door. A bell at the top clanged, announcing his arrival. Gus quickly cut his eyes around the premises; there were window displays and buckets of flowers neatly arranged in the shape of pyramids; a customer service counter sat in the middle of the room. Greeting card racks and a wrapping station stood adjacent, providing a bit of cover. The shop presented a high-end, Parisienne vibe. There were three customers ahead of him, in various stages of placing their orders.

Gus pretended to shop the selection of flowers but carefully observed the sales clerk as she worked. The woman documented each order in detail, hand-wrote a receipt, and then tearing the perforated, bottom portion, handed it to the customer as proof-of-purchase. After that step, the clerk went to the back room where the commercial coolers were kept. After a moment or two, she would return and repeat the cycle with the next customer. Gus deduced there must be at least one other employee in the back, more than likely the floral designer. As each order was taken, the date, time, customer name, phone number, and payment method were documented in the sales book. This would be where Gus would find what he was looking for. Hopefully, it would prove to be a motherlode of information.

Just as the clerk completed the transaction with the customer ahead of him and turned her attention to Gus, another customer arrived. Smiling courteously and insisting he wasn't in a hurry, Gus waved the new arrival ahead of him in line. He needed to watch one more transaction in order to get the rhythm right. Just as with the other three customers, the clerk repeated the identical process. Gus estimated he'd have about a minute -maybe a minute and a half- to rifle through the book for what he needed. He'd have to quickly scan dates to get to the right section of receipts.

The young woman looked at Gus and smiled. "Your turn now, Sir! Welcome to 'Blossoms, Dearie'! How may we help you today?"

"Well..." Gus replied, smiling slightly at the Jazz pun. "My golfing buddy just passed, and I'd like something special for the funeral."

The clerk made a sad face, and it appeared she was actually sincere. "I'm sorry for your loss, Sir. What kinds of flowers did your friend like? What church is hosting the service?"

The second question was going to provide the time wedge Gus needed. "Daisies and roses." He answered. "And the name of the church escapes me at the moment. It must be the shock and grief!"

The clerk, eager to be of comfort and use, nodded efficiently. "That often happens. What's your friend's name, Sir? We're supplied with a daily listing of all upcoming local funeral services. I can look it up in a jiffy."

Gus feigned profound appreciation and gave the name 'Marion Morrison.' "Marion with an O." He added sorrowfully.

Stepping away from the service counter, the clerk excused herself 'for what would be two or three minutes.'

Wasting no time, Gus seized the opportunity. Looking around the store and finding himself alone, he carefully -and quietly- searched the pages. The shop was a busy one, and even though it had only been a couple days since the delivery in question, he had to go back several pages to get to the right section. Flipping pages quickly, Gus kept one eye open for the clerk's return. Suddenly, there it was—an order for four gardenias to be delivered to Angie's address.

Grabbing the page, Gus ripped it from the book, stuffed it in his pocket, and beat it out the door. He drove away quickly, just as the clerk returned to the counter, prepared to tell him the bad news that no services were scheduled anywhere for his friend, Marion.

Pulling into a parking space at City Hall, three blocks down, Gus killed the engine and grabbed the prized piece of paper from his jacket pocket. Unfolding it, his eyes scanned carefully. 'Four gardenias delivered to DeAngelo's Truck Farm. Sender: A. Smith'. Gus sighed in exasperation at the alias. But then, he noted the phone number... area code 646. The order had been paid with cash, so no additional information was gleaned from his thievery.

He was now armed with the exact day and time the delivery was placcd and a juicy, mysterious phone number just beckoning to be called. Stuffing the receipt back in his pocket, Gus started the car, reaching for his cellphone as he drove.

Chapter Fifteen

Gus was just about to call Jack when his cellphone chimed, announcing the arrival of an incoming text. Keeping one eye on the road, he glanced at the message. It was from Nick. There were two images contained within the body of the text, and Gus immediately knew what they were. Wanting to check out the images as quickly as possible, he began to look for a place to pull off the highway.

Catching sight of an approaching roadside rest area, Gus decided this would be the perfect opportunity to stretch his legs, hit the head, and then check out Nick's new lead. Making his way into the parking lot, he guided the car to a stop and surveyed his surroundings; a few long-haul truckers and three cars carrying traveling families. Exiting the vehicle, Gus stretched, drew a deep breath, rolled his shoulders a time or two, and then made his way to the restroom.

Returning a few minutes later, Gus again cast his eye around the parking lot. Feeling confident all was well -or at least as well as could be- given the circumstances, he glanced at his watch and next turned his attention to his phone, reaching in his shirt pocket for a smoke as he did so. Drawing a hefty drag and enlarging the image, Gus scanned the advertisement for the five-city Billie Holiday singing competition Nick had told him about. Just as described, Gus read the cities listed. He then pulled focus on the ad as a whole. It was rather lackluster and subdued for an ad promising the chance to be 'discovered' and made 'rich and famous.' Black and white and featuring a clip art image of a spotlight and microphone, the ad fell flat in an odd sort of way. Gus read the print: *'Your Big Break Is Here! Win Large Recording Contract! Enter Today! Call Anton for personal interview and audicion.'* This auspicious message was then followed by a phone number.

Gus held his gaze on the ad for a few moments as several things became clear to him. The first being: *'Win Large Recording Contract...'* Gus mumbled the words aloud three times. Could be this was written as it was to keep the ad tight and more affordable, or could be a vernacular issue...written by someone for whom English wasn't a primary language, perhaps? Impossible to tell, in and of itself.

The second thing Gus noted: *'Call Anton for personal interview and audicion...'* Gus's lips pursed as he pondered this next clue. *'ANTON.'* No last name given. Gus had only met two Antons in his life. One was an old Army buddy, an African American man with a hearty laugh, and a French mother. The other, Mary's uncle. Mary Elizabeth Barnick Walker was a first-generation American. Her parents had fled the Eastern Bloc shortly before her birth, and Gus had enjoyed Mary's family and their traditions, food, and culture. Uncle Anton had been extremely kind to Gus and Gus had genuinely liked him. Pondering this option, Gus reached into one of the bags on the passenger seat and located a packet of peanut butter crackers and a small bottle of water in the stash of supplies Jack had provided. Tearing into the package, he pulled a cracker from the sleeve and slowly chewed, his attention still focused on the ad in front of him. 'Anton,' in and of itself, wasn't necessarily a great lead, but coupled with the first oddity and then the misspelling of the word 'audition,' it was aligning to form an interesting picture.

The next thing that caught Gus's eye and had him questioning: 'If this was a legitimate, vast, five-city audition, why was there only one man in charge of handling interviews? Why was no business entity or sponsorship listed? No last name even?' Gus then glanced at the phone number—646 area code.

Reaching for another cracker, Gus turned his attention to the listing of the publications where the ad had appeared. Two listings had been placed in a street publication listing all manner of services for the more 'down and out' social sphere. One listing in a 'Free and Fabulous' newspaper that routinely advertised used 'buy, sell and trade' merchandise. A final listing had been placed in an adult entertainment publication frequented by Johns and drug dealers. Gus found himself wondering how Tony and Samantha could've ever felt right about directing Lindy to such a sordid opportunity. A whole lot just wasn't adding up. Eating the last cracker and taking a gulp of water, Gus took another long drag and snuffed out his remaining smoke. He knew there was only one thing to do: call Anton and have a chat.

Twenty miles later, Gus exited the highway and pulled into the heart of town. He wasn't sure exactly where he was but knew in about another two and a half hours, he'd be pulling into the small community that housed Jessie's brother's vacation cabin. It would probably be dark by the time he arrived, but he'd call ahead to work out the details and alert Jessie he'd be coming. It had been a few years since he'd been at the cabin, and knew finding it in the fading light was going to prove tricky. In the interim, Gus entered the parking lot of a local coffee house. Exiting the car and walking inside, he was met by a young woman serving as Hostess.

"Hi, Sir. Welcome! How many?"

"Just me." Gus answered.

"Would you like the counter or a table today?"

Gus glanced around the establishment. It was in between lunch and dinner, with only a few people inside.

"Counter will do fine. Thank you." He replied and took a seat on one of the swivel chairs.

"Howdy." The cook behind the counter nodded with a half-smile. "Coffee while you look over the menu?"

"That would be great." Gus answered and then added, "Black, please."

The cream-colored, cafe ware, porcelain cup was brought, topped up and steaming, and Gus raised it to his lips, drawing in a sip. The coffee was piping hot, rich, and revived him at a cellular level.

After a few minutes, looking over the selections, Gus ordered the turkey swiss on rye and a cup of cream of tomato soup.

"Sure thing!" The cook responded.

Thirty minutes later, meal eaten and finishing his third cup of coffee, Gus knew he was fortified enough for his next task: calling the number in the ad.

"Is there a pay phone here, Mister? My cell is out of juice."

The man behind the counter shook his head, 'No.' Seeing Gus's disappointed and frustrated expression, he added by way of afterthought, "You can use the one in the office. I gather it ain't local..."

Gus nodded and spoke with sincerity in his voice, "Thank you, Friend. I'll leave money to cover the charge."

The man winked slightly in acknowledgment of their arrangement. "Right over there - door marked PRIVATE."

Gus paid his bill and left a generous tip. Walking to the office door, he opened it, finding a cramped and cluttered room laid out in front of him. Toward the back was a desk covered with receipts and piles of loose ketchup, mustard, salt, and pepper packets. And underneath all that, the telephone. Closing the door behind him, Gus collected his thoughts - and his nerve. He'd made these calls a million times as a cop working cases, but this time was different. There was a high likelihood the person he was about to speak to had a big part to play in the trail of murders Gus now found himself mired in, including Angie's and Arlo's. Gus also knew that short as it would probably be, by conversation's end, he would know for certain if they were on the right track with their new leads and theories. Part of him was afraid to find out.

Steadying himself, Gus picked up the receiver and dialed the number. After several rings, a heavily accented man answered with a gruff, "Yeah?"

Immediately Gus began, "Uh, yes. I'm calling to speak to A. Smith, please." Gus was kind, solicitous, and overly pleasant.

After a pause, the man on the other end replied, "Nobody here by that name."

Sensing he was about to be hung up on, Gus went all in. "I mean ANTON. Is ANTON in?"

Gus could hear the man on the other end clear his throat. After another moment, Gus got what he was hoping for.

"What'd you vant? Who calls?" There was a growing suspicion and an agitation present in the voice.

"Well, Sir, this is Bert McKenzie. I'm the floral designer at 'Blossom's, Dearie' in Andover." Gus heard a grunt of acknowledgment and quickly continued, knowing time was not on his side in this exchange. "You see, Sir, we show you ordered four gardenias for delivery the other day - ummm...to a... DeAngelo's Truck Farm. The shipment of gardenias we got last week was defective, so to speak... had a fungus..." Gus lied and kept on going. "The gardenias just weren't up to snuff and wilted way too soon! We're calling all our customers who ordered gardenias and are providing one hundred percent money back - no questions asked. Do you have a credit card you'd like your refund applied to, Sir?"

Anton grew impatient, grunting adamantly a word Gus recognized that sounded like 'Nii!'.

Gus made note and pressed on in his overly solicitous tone. "Ah, I see. How about we mail you a check, then? Who should we make it out to, and where would you like it mailed, Sir?"

"Leave it be! No refund needed!"

With that, Anton slammed down the receiver, leaving Gus sitting in silence. Short conversation, but he'd gotten what he needed - and had hoped for.

He'd just talked with the man himself, ANTON. And Anton spoke like he had a mouth full of marbles - rolling his words around in his mouth before spewing them out forcefully. Just like Mary's Uncle Anton. Gus also now knew Anton had been involved in the ordering of the gardenias. But even more crucial, Gus knew hands down Anton was definitely Eastern Bloc and felt confident he was of Ukranian origin. The way he'd grunted what sounded like 'Nii', Gus recognized as Ukranian for 'No.'

Setting the receiver back in place, Gus stood and reached for his wallet in his pants pocket. Suddenly, his knees buckled, and he lowered himself back onto the chair.

His eyes widened, his heart pounded, and his mouth grew dry. There, flashing through his mind's eye, was the image of Angie dead in his arms and the three letters she'd scrawled on the kitchen floor in her own blood: U K R. She had known and had tried to warn him.

"Dear Christ, Almighty..." Gus whispered, a chill of dread overtaking him.

Chapter Sixteen

Tossing a twenty on the counter, Gus nodded at the cook on the way out. "Thanks again, Pal. This should cover it."

Without waiting for a reply, he made his way quickly to the car, unlocked the door, got in, and took cellphone in hand. Trembling slightly, he placed the call and, as he waited for Nick to answer, tried to calm his mind. How had Angie known it was the Ukranian Mob they were up against? Why hadn't she said anything to him? As his thoughts raced, Nick's voice spoke on the other end.

"Nick. Gus. Where are you now?" Gus wasted no time initiating conversation.

Nick sounded a bit confused but maintained a low, calm voice. "I'm waiting to pick up 'Uncle Manny', Mom. He landed just a few minutes ago. Am meeting him at Baggage Claim as planned." There was questioning in the young detective's voice.

"Nick, when you two connect, get someplace private fast and call me back ASAP. ASAP SON."

"Uh, yeah, Mom. Sure thing. Here he comes now!"

With that, Nick disconnected, leaving Gus alone in the parking lot, pondering his next move. He wanted to call Jessie and Theresa but knew there wasn't time. Instead, Gus sat a moment, pulling focus.

It wasn't like Angie to withhold intel from him. Why had she done it this time? Had they gotten to her some way? How? Angie wasn't one to be bought. Had she really even known the truth? Perhaps not. Maybe Gus was reading more into the situation than he should. If Angie hadn't known, what tipped her off at the end, causing her to leave the cryptic letters in blood as she lay dying? Too many questions percolating all at once - and all of them crucial.

Gus instead turned his attention to his surroundings. He was closer to Jessie, Theresa, and the cabin than he'd recognized. Glancing at his watch, Gus calculated that, all going smoothly and with no untoward activity along the way, he'd actually be arriving in the heart of Lake George around five PM. That ETA sat better with him than wending his way up the remote lane in the dark of night. Just as Gus began to fidget with impatience, his cell rang. It was Nick calling back as instructed.

"Hey, Gus..." Nick spoke. "What gives?"

"Are you with 'Uncle Manny' somewhere private - and safe?" Gus fired back, an edge in his voice.

"Sure thing," Nick replied. "Found an unlocked utility closet off Baggage Claim."

"Good. Put me on speaker and listen close."

Huddled together in the small space, Nick and Jack listened intently as Gus revealed all he'd learned in the last few hours. There was a lot to take in, and Nick's eyes widened as the information flowed.

Jack stood motionless, eyes fixed hard on the floor. Finally, Gus's voice trailed to a close. After a long moment of silence, Jack spoke. His voice was low and emotionless. "Christ, Augustus. We're in it, man."

Nick stared into Jack's heavily disguised face, his color slightly fading. Realizing the need to collect himself, Nick spoke in a professional air. "By way of recap, Gus, we're ass deep in an international, Ukrainian mob run, sex trafficking ring."

"Affirmative." Gus acknowledged.

"So, all these hits have come from them..." Nick continued his assessment.

"Certainly seems that way." Gus again answered.

"Why the gardenias, Gus? I don't follow." The young detective again questioned, a tone of frustration and alarm growing in his voice.

"Simple." Jack chimed in. "Billie Holiday's favorite flower was a gardenia. Sure seems like a big bother to make that your calling card, though... bit of a cheek, I guess, but an expensive one. They're hard to get - this time of year especially."

"I get the Billie Holiday connection, but why bother to leave these scattered everywhere?" Nick pressed.

No one spoke, and Jack continued. "Who knows at this point. The big questions for us now are: When did Angie know, and why didn't she come clean? Are these apes using the ports to get these girls out of the country after scooping them up from these singing competitions? Are they holding these women somewhere first or streaming them through the ports in live time as they snare them? And..." Jack continued after a pause, "what happened to make them kill three of these women - and try to whack a fourth? Who wants to damage their merchandise like that? Seems risky and expensive."

"Indeed. And the real question after that becomes," Gus stated in a disturbed tone, "How the hell long have these bastards been working under our noses like this?"

"True." Jack responded and then added, "Judging by appearances, My Brave Friends, the tentacles of this racket go long. If Dirties are involved - and at this point, it's safe to assume, they ARE - they've probably been operating this little enterprise for quite some time - and with total impunity."

"There's gonna be alot of big players, big mad." Gus spoke, deep in thought.

Nick spoke next, "What I wonder is this: if this singing competition racket has been used successfully for procuring their 'merchandise,' what other entertainment-based genres are they tapping? Everybody wants to be a star...Modeling agencies? Film and TV talent agencies?"

"Indubitably..." Jack replied.

Nick swallowed hard and shot a look at Jack. Sensing Nick's dread, he shot him a quick wink. "Ah, what the hell, Son. You only live once. Might as well not be bored while you do it!" Nick didn't smile.

"Fellas," Jack said emphatically, "The only way out is through. Gus, I'm glad you caught us when you did. Your intel gives us much more to go on - and accelerates our mission tremendously. We're gonna head out now. Where are you headed, and what's next?"

Gus replied, "Five PM ETA for the cabin. Will try to snap our vic to quick. Will report tomorrow morning at ten AM. Oh, and Jack, can you dispatch a nurse and trauma Doc to us there forthwith? We're going to need all the professional help we can get."

"Sure thing." Jack answered. "Will have all that info for you at our ten AM recon and will have them already enroute by the time we talk tomorrow."

"Thank you." Gus breathed with relief.

"Augustus... one last question to leave you with," Jack began. "Would Angie really withhold from you - and if so, why? And if not, what would she do to attempt to get info to you? Now, we gotta jet. Ten AM recon call tomorrow! Stay safe." With that, the call ended.

Gus sat a moment more, letting the conversation -and Jack's questions- track.

Finally, picking up his cell again, he dialed Jessie. After three rings, Gus heard Jessie's voice. It was like oxygen to him. "Hi." He heard himself say.

"Hi, Gus..." Jessie replied. "You sound tired."

"Little bit." He answered. "Everything OK there?"

"So far," Jessie answered. "We got here a few hours ago. No one tailed us. Picked up supplies and are getting settled in. Lindy's in bed but showing signs of coming around."

"How are you and Theresa? Gus asked with concern.

"Hanging In." Came Jessie's answer.

Gus could hear fatigue and a bit of dread in her voice.

"I should be there around five this afternoon, Jess."

"Praise God!" Jessie responded with relief and a sincerity that hit Gus straight in the heart. She continued, "It will be so good to have you with us, Gus. Theresa will be so relieved."

"Where is she now?" Gus asked.

"Asleep on the couch. Bless her heart, she's worn out."

"I bet!" Gus spoke and then added, "Jess - we're in deep. Way deep. And way bad. Lots to tell."

"I know." Came her reply. "Just get here, Gus. Just get here...."

CHAPTER SEVENTEEN

As Gus steered the car for Lake George and the last leg of his journey -for the time being- another car was easing to the curb just outside the Embassy Suites in Manhattan. Nick pulled the car to a stop, exactly as Jack had directed. The two men sat for a moment, taking in their surroundings. Finally, Jack spoke. "Nick, I know you're a damn good cop, so this little reminder isn't meant as an insult." Nick glanced at Jack as the older man continued, "Once we exit this car, the game is seriously afoot - and for all we know, we've already got eyes on us." Nick nodded his understanding. "The slightest slip-up, Son, we're dead. Hear me?"

"Copy." Nick answered, his voice registering a clear grasp of the situation.

"Now," Jack reassured, "I've played this game plenty in my career, and I've made it this far. You get in a situation you're unsure about, punt. I'll be there to cover."

"Yessir." Nick again replied, his hands growing sweaty as they instinctively gripped the steering wheel.

"Now, pull us up to the entrance, and let's get this show on the road."

Nick eased the car up to the sliding doors of the hotel lobby. Jack stepped out of the passenger side, making a show of stretching himself and rubbing his protruding belly. "Get my bag, Nephew. Your 'Uncle Manny' is checking in."

Nick moved to the trunk of the car and watched as 'his Uncle Manny' waddled into the hotel lobby - a far cry from the man he'd met back at the Lamplighter Motel in Scranton.

Following behind, Nick placed 'Manny's' suitcase next to him, as they stood side by side at the front desk.

Pulling a cigar out of the leather case clipped in his shirt pocket, 'Manny' stuffed the stogie decisively in his mouth and was immediately met with, "Sir, we do NOT allow smoking here! We're a non-smoking establishment!"

Unfazed by the smug tone in the clerk's voice, 'Manny' responded bluntly,

"How 'bout SUCKING? You allow SUCKING here, or are you a non-sucking establishment too??!"

The clerk's eyes widened, and he sputtered in embarrassment, color flushing his cheeks.

"Wasn't lighting up." 'Uncle Manny' continued. "Just givin' it a chew. I need my jangled nerves soothed, Capiche? This is my pacifier... kinda like a tit!"

The clerk chuckled uncomfortably, trying to regain a pleasant tone and dignified demeanor. "Rough trip for you today, Sir?"

'Yeah." 'Manny' grunted. "Here to bury my murdered brother, God rest him..."

The clerk's face contorted into a look of shocked sympathy. "My deepest condolences, Mr... Spinoza..."

'Manny' grunted acknowledgment.

"Here's your room key. Fifth floor, down the hall on your left. You can't miss it. Your suite is at the end of the hallway. Do let us know if there's anything we can do to help during this most difficult time."

'Manny' chewed on the stogie and nodded, placing his credit card back in his wallet. "Come on, Nephew." He commanded, and Nick obediently followed toward the elevator, bag in tow.

Arriving on the fifth floor, 'Manny' and Nick stepped off the elevator and made their way down the hall as directed. Sure enough, Room 550 was right where they'd been told it would be. Slipping the key card into the reader, the door clicked open unceremoniously. The room was good sized, well appointed, but sterile in feel. It smelled of HOTEL. The door slammed closed with a solid 'bang' behind them. 'Manny' made his way over to the window and gazed at the late afternoon light, chewing on his cigar and rubbing his hands over his gut. "Unpack my case, will ya, Nephew? I'm gonna make some coffee."

Nick tossed the heavy bag on the bed as 'Manny,' his back turned, located the coffeemaker and pods. "Wanna cup?"

"No thanks." Nick replied, unzipping the suitcase and opening it wide. Nick proceeded to remove a stack of perfectly folded shirts. Next, he lifted three cashmere sweaters from the bag, each neatly folded with sheets of tissue paper in between. "This case weighs a ton!" Nick commented, half joking. "Mighty heavy wool!"

Taking his cup of coffee in hand, 'Manny' walked over to where Nick was standing and without a sound, pulled a tab hidden in the side of the case. Up popped a panel, revealing a stack of cash, two 9mms, a .357, several pre-loaded magazines, a small batch of documents and business cards, and a navy-colored Dopp kit containing what looked to be a bottle of spirit gum and several pots of makeup. Nick's eyebrows raised, and he cut a look at his 'Uncle Manny.' "Sweet arrangement. I take it 'Uncle Manny' is in this blue bag?!"

'Manny' winked, drawing a sip from his cup. "Go on." He motioned to Nick.

Nick cast his eyes over the stash and, picking up one of the business cards, studied it carefully. The card was of quality stock, simple but refined. White with glossy black and gold lettering, it read simply, 'Manny Spinoza, Textile Engineer - FL, Rome, UK' On the bottom right was a phone number.

Setting his coffee cup on the bedside table, 'Manny' reached up and removed the picture from the wall. Carrying it to the bed, he sat down and placed the picture, glass side up, on his lap. Motioning for Nick to turn on the clock radio, he took out a piece of paper and a pen. He then motioned for Nick to sit beside him. Nick sat silent, music playing, as Manny wrote:

1: First stop Morgue.

2: Second stop Squirrel Cage.

3: Late dinner - preferably steak.

Slipping the paper to Nick, 'Manny' waited for the young man's acknowledgment and then scribbled in large letters: 'BALD SPOOK IS MINE.'

Nick cut a sharp look and held 'Manny's' gaze.

"Capiche, Nephew? I mean it." He spoke low and forcefully.

"Yes, Uncle." Nick replied. It was clear he wasn't keen on this portion of the plan.

'Manny' patted the young detective on the back and then ripped the paper into shreds, flushing it down the toilet. He then flushed three extra times for good measure.

Speaking out loud, in a commanding tone, 'Manny' then announced, "Nephew, the time has come. I need to see my brother's body..."

The two men walked solemnly back down the hall, took the elevator to the lobby, and returned to their car.

***

As the low light shifted, casting long shadows around him, Gus pulled into the heart of Lake George. Driving through town, he exited onto a small road and skirted the shore for a couple miles. Turning inland, he then made his way into the wooded hills. It was deep into the off-season. Traffic was light, and a cold drizzle began to dampen the windshield. Gus drove past a handful of houses; some cozy and inviting, inhabited by year-round residents, and others, boarded up, empty, and devoid of life - awaiting the return of their wealthy summer inhabitants. Hitting the wipers, Gus watched carefully for the mile marker he needed. After a couple more miles, it appeared. Taking the curve, he guided the car down a heavily wooded lane. It was growing dark.

It had been four years since Gus had been to Jessie's brother's 'cabin'. The last time had been with Mary, and they'd made the trip to celebrate the long Fourth of July weekend with several of Gus's law enforcement colleagues and their families. Gus smiled faintly as he recalled the patriotic revelry of that gathering. A lifetime ago and a world away now, it seemed.

Continuing down the darkened lane, Gus came to the driveway as the road became a dead-end. He immediately recognized the property. Hardly a cabin by anyone's standards, the dwelling was more Bed and Breakfast material. Two stories and sprawling, the wood and log house contained three fireplaces, a picture window that looked out over the wooded forest beyond, a welcoming, covered porch, numerous bedrooms, and baths, and was still stunning despite its advanced age. Although rarely used by Jessie's brother and his family, they maintained it lovingly and spent what time away from the corporate grind schedules would allow.

Letting out a sigh of relief and glancing in the rearview mirror one last time for good measure, he guided the car to a stop, turned off the ignition, exited, and stretched. The air smelled sweet, and all around him was quiet, just the sound of raindrops splashing on the ground and leaves around him. He stood a moment collecting his thoughts and looking at the house.

Suddenly, the silence was broken by the sound of a woman's voice. "Gus! You made it! The old house is still standing, Grand Dame that she is!"

Gus turned to see Jessie walking briskly toward him. With arms outstretched, she grabbed Gus and hugged him. He hugged back. Looking back at the dwelling and standing next to him, Jessie quipped with a half laugh, "Every time I come up here, it makes me sorry I chose Bounty Hunting as my career path... must be nice, huh?"

Gus grunted his agreement with a slight smile. Jessie's voice and demeanor then turned serious. "I wasn't sure we'd make it this far, Augustus."

Jessie looked at him with wide, brown eyes. Her short, brown hair curled into ringlets in the drizzle, and she wore a red and black buffalo checked flannel jacket over a black turtleneck and jeans. She was the best-looking thing Gus had seen in days. Grabbing a couple bags from the car, she looked up to catch Gus's gaze. "It's good to see you, Gus. I was worried."

Gus smiled a soft smile. "It's good to see you too, Jess. I know... me too. We're in for it, Partner."

Jessie nodded her understanding and then spoke again. "Plenty of time for that. Come in and get settled first. Theresa will want to see you, and I've made stew and cornbread!"

"Heaven!" Gus replied, grabbing more bags out of the car and following her into the cabin.

The interior felt like a haven, fire crackling in the river rock fireplace, the smell of homecooked goodness simmering on the stove, and the radio on the kitchen counter playing Frank Sinatra's 'In the Wee Small Hours'. It was almost like life had gone back to normal, and Gus hadn't been notified. Just then, Theresa came out of the bedroom. Seeing Gus, she ran to him, crying in relief and joy. "Dad! Dad!! I didn't think I'd ever see you again!"

Clinging tightly to Gus's neck, Theresa sobbed. Gus hugged her tight. "There... there." He soothed as though comforting a small child. "I'm here now."

After a moment, Theresa composed herself. "What now, Dad?"

Just as he was about to answer, Jessie chimed in.

"Grab a shower, Gus. Dinner will be ready in thirty. Help yourself to some of Brian's things if you need. Clean towels are in the bathroom closet!"

Gus glanced at Jessie and smiled. It had been days of living on crackers, peanut butter, diner coffee, cigarettes, and tepid showers with cheap bars of soap. He was disheveled, stubbly, and smelled less than inviting. All that, coupled with minimal sleep and high stress, had him feeling undone. Too much like he used to feel on long stakeouts at the beginning of his career. He didn't miss those days or this feeling.

"Thanks, Jess." He answered. "Don't mind if I do. Jack supplied me with some fresh duds and a razor... in these bags somewhere. Back in a few!"

Hugging Theresa one more time, Gus made his way down the hall toward the bathroom. Passing a partially opened door, he instinctively glanced in.

There in the dim light of the bedroom, his eyes made out the shape of a pale and bruised woman lying propped up on pillows, a comforter and quilt pulled over her, folded neatly at her chest.

The sight startled him. Fighting the urge to walk in for a closer look, Gus paused for a brief moment and then continued toward his rendezvous with the shower.

And, just as Jessie had stated, there would be plenty of time to assess their dire situation and lay the next plans. For now, there was a hot shower, a nourishing dinner, and, hopefully, some stolen moments of peace and safety to be had before death attempted its return.

Chapter Eighteen

Gaining entry to the morgue and obtaining permission to view Pete's body had been easier than Jack anticipated. Nick had had to accompany him, and Jack regretted having to put the young man through the awful ordeal a second time. On their way to the precinct, Jack acknowledged his concern and regret.

"I'm sorry you had to see Pete like that a second time, Nick. No way around it. It had to be done."

"Yes, I know." Nick replied, a tone of sadness and determination in his voice.

"Good thing we caught them when we did. Once the mortician steps in, they seem to really loosen the rules and regs. We got lucky with the timing."

Nick nodded and continued driving.

"Anything interesting catch your eye back there, Detective?"

Casting a gaze out the window, Jack watched the city lights pass by and waited for Nick's answer. He didn't have to wait long.

"Yessir..." Nick responded as he merged into the left lane, preparing to turn into the parking lot of the station house. "Powder burns are heavier than I remembered them..."

"Anything else?" Jack again questioned.

"The size of the wound seems irregular to me. I noticed it right off when I viewed Uncle Pete's body the first time."

Jack nodded and continued his line of questioning. "Either of these things jibe with anything unusual at the crime scene? I need you to be my eyes there since I didn't see the scene myself."

Nick eased the car into a parking space and killed the engine. Taking a long breath, he stared off into the distance, replaying the grim scene he'd viewed at Pete's office. Finally, after a moment, he spoke.

"At the time of the shooting, Uncle Pete had a full cup of coffee -with cream in it- sitting in front of him on his desk. He always took his coffee black. And... not one thing was out of place in his office or on his desk when they worked the scene. Stapler... pens... sticky notes... everything perfectly in place."

"Anything else?" Jack asked in a gentle but prodding tone.

"Yes." Nick replied. "There were no folders or papers on Uncle Pete's desk when they found him. Why weren't there any papers - or some type of work there? Where was his laptop? It wasn't like Uncle Pete to not be working on something all the time! And why would he just be sitting at his desk, in the middle of the night, NOT working, drinking coffee a way he didn't like?"

Jack sat in silence a moment and then proceeded, "So - what do you think, Nick?"

"There's only one thing to think. The scene was scrubbed, and whatever Pete was working on had been removed. Whoever was involved in scrubbing, didn't know Uncle Pete very well in terms of his behaviors and preferences."

"Yes." Jack stated simply, and then continued as an afterthought, cutting his gaze to Nick and watching the young man closely, "Given the wound,

Nick, I'd lay odds whoever did your uncle knew him well and had been perceived by him to be a friend - or at the very least, a trusted associate. They caught him completely unaware and he had his guard down. Total ambush. But the wound indicates he turned his head slightly just as the shooter pulled the trigger. Why?"

"Yeah... why?" Nick half whispered and then, cutting his eyes to Jack, continued with the next realization, "We're looking for two different people... Shooter and Scrubber?"

"Quite possibly." A moment more passed. Jack inhaled deeply and then spoke again. "So, back in the game we go, Nico! You think this bald Dick will be on duty tonight?"

"No way to know for sure since I've missed a couple days. Only way to find out is to go inside and look around."

"Better get in character!" Jack winked, taking another stogie out of his shirt pocket and stuffing it firmly between his teeth. "Now, keep your eyes peeled. I'm gonna be layin' it on thick."

Nick looked over at Jack and smiled a tired smile. "Thanks, 'Uncle Manny'. My family and I are really grateful."

Jack replied in his best, most gruff 'Manny' impersonation, "Fuhgeddaboudit!"

Nick shook his head with a faint laugh.

Together, the two men walked up the steps to the station house, Nick leading the way and 'Manny' shuffling behind. Once inside, Nick escorted 'Manny' past the information desk and waiting area, and then into the bullpen. Phones rang, an agitated voice yelled, and the smell of stale pastries and coffee wafted through the air.

"Sit here, 'Uncle Manny'," Nick said, motioning to a chair by a desk. "I'll go see if I can find who you need to talk to."

With that, Nick walked out of the squad room, leaving 'Manny' on his own, sitting quietly, chewing on his cigar, and taking in every minute detail of his surroundings.

At one point, a man approached and asked if he could be of assistance.

"Nah." 'Uncle Manny' responded. "Here about my murdered brother, God rest his soul. Waiting on my nephew Nick to get back from the can."

"I see." The man replied. "I'm sorry for your loss."

'Manny' nodded his head and dismissed the man with an irritated wave.

A couple minutes later, Nick returned, looking frustrated. "He's not here." Nick whispered and looked at 'Uncle Manny' in disgust.

"Don't stress, Kid. Could be a good thing. You know this Dick's name?"

"Dirksen." Nick replied. "Detective Randal Dirksen."

"So, where's he come from, this guy?" 'Manny' questioned.

"Looks like they shipped him in from Staten." Nick muttered.

"Why?" 'Manny' queried.

"No clue." Nick replied. "Why indeed. Looks like that's the big question. He just appeared."

"Gimme a paper and pen, Nephew."

Nick did as instructed, and watched as 'Uncle Manny' penned:

'Came to see you tonight re: murder of my brother, Pete. Want info and a meeting ASAP. Leave in three days. Embassy Suites Downtown, Room 550. -Manny Spinoza.'

Manny then reached in his wallet, removed a business card, and, using the stapler on Nick's desk, drove a staple forcefully through the card, attaching it to the note. Folding the paper and handing it to Nick, he then whispered,

"Stuff this in Dirksen's cubby, and let's see what breaks loose. Let's blow Nephew. I need meat."

Nick placed the note in Detective Dirksen's message box and the two men made their exit.

Nine thirty PM found them seated at a table in Arno Restaurante, finishing up the last remnants of an excellent dinner. 'Manny' had ordered the Delmonico steak, and Nick had picked his way through a plate of Rigatoni all' Amatriciana. His heart wasn't in eating, so as 'Manny' sat savoring his second glass of Malbec, Nick nursed a beer. It had been the meal 'Manny' had dreamed of all day.

Conversation had been kept to a minimum, pending return to the privacy of the car, and now, bill paid, they made the very short ride back to the hotel.

"So..." Nick finally spoke. "What's next?"

"Well, I'd give my right nut to get out of this disguise, but until Dirksen shows, 'Uncle Manny' will have to keep his battle rattle on full display!"

Nick's eyebrows raised at the realization that Jack must be getting extremely uncomfortable in his latex facial appliances, makeup, hair piece, and fat suit.

"It's all pretty amazing." He replied with a bit of a laugh. "I never would've recognized you at the airport if you hadn't prepared me!"

"That's the whole idea, Kid." Jack laughed. "Alot of these cops at least know of me, so I can't look at all recognizable - but man this shit itches after a while! Almost as bad as the decoy granny disguises I used to have to wear during purse-snatching ops in the old days..."

"Oh man, that's an image I don't need in my head!" Nick snorted.

"Seriously, Nick," Jack spoke again, with sincerity. "If Dirksen's not crooked, we'll get a nice, polite call from him tomorrow -either by phone or in person- at a reasonable hour. If he's dirty and up to bad, my bet is, he'll be banging on our door by seven AM at the latest. You know the game and how it works, Detective."

Nick looked at Jack, forehead furrowed, and nodded.

"We'll know soon enough, Son. I lobbed a grenade down his shorts with that note. One way or another."

Returning to the hotel, Nick went into the bathroom, and then returned, ready to grab some sleep before the next wave of action. "Thank you for dinner. I'll take the couch, 'Uncle Manny.' You've had a long day."

"Thanks, Son. You do your Momma Cecile proud." Jack replied with a wink, rolled over, and stuffed a pillow under his head.

In a matter of moments, they were both asleep.

Chapter Nineteen

At exactly six AM, Nick and Jack were startled by a heavy-handed knock on the hotel room door. Nick jumped up from the couch, shaking his head clear, and reached for his gun, only to find 'Uncle Manny' sitting in the predawn darkness, fully dressed, calmly drinking coffee, and ready for action. He motioned for Nick to center himself. Taking another sip of coffee, 'Manny' allowed the knocking to continue for a moment more and then, standing, turned on the bedside lamp, mussed his silver hairpiece to appear sleep-disheveled, and made his way to the door. Opening it, he shielded his eyes from the bright light of the hallway, further adding to his sleepy appearance. Standing in the hall was a tall, broad-shouldered, bald man, wearing a scowl on his face.

"Manny Spinoza? I understand you're looking for me."

"Depends on who you are, Mister." 'Manny' shot back. "You got a name, or am I supposed to intuit your identity?"

"Detective Dirksen, NYPD."

"Ah, Randy..." 'Manny' retorted.

"RANDAL." The bald man corrected.

"Whatever." 'Manny' dismissed. "Come on in. You know my nephew, Nick? He's one of you guys too. Coffee?"

Surprised by Nick's presence, Dirksen walked over, eyeing him as he reached to shake hands. "No coffee for me. Thanks." Dirksen curtly replied.

"Detective." Nick acknowledged, reaching to shake Dirksen's hand, maintaining solid eye contact with him as he did so.

"So, you boys work together at the same house?" 'Manny' asked, making himself another coffee.

"You're new to the precinct, aren't you? I've only seen you a couple times." Nick queried, continuing to watch Dirksen closely as he spoke.

"I'm here now." The Detective commented, a tone of challenge in his voice.

"So— enough of Old Home Week." 'Manny' shot back. "I wanna know who the fucker is that killed my little brother, Pete. You got any leads?"

Dirksen cut a gaze 'Manny's' direction. "No, Sir. A terrible thing. Sorry for your loss..."

'Manny' waved off the feigned sympathies. "Some jerk wad shoots my brother in the head, at his office, in the middle of the night, and you got no leads? How's that? He had a security camera outside his office, didn't he?"

"This is a big city, Mr. Spinoza. Lots of crime - and limited resources. These things take time. And the camera wasn't working at the time of the shooting."

"How effen convenient!" 'Manny' growled. "So, tell me what you DO know then."

A smug smile curled the left side of Dirksen's mouth, and he moved closer to 'Manny'. "Well..." Dirksen spoke in a slightly menacing tone. "One thing I DIDN'T know was that Pete Spinoza had a brother - or that

Nicky here had a second uncle. That fact isn't mentioned in any part of the report. Then, on the other hand, what I DO know is that when I called the number on your business card and asked to speak to you, the woman on the other end told me there was no one there by that name. Odd, huh?"

Dirksen hissed the last part like a snake. Nick stood behind Dirksen, trying to keep his expression steady and unfazed. He had a bad feeling the situation was about to take an unexpected turn.

"For fuck's sake, Man, if you called before you came here, that was the answering service you talked to. We're not twenty-four-seven in the fabric industry, for chrissakes!" 'Manny' grunted with a heavy tone of sarcasm. Glancing at his watch, he then picked up his cell and began to dial.

"Not so fast!" Dirksen challenged. "Allow me."

Taking the phone from 'Manny's' hand, the Detective dialed the number printed on 'Manny's' business card, placed the call on speakerphone, and handed it back to 'Manny.'

"Be my guest." Dirksen said with a wry smile.

Nick stood in rivetted silence, watching the scene unfold. After four rings, a woman's voice answered, "Manny Spinoza's office. How may I help?"

"Rachel?" 'Manny' spoke with a slight cough. "Just checking in. Any messages I need to know about?"

"No Sir, Mr. Spinoza. How's your trip? You sound like you have a cold!"

"Trip's Ok. Yeah, fighting off a cough. Damn airplanes! Flying germ crates! Will be back next week still. Thanks for holding down the fort. I'll touch base again later."

With that, 'Manny' abruptly ended the call. Detective Dirksen looked bested and annoyed.

"We seem to have gotten off to a bad start." He finally spoke.

"Yeah. Seems that way. Any special reason why? I mean, Christ - I'm the innocent victim of a tragedy here. What gives? You're treating me like... like you have something to HIDE!"

"Guess I'm sensitive to criticism." Dirksen half-joked, ignoring 'Manny's' implied accusation. "It read a bit like you were sizing me up."

"My brother's been whacked, and I want answers! You're the Dick in charge. Damn straight, I'm sizing you up! You ARE running this investigation, right? Seems to me you're gettin' nowhere fast. In the meantime, my sister Cecile is heartsick - and my nephew... my nephew... poor boy....lost his favorite Uncle, hands down. I want answers, and I'm gonna be on you like white on rice 'til I get 'em! I want the name of your superior too. I ain't screwin' around!"

This last part, 'Manny' all but yelled. Dirksen nodded his understanding, cutting angry eyes at Nick. "Guess I better get digging then." He replied.

Excusing himself, Dirksen strode to the door. 'Manny' followed close behind.

"What precinct did they ship you in from, Detective? I got a right to know."

Dirksen clenched his jaw, his eyes narrowing. After a moment, he merely answered, "Staten."

'Manny' rolled his eyes and then continued, "And another thing, Randy, just to be clear, I'm the black sheep of the family. Hadn't seen Pete in a good twenty years. My loss now. Last time I saw Cecile was on her wedding day, a long damn time ago. But as you stated at the start of this soiree, 'I'm here now.' "

Opening the door, he bade Detective Dirksen goodbye.

"You'll be seein' me, RANDY. Be watching." 'Manny' growled after the man and, with that, slammed and locked the door, turning to find Nick staring at him incredulously.

"How..." Nick began to speak but was immediately interrupted when 'Manny' raised his hand to silence him.

"Not now, Boy. Not here. Your 'Uncle Manny' needs a real coffee. No more of this pod shit. Let's head over to that coffee place across the way, and I'll be happy to answer all your questions - plus, I got some news for you."

Nick nodded, placed his wallet in his jacket pocket, and followed 'Manny' out the door.

A few minutes later, coffee in hand, Nick and Jack sat at a table in the back of the establishment. So as not to blow his cover as a civilian, Jack allowed Nick the seat against the wall and kept his back to the front door and the patrons sitting scattered around the room. He then checked his watch. "We have an hour before Gus checks in. Lots to cover in the interim!"

Nick nodded, taking a sip from his cup. "First thing I have to know..." He started to speak.

Jack interrupted him with a look of care and warmth. "Your family is doing fine, Nick. Or as fine as can be expected given the circumstances. I was checking in with my team by text when Dirksen came knocking this morning. Your mom sends her love and says to be careful."

A huge look of relief swept the young man's face. "Thank You." Nick replied with deep sincerity, tears welling in his eyes for a brief moment. He looked embarrassed by the unplanned display of emotion.

Jack smiled and nodded.

"Next thing I gotta know..." Nick spoke again, this time with incredulity, "Who the hell did you call on the phone in front of Dirksen? I wondered how the hell we were going to get out of that one!"

Jack chuckled. "Pays to have friends in high places! That was Rachel. I call her in when I need her...talents."

Nick raised his eyebrows and questioned, 'Her TALENTS??"

"Not what you think, Son!" Jack laughed. "We route numbers through to her at times. She's a helluva fake receptionist. Always knows her lines - although I don't know why she didn't catch the line when Dirksen called the first time. Would've been bad if she'd screwed us the second time when I called. Will have to get the scoop on why she misfired."

Nick's eyes widened a bit at the thought of what could've happened in that particular scenario.

"Don't sweat it!" Jack reassured. "Your 'Uncle Manny' always has an extra trick or two up his sleeve."

The two men sat drinking coffee in silence for a bit, and then conversation picked up again. Jack cut a serious gaze at Nick. "Dollars to donuts, Dirksen takes his coffee white."

Nick set his cup down and met Jack's look. "Shooter or Scrubber?"

"Still not sure." Jack answered and then continued, "But it's mighty interesting to me he first showed up when you fellas were investigating the alley where our last vic was found. Sounds like, from what Gus told us, Dirksen knew where he'd find the evidence that needed to be scrubbed there. A really keen and stealthy eye for detail, or something more? Up until then, had anyone even heard of him before?"

"True." Nick nodded. "Not sure about his connections or how he ended up transferring in."

"That," Jack replied, "will be our next mystery to solve."

Glancing at his watch, Jack motioned for Nick to follow him outside. The air was chill, but the sky shone blue, despite rain clouds threatening off in the distance. There was a vague sense of spring trying to arrive, but winter still held its firm grasp.

"Let's take our call with Gus and then get back to the room. I'm gonna need you to stand watch while 'Uncle Manny' disappears for a bit. Man, I need a shower!"

"Gotcha covered." Nick stated his understanding.

After several minutes, Jack's cell rang. He answered while Nick stood beside the bench on which Jack was sitting. The call was kept off speaker, and Jack focused, speaking low and listening intently, while Gus provided his update.

"Nothing too new to report from here, Jack. I'm at the cabin with Theresa, Jessie, and Lindy - our vic."

"How's everyone doing?" Jack asked with concern. "Did the girls ditch Silvers effectively?"

"Theresa and Jessie are Ok. Getting a bit of rest - and yes... they ditched her at a convenience store while she was in the can - with her phone..."

"Nice gal." Jack responded with sarcasm.

Gus continued, " Our vic isn't doing too well. No luck snapping her to yet..."

"About that." Jack chimed in. " By noon, you should be getting visitors, Augustus. I've sent you a trauma doc - Dr. Abram Jackson. One of the best around. African American fella, tall. A psychiatrist who specializes in violent sex assaults. Dr. Anna Paulsen. Female, Caucasian, blonde/blue. You can't miss her. Not only will she be the only female in the bunch, but if 'Psychology Today' had a centerfold, she'd be it. A little odd, given her field, but I digress... if Lindy comes to, she's probably going to be severely unhinged - and all kidding aside, Dr. Paulsen is top-notch in her field. Next up, Dohr Moreno - one of my best pals, will make Three: helluva bodyguard and a mountain of a man. Trust me when I tell you, you'll know him on sight. He'll work security detail so you all can let your guard down a bit. They'll present one at a time and hand over their credentials at the door. Code word: 'PLATYPUS'. They don't present; shoot them on the spot."

"Copy." Gus responded and then asked,

"Enough from here. What do you and Nick have?"

"It's coming along." Jack answered. "Our bald Dick is named Dirksen. Randal Dirksen. Transferred in from Staten, but why and on whose order is anyone's guess. Got a real winning personality... came door knocking at six this morning."

"Huh..." Gus grunted.

"Yep." Jack acknowledged. "Pete's crime scene was scrubbed - excessively." Jack continued. "Wrong coffee put by his head, evidence completely pulled. According to Nick's input, by the time whoever did the scrubbing got through with the task, the scene pretty much looked like Pete was just sitting at his desk in the middle of the night, drinking coffee and diddling himself! Gunshot wound to the temple is irregular too."

"So, they either did a really unprofessional job of scrubbing or had so much of importance to hide they didn't care it was an obvious job." Gus replied.

"Correct." Jack confirmed.

"Nick, OK?" Gus asked, "How's his family?"

"All Ok." Jack answered, glancing at Nick and nodding at him. "He's trooping along. Any thoughts about Angie, Gus?"

"No." Gus responded. "I've wracked my brain, and I just can't come up with any reason she'd withhold intel from me. Also, can't come up with any way she would've tried to get intel to me. I'm at a loss - and it's a big one. It's just too out of character for her. Way out. Something's just not adding up."

"Stay on it." Jack urged and then continued, "Well, Pal, 'Uncle Manny' needs a serious break. Text me when your 'guests' arrive. Next recon same time tomorrow?"

"Same time." Gus replied. "Unless sooner becomes necessary."

"Roger That." Jack responded. "Take care!" With that, Jack ended the call and looked at Nick.

"Son, when we get back to the room, draw the blinds, grab a seat, pull your weapon, and keep your eyes on the door. 'Uncle Manny's' due for a nice, long shower, and he's gonna disappear for a couple hours!"

****

The afternoon passed without incident. Nick pulled guard duty while Jack took a much-needed, long shower and temporarily freed himself of the 'Manny' disguise. The two men remained in relative silence with the curtains drawn while Jack sat thinking. After a bit, he walked over to the picture on the wall, removed it, again turned it glass side up, placing it on his lap. He then took out a piece of paper and a pen. After writing for a few minutes, he handed the paper to Nick.

It read:

' 'Uncle Manny' heads out day after tomorrow. Think I've gotten all I need here.

1: We meet with Dirksen tomorrow early AM at coffee place across street. Not optional so must make happen. Will make appt.

2: Recon Call #2 with Gus tomorrow, 10 AM. Must be clear of Dirksen before that time.

3: Need to know who gave order to move Dirksen in from Staten.

4: 'Uncle Manny' is about to suit up. Let's stick close to home tonight.'

Nick read the note twice, nodded, and handed it back to Jack, who then tore it into tiny pieces. Standing and stretching, Jack walked to the bathroom to flush the pieces down the toilet and transform back into 'Uncle Manny'. Barking over his shoulder as he went, "Nephew, snag me a fresh shirt and cardi from my case. I'm gettin' hungry! Let's hit the restaurant downstairs!"

Chapter Twenty

The previous evening at the cabin had been uneventful and welcomed. It was good to be with Jessie and Theresa again. Gus felt almost human after his shower and Jessie's dinner. Afterward, the three of them sat in front of the fireplace with a bottle of wine, discussing their options. There didn't seem to be many, and after mentally exhausting themselves, they finally turned in. Gus took the couch in the den by the front door and dozed lightly, his .38 at the ready.

Fortunately, the night had passed without incident, except for the few times Jessie and Theresa took turns checking on Lindy.

Awakening the next morning to Jessie's touch on his shoulder, Gus opened his eyes as she offered him a cup of coffee. "Room Service!" She quipped with a smile.

Taking the cup, Gus gave a slight smile, took a long sip, and stared out the picture window for a moment.

"What are you thinking, Augustus?" Jessie whispered.

Turning to face her, Gus locked eyes. His answer came in a monotone voice. "Jess, I just can't see a way to get us clear. No matter what angle I try, we're cooked..."

"I know." Jessie answered and drew a sigh. She then continued, "Come on, Gus. It's not like we haven't been here before, working cases. We've always made it through - sometimes just barely, but still..."

Gus took another swig from his cup and nodded silently. He finally spoke. "True, but Jess, never this bad. My gut is screaming. This is a beast of a different sort. Too many players - most still unknown, too many angles, too many variables, too many questions, and precious few answers. You and I both know it's a miracle we've made it this far. Christ Almighty, if it wasn't for Jack, we'd be dead by now!"

Jessie sat next to Gus and reached for his hand. A soft smile curved her lips, and she looked at him with warmth in her eyes. "It sounds like a mighty fine cop has lost his confidence somewhere along the way. Don't go there, Gus."

Gus drew a breath and fought the tears he felt forming. "Shit - I've lost more than just my confidence..." he muttered under his breath. "Jess, I'm half the man I used to be - if even that."

Jessie sat in silence for a moment and then replied with a gentle grin that quickly faded into sincere concern. "Gus, I told you at the start of this mess, and I guess I'll have to tell you again, so listen and listen good: I've been in this business a long time, and I've never known a better cop than you. You've been hit -and hit hard- the last two years. You'll bounce back and get your bearings, but it will take time... longer if you let the doubts consume you. You know this. It's all still in there, Gus. It's all still in there!"

Gus returned his gaze to the view out the picture window. A tear formed and rolled down his cheek, hot and wet. He let it. Jessie reached up and wiped it away with her hand without speaking.

"I could get you and Theresa killed..." Gus whispered.

"True." Jessie whispered back. "Or not. Only God knows, Gus. Why don't we place our trust in Him for a while? Let's take it one step, one break, one prayer at a time."

Gus instinctively nodded his head in agreement.

"And besides, this isn't the Dark Ages!" Jessie continued. "I know you're a man and all, but it's not your job to look after us 'little women!' Theresa and I are pretty savvy on our own, ya know...except for that time we were on the lam, and the enemy was actually in the car with us..."

Jessie chuckled and nudged Gus to raise a smile. It almost worked.

"Now," she began again, speaking with softness in her voice, "You keep making me talk this way; I'll have to assume you're just fishin' for compliments!"

With that, she leaned against Gus's arm and gave him another playful nudge. Raising the back of her hand to his lips, Gus placed a kiss of appreciation there.

The morning passed.

Now almost noon and his first recon call with Jack and Nick behind him, Gus turned his attention to the long, wooded drive leading to the cabin. Standing on the porch smoking a cigarette, Gus heard gravel crunching in the distance. Snuffing out his smoke and quickly concealing himself in the shrubs by the door, Gus drew his weapon and waited.

Moments later, a car rounded the curve, coming to a stop in front of the cabin. Gus watched as a tall black man exited the driver's side, walked to the back of the car, and retrieved a medical bag. He then made his way to the porch, pausing at the door.

Just as he was about to knock, Gus pointed his gun at the man and spoke low from his hiding place. "Hold it right there. Don't move. I think you have a word for me, Friend."

The man swallowed hard and kept his eyes fixed on the door directly in front of him. "Yes, yes, I do, " he answered quickly. PLATYPUS."

"Hand your ID over to me - SLOWLY." Gus directed, thrusting his hand out to receive the credentials. The man slowly reached into his shirt pocket and, again, without making eye contact, handed the card to Gus. Grabbing it, Gus looked at it closely, keeping his gun trained on the man's head the entire time.

"Sorry, Dr. Jackson." Gus spoke with sincerity, stepping from his hiding place and greeting the visitor.

"Quite alright," the doctor replied. "I understand you have a very troubling case here, and safety is paramount."

"Yes," Gus answered. "We're very glad you're here. She needs you. Let's get you inside and introduced to Jessie. She'll get you settled while I check out your colleagues."

"Just take me right to the patient." Dr. Jackson requested. "There'll be plenty of time for settling in. First things first."

Nodding, Gus opened the door and introduced the man to Jessie. He then returned to the porch, where he waved another passenger from the car to come forward.

Next came Dr. Anna Paulsen. Tall, blonde, and willowy. Just the right amount of makeup to maintain a professional demeanor, well pulled together, and quite attractive. Gus figured her to be around forty or forty-five. She fit Jack's description but in a less blatant way than Gus was expecting. Taking no chances, he repeated his vetting process, complete with a well-aimed pistol. Dr. Paulsen whispered the code word 'PLATYPUS' and then turned to face Gus.

"It looks like perhaps there's more than one person here in need of a bit of trauma relief."

She spoke coolly but looked at Gus with bright blue eyes, displaying a hint of kindness and concern. Gus raised his eyebrows, nodded in agreement, and responded. "I suppose that's an accurate assessment. It's been a really rough week... on top of a really rough two years - or so."

Dr. Paulsen touched Gus on the arm. "Perhaps there will be time to chat about that as things progress here."

Gus nodded and opened the door to the cabin, allowing her admittance. Once introductions were made and Jessie received their new visitor, Gus returned to the porch and waved to the lone figure still sitting in the car. He watched as a tall, muscular man exited and walked toward him. The man was immaculately well groomed and smelled of expensive cologne. Reaching Gus, he seemed totally unfazed, finding himself on the business end of Gus's gun.

"Hey." The man spoke. "Dohr. Dohr Moreno. 'PLATYPUS', Friend. 'PLATYPUS'."

Holstering his weapon, Gus reached out and shook hands with the man. "Glad you're with us, Dohr. We're greatly in need here." Gus spoke sincerely and then added, "Jack speaks very highly of you."

Dohr nodded, and a faint smile lit his stern face. "Comin' from the likes of Jack, that's high praise indeed!"

"Indeed." Gus replied.

"Let's get inside and get this show on the road," Dohr spoke with a blunt, professional air. "Time's tickin', and we never know how close the danger is!"

"True that." Gus replied, opening the door and escorting him inside.

Introductions made, the team immediately began their duties, bringing a slight sense of much-needed relief to Gus, Jessie, and Theresa.

Dohr scanned every inch of the cabin, noting its security vulnerabilities and assets. Dr. Jackson had immediately started an IV on Lindy and stood carefully examining and assessing her injuries. Dr. Paulsen sat in the den, interviewing Jessie and Theresa regarding every aspect of Lindy's case they could detail. Looking up and seeing Gus watching from across the room, Dr. Paulsen spoke in a commanding voice, "You'll be next, Mr. Walker. Please make yourself available."

She smiled efficiently as she spoke, and Gus smiled back, nodding his agreement. Jessie glanced at him and her right eyebrow raised slightly. She then turned her attention back to the discussion at hand.

Breaking for a late lunch of sandwiches and coffee, Dr. Jackson returned to Lindy's bedside. Jessie entered the quiet room and found him monitoring vitals. Meeting the doctor's gaze, Jessie whispered, "How is she, Doc?"

The concern on his face was reply enough. After a moment, he spoke. "I think her injuries are healing well enough, but they've given her a near-fatal amount of drugs. It remains to be seen how she'll be when she comes around."

"Will she??" Jessie sought reassurance.

"Well-" Dr. Jackson spoke again. "She's severely dehydrated and extremely weak. We'll have to see what the IV fluids are able to accomplish. I'm hopeful she'll start reviving within the next few hours. As she hydrates, her body will hopefully start flushing the poisons."

"Do you think she'll be cognitively able to function, Doctor? She's taken one helluva beating..." Jessie looked across the bed and locked eyes with Dr. Jackson. "Doc... we need her."

The doctor nodded his understanding. "Only time will tell. I'll do everything I can." He replied softly and then added, "I have a supply of adult diapers in the trunk of the car. Can someone bring them to me, please? I'd like to get Ms. Abrams bathed and diapered so as the fluids start reactivating kidneys and bowels, she'll be ready."

Jessie nodded her understanding of the plan and responded, "Theresa and I have been doing what we can to keep her clean. We have a small stash of them in the bathroom cabinet. Stopped and bought them on the way here. She's terribly bruised in her crotch area, thighs, and buttocks, Doctor. I'm sure you've already noticed."

Dr. Jackson nodded his awareness. Jessie continued in a whisper, "The only time she's shown any signs of recognition or acknowledgment of us is when we've changed her undergarment. She seems to get a bit agitated, if you can actually call a person in a vegetative state that..."

Dr. Jackson looked up and made eye contact with Jessie as she spoke. He whispered in an unemotional tone, "You've done well. I suspect the action of removing her underpants is triggering a terror response."

Jessie stood silent, looking back at Dr. Jackson, tears coming to her eyes. "Yes..." She finally spoke. "God Bless Her."

Making her way back to the kitchen, Jessie found Gus pouring a fresh cup of coffee.

"Want a cup?" He asked.

"That would be great. Thanks. I could sure use one." She answered and then tossed in for good measure, "How'd it go with Ms. Freud?"

"Fine, I guess. Nothing special. Just a typical psych interview." Gus replied, handing a cup to her and catching her eye.

Jessie took the cup and looked away, somewhat distracted. Walking over to a kitchen cabinet, she opened it, speaking as she did so. "Gus, I've been meaning to give you this. I hope it won't make you sad - but back when Theresa and I had to ditch the Mustang, I grabbed everything out of the back. Didn't realize I had this until the other day. I know how close you and Angie were, and this was the bag she packed for us when we went back to the City, so..."

With that, Jessie placed Angie's plaid thermos bag on the counter next to him. She watched as Gus reached out and touched it reverently.

"Given what happened, I didn't want to pitch it..." Jessie spoke again with care.

"Thanks, Jess. No room for sentimentality now, but it's nice to have a bit of her still with us. That was considerate of you."

With that, Gus stood, coffee cup in hand, and started toward the den. Halfway there, he whirled around, sending the cup clattering to the floor, coffee spilling everywhere. Jessie stood, eyes wide and questioning, as she watched Gus race back to the counter. Grabbing the thermos bag, he forcefully emptied the contents onto the countertop.

"Gus, what the..." Jessie stopped herself as she observed his face.

Eyes focused, forehead deeply furrowed, and jaw set, Gus ran his hands frantically around the inside of the bag. Racing to the utensil drawer, he quickly rifled through it. Armed with a paring knife, Gus set to work carefully slicing through the bag's inner seams. Neither spoke. Jessie stood in silence, watching his every move. His hand plunged deep inside the bag, and with a look of intense concentration on his face, Gus suddenly burst forth with a relieved, euphoric smile and a 'EUREKA!!' "God love ya, Angie! I knew you wouldn't let me down!!"

Lifting his hand, Jessie saw it contained a white, letter-sized envelope with Gus's name hand-printed in black Sharpie. Gus met Jessie's gaze, and she observed a flushed look cross his face.

"Gus...?" She whispered.

"Give me a minute, Jess." He replied breathlessly. "If this is what I think it is, our prayers have been answered!"

Jessie nodded and stood by in total silence as she watched Gus's eyes scan the page. Minutes passed, and then, without a word, Gus handed her the letter. As she read, her mouth began to grow dry, and her throat tightened.

'My Dear Augustus, I hope you find this, my boy. It's the only way I can think of to get this intel to you. Gus, I suspect soon I'll be dead. If that happens, you'll need to know the whys and hows.

The fact that you've shown up at the farm as you have, tells me time is not on my side - or yours. I'll cut to the chase.

About six months ago, Bette -one of my old Girls- showed up here pretty banged up. She'd had a helluva fright. Kept talking about some group of foreign suits she'd encountered while working some fancy party on Park Ave. Real hot shots, and she was supposed to make big money there that night dancing and letting them snort coke off her ass. Instead, she wound up gang-raped and held against her will several hours. You wouldn't think monied folks would be so devilish, but perhaps they got demons worse than regular folks. Anyway, they finally let her go, and she ran to me.

She stayed here about three weeks, and I managed to get her put back together - relatively speaking.

A month later, she shows up again, this time with a fifteen-year-old in tow. Them young ones really get me. Way too young to be in the game, and this one was already way far gone. Pregnant – about five months along - and real sickly. Terrified out of her wits. Bette had sprung her from what sounded to be a baby farm. According to Bette, the same guys were running this show as were at the party that night. Bette and Kimmy stayed here about a month.

I got the goods as best I could, but there's a lot of holes in what I know.

We managed to get Kimmy into the system so she could get prenatal.

Gus, Bette was stabbed to death outside Andover a couple weeks ago. Nothing came of the investigation - just wrote her off as a Trick gone bad - but I know different. She was on her way here and I'm convinced she was running for her life—hard.

Somewhere back in the City, you'll find a warehouse or some such place, filled with stolen women -all colors, all ages- all walks. Word is, they're using them for sex, baby-making, and organ harvesting. Shit, Gus - I just can't bend my mind around that. Right here in our own country! Selling sex is one thing, but Dear Great God Almighty, treating babies like products and women like living organ donors?? Pure EVIL!

Gus, you gotta stop them!

It's obvious a Mob - and Bette says they talk funny. Not a language she's ever heard before. She also says she saw certain people at that Park Ave party, and they were BIG. BIG people, Gus. Like City Hall and beyond Big. You get my meaning? There were little boys and girls at that party, too, all sexed up in skimpy outfits. CHILDREN, GUS! At a sex party!

Do what you can and go with God, Augustus. You was always a bright spot in my life. A rose among the thorns. I have treasured you.

Please don't let this go, Gus. A lot of people's lives depend on you now. I know you won't let me down with this. You never have.

If I die, so be it. I'm old and have done wrong most of my life. Spent the last several years trying to get right with the Almighty, so I expect he'll accept me Home. Don't fret over me.

If you make it out, Gus - live happy. You've got it comin'.

Ange.'

"My Dear God..." Jessie whispered, raising a hand to her mouth, her brown eyes wide. Gus came around the counter, wrapping his arms around her and holding tight.

"What in the world are we going to do?!?" She again whispered, raising her face to look him in the eye.

Glancing at his watch, he reached for his phone. "I'm calling Jack. You go get Dohr-quickly."

With that, Gus dialed as Jessie left the room.

Chapter Twenty-One

Nick and 'Uncle Manny' had just been seated for an early dinner in the cafe outside the hotel and were perusing menus when Jack's cell rang. "Spinoza here." Jack answered, flawlessly in character.

Nick watched as an expression of concentrated concern flashed across Jack's disguised face. Holding the phone tight against his ear, Jack spoke low and in concise sentences. There was no wasted conversation or pleasantries. Jack spoke so low, Nick only clearly made out one sentence: 'Good God. So now we know...'

That was then followed closely with, "Put Dohr on the phone ASAP."

Nick watched as Jack waited intently, looking up only long enough to catch Nick's gaze. Jack's mouth was pulled tight, and his look stern. Nick noted that for the first time since meeting him, Jack was fidgeting, thumping his fork quietly against the table, and repeatedly repositioning his knife next to his plate. Finally, he spoke. Nick listened carefully.

"Man, yeah - quite a pickle. Call in any help you think you might need. We'll pull out after our meeting early tomorrow morning and will head that way. STAY IN CONTACT."

There was no mistaking that the last part was a direct order.

Disconnecting from the call, Jack exhaled, long and slow.

"Bad news?" Nick asked.

"Only the worst." Jack retorted. "But The Worst is my business! Let's get out of here, Nephew. Change of plans... a big one."

Jack tossed some cash on the table to cover the drinks they'd ordered, and together, the two men made their way into the chilly twilight. Keeping a sharp eye on their surroundings, Jack guided Nick into a neighboring wine bar just down the block from the hotel. Business was brisk with lingering Happy Hour patrons. Taking a bistro table toward the back of the establishment, Jack motioned for Nick to sit; all the while, Jack's eyes scanned the room. He seemed agitated. After ordering two glasses of cabernet and appetizers, Jack waited for the attentive waitress to leave. He then turned his full attention to Nick. The young detective was unnerved by the intensity of Jack's demeanor. Finally, Jack spoke. "Kid, what I'm about to tell you is really neither here nor there..."

Nick looked confused and quizzical. "I don't follow." He simply stated.

"Well-" Jack continued on, "what I mean is, it doesn't even really matter at this point because we're in so deep now, there's zero backing out - even if we could. We're what they call 'FULLY COMMITTED'."

"Go on, 'Uncle Manny.' Say what you have to say." Nick braced himself for what was to come. He already knew he didn't want to hear it.

Taking a sip of wine and another breath, Jack laid it on the line. "Well, Son, we're ass deep in evil, and I mean EVIL. And it goes all the way to the top. And I mean the TOP. We are, for all intents and purposes, now living on seriously borrowed time."

Nick swallowed hard and said again, "I still don't get what you're talking about, 'Uncle.'"

What I'm talking about is international trade, just like we thought, but the full meal deal: sex, babies, organs. Mob. And..." Jack paused before continuing, "players so big we probably won't believe it."

"Shit." Nick groaned, wiping his hand across his mouth incredulously. "Is my family gonna be OK?" The young man finally spoke once more.

"I need to do some quick shoring up in that regard, Nick." Jack didn't mince words. "Already on it."

A look of aching dread washed across Nick's face. Jack continued, "'Uncle Manny' needs to bail fast - and his beloved Nephew's coming along for the ride."

"But - I can't!!" Nick blurted in whispered frustration, casting a glance around to ensure he wasn't being overheard. He was clearly distressed and angry. "My family needs me! My job! SHIT! I have a life here, Jack. Responsibilities. I can't just turn tail and run! I'm already two days into sick leave. They're gonna pop me, but good."

"SIMMER, KID." Jack shot a stern warning and followed up with a glare. "Take a breath and collect yourself. Son, they may be watching us right now. I'll protect your family; you have my word. They'll have only the best. Dohr is handling that now."

"Who the fuck is 'Dohr'??!" Nick hissed in reply.

"Only the best commando in existence," Jack answered curtly. "He's on my team now and brings with him powerhouse assets. I promised the best of the best, and that's what you're getting. Nicholas - deep breath, listen close and trust me. You stay here, you're a dead man. You walk in that stationhouse tomorrow, I guaran-damn-tee you, you won't likely live to hit the parking lot for the ride home tomorrow night. Dirksen is in on this BIG. I think he's planning on scrubbing YOU. We need to meet him tomorrow morning as we discussed, and then, immediately after that, we get the hell outta Dodge."

"Where?" Was all Nick could muster the strength to ask.

"You'll find out." Jack answered, draining the last of the wine from his glass.

Catching the eye of the waitress, Jack raised his chin and stuck two fingers in the air. She nodded, and he then continued. "Son, once we're on the road tomorrow safe and sound, I'll tell you all I know. For now, it's too risky to discuss. Just know your entire precinct is a cesspool. They need you gone. Seriously gone. I'd rather have you 'gone' my way than theirs."

Nick nodded his reluctant understanding and agreement. "We gonna make it out?" He asked with concern.

The answer wasn't the one he wanted.

"Nephew," Jack spoke in his best 'Uncle Manny' persona, "there comes a case in every cop's career that's the one that potentially takes him out. This very well may be ours. But hell, what'd you take on that gold shield for if you weren't willing to deliver the goods when it came knockin'?"

There was nothing Nick could say to counter Jack's point. He was completely right. Picking up his glass, Nick emptied it with two large swallows. Looking at 'Manny,' he simply replied, "SALUT!"

Taking out his phone, Jack dialed Detective Dirksen's number. It rang several times, and Dirksen finally answered. "Yeah?"

Immediately, Jack slipped into character. "Randal, Manny Spinoza here. Say, listen, I'm blowing town tomorrow and feel real bad about how we got on. I'd like to treat you to coffee tomorrow morning before I go. You know - man to man. Just a final recap of Pete's case before I leave it to you. I'll be leaving it completely in your hands from here. Me and my Nephew gotta focus on Pete's arrangements and final wishes & all. Would be most obliged if I knew we were ending on friendly terms. Say eight AM at the coffee place across from my hotel?"

There was an uneasy silence on the other end. Jack jumped in, reassuring, "I know how busy you are, Detective. Will only keep you a few minutes. Spare that long for a sad and grieving old man?"

"Well, sure, I guess I can do that." Dirksen finally replied.

"Great! Thanks, Randal. Most appreciated."

Jack disconnected and sat a moment, looking somewhat spent. Taking his last swallow of wine, he then said to Nick, "Come on, Nephew. It's going to be a long night - and an even longer near future, at this stage. Let's get outta here. There's work to be done."

While Gus had been talking to Jack on the phone, Jessie stood next to Dohr. She handed him Angie's note. Dohr stood silent, eyes scanning the page. No expression crossed his face.

As Gus ended the call and placed his cellphone on the kitchen counter, Dohr finally spoke. "Fuck, Man. I'm gonna need a pay increase."

Gus's face turned red with barely contained rage. "Jack didn't tell me you were a fucking low-life mercenary. Get your shit and get out now!"

Jessie stood in silence, watching the two men. Suddenly, Dohr's expression turned to shocked embarrassment.

"Whoa-whoa-whoa! Mr. Walker, I was just joking! My apologies, Sir. I use humor to diffuse hard situations... comes from working with Jack so long! Trust me. I was only making a joke... albeit a bad one. I am ALL IN on this - whatever is needed!"

Jessie looked at Gus. Now it was his turn to look sheepish. "My apologies, Dohr. I'm pulled a little tight at the moment." Gus replied.

"Understandably." Dohr reassured. "This is a truly bad hand we're playing. No two ways about it."

"Well... what's next?" Jessie questioned, looking at Gus. "What does Jack say?"

Gus exhaled. "He and Nick are bugging out of the city tomorrow morning after they meet with Dirksen at eight AM. They'll be heading here."

Dohr chimed in, "I've been instructed to call in reinforcements for Nick's family at the safe house. Doing that now. I'm thinking we could use at least one more gun here, too."

Gus nodded. "Probably wise." He agreed.

"I'll go get on it." Dohr stated and, cellphone in hand, turned to leave the kitchen. As he did, he stopped and turned back to face Gus and Jessie. "My apologies for the bad humor and the angst it caused. You have my word; it won't happen again."

Jessie smiled at Dohr, and Gus nodded his head in appreciation.

Standing alone in the kitchen once more, Jessie looked at Gus. "What time will Jack and Nick get here tomorrow, Gus?"

Glancing at his watch, Gus calculated. "Well - an hour for their meeting with Dirksen, padding for evasive maneuvers and losing tails, I'd say by one or one thirty tomorrow afternoon."

Jessie nodded in acknowledgment. "We'll need more supplies."

Chapter Twenty-Two

After a night spent barricaded in their hotel room, taking turns standing watch, eight AM found 'Uncle Manny' and Nick sitting at a table in the coffee shop across from the hotel. They'd been there all of five minutes when Detective Dirksen arrived. As he walked to the table, 'Manny' stood, extending his hand in greeting. "Detective, so glad you could make it. We appreciate the time."

Dirksen nodded, glancing over at Nick. "Detective." He said stiffly, acknowledging the younger man's presence.

Nick nodded his head in response.

"Tell ya what, time is short. Let's not dilly-dally!" 'Manny' spoke with enthusiasm. "Let me get our coffee orders turned in. Nephew? What'll you have?"

"An Americano, please, Uncle Manny."

"One Americano." 'Uncle Manny' repeated and then added, "Just a boring drip for me!"

Turning his full attention to Detective Dirksen, he then asked, "And for you, Detective?"

Dirksen looked at 'Manny' and replied, "Nothing for me. I'm good. Thanks."

"Nope! Won't hear of it!" 'Manny' shot back, overly solicitous. "My treat! A parting peace offering. I insist. Besides, it's cold out this morning. A good cuppa coffee will warm you up!" 'Manny' made eye contact with Dirksen and smiled.

Dirksen sat a moment, raised an eyebrow, and then conceded. "Well— if you insist. I'll do a tall drip To Go then."

'Manny' nodded, drew a breath, and went for the kill. "You take it black, right?"

"No. No. Room for cream—about an inch. Nice and white! Thanks," Dirksen replied.

"No. Thank YOU." 'Manny' responded, cutting a glance at Nick as he made his way to the counter to place their orders.

Nick sat across from Dirksen but didn't speak or make eye contact. He could feel Dirksen's gaze boring into him.

"So..." Dirksen began. "When you coming back to the cage?"

Just as Jack had instructed, Nick shifted his posture toward Dirksen and spoke. "My Mom's not doing too well right now. Uncle Pete's death hit her pretty hard. I'm dipping into my sick days to tend to her. Should be back to work next week."

"I see. Sorry to hear that." Dirksen replied and then added, "The squad wanted to send your mom flowers, but no one answers at her house..."

Nick cut a hard look at Dirksen, his eyes narrowing. Holding his nerve, he merely stated, "Mom's staying with her friend, Inez. Flowers aren't necessary, but thanks all the same."

Detective Dirksen sat in silence, slowly nodding his head.

At that moment, 'Uncle Manny' arrived back at the table, coffee in tow. "One Americano for you, Nephew. One black drip for me, good and strong... and...one To Go for you, Detective, white as snow!"

"Thanks." Dirksen replied, taking the cup in hand and then adding, "I'd better get going."

Standing, Detective Dirksen extended a handshake. "Again, Mr. Spinoza, I'm sorry for your loss. You have my word; I'll be doing all I can to find out who killed your brother. I'll phone you with any updates."

"About that..." 'Manny' replied, "I have a three-week buying trip to Italy I have to make, so I'll be out of pocket a bit. Gotta get the family all settled before I leave. Feel free to leave info with my receptionist, Rachel, while I'm gone. She'll keep me informed."

Yes'sir. Will do." Dirksen spoke again. "I'll be looking for you next week, Nick. You take care now..."

With that, Dirksen exited the establishment.

"Well, well..." 'Uncle Manny' spoke, watching Dirksen stride to his car. "DING-DING-DING- we have a winner! Just like I thought, takes his coffee 'nice and white'."

Nick looked at 'Manny,' eyebrows raised and face drawn. "He's been calling my mom's house."

"Figured as much," Jack replied. "Let me guess—'just a courtesy call from the Department because we care...' or was it 'we need to speak to you about Pete's life insurance benes...'?

"Flowers." Nick replied flatly. "They 'want to send flowers'."

"Crap, that's so nineteen fifties MAFIA! Why don't they just send her a dead fish, for crap's sake, and be done with it!?" Jack snorted sarcastically. "Don't worry, Son." He then stated in a low voice, touching Nick on the shoulder as he spoke. "They'll never find your mom. She's so deep now, Santa Claus couldn't deliver."

Nick bit his lip and cut a look Jack's direction. "Come on - let's blow. We gotta get on the road."

Having checked out of the hotel prior to meeting with Dirksen, 'Manny' and Nick were soon in the car, buckled in, and on their way. It wasn't long before there was trouble. Glancing in the side mirror on the passenger side, Nick reported, "We have a tail three cars back. White SUV."

"Yes, I know," Jack replied without inflection. "He was on us a couple seconds after we pulled onto the road. Good catch."

Jack cut his gaze to the rearview mirror. "My take is two behind us at least. Probably three. A minimum of one to stay on us once the white one pulls away and another to tag on the side. My money's on the green sedan and the tan pickup."

"Yep. They're running a traffic stakeout on us, for sure." Nick said emphatically.

"So they are." Jack stated. "Aren't we special!"

Reaching for his phone, Jack dialed with his right hand while steering with his left. "Nick, give me cross streets as we pass them, please."

Nick squinted to get his bearings. As he did, he heard Jack speak.

"Hey, Sylvesto! It's Jacko-lantern! Long time no speak, My Man. Yeah - I know. My apologies. I'm in a fix, Pal. Coming in hot and need to shake a tail. Got unmarked Boys In Blue pulling a traffic shakedown. Yeah, here in town a couple days workin' a case. The entrance to the bakery still work? Excellent. We'll be there in..." Jack snapped his fingers at Nick, requesting cross-street info. Nick answered quickly. "We'll be pullin' in in about five to seven. See ya soon!"

With that, Jack disconnected, proceeding to drive casually and in a relaxed manner.

"So— what's your plan?" Nick asked, continuing to look at the side mirror.

"We're heading to Powell's Bakery. Just a few blocks up. We'll park in their lot and go check out the pastries. I could use a good cream puff!"

Jack glanced over at Nick and shot a quick wink. There was a slight twinkle in his eye that had all but disappeared over the course of the past twenty-four hours. Nick looked puzzled but knew not to question. Exactly six minutes later, Jack pulled into the corner lot of Powell's Bakery. The white SUV continued on down the street and the green sedan parked down the block, curbside.

"Yep. Real Smooth." Jack snorted sarcastically. "When we get out of this mess, and you get big-time promoted, tell 'em they really need to teach you guys how to pull off more successful stakeout maneuvers!"

"Yeah - that's pretty lame!" Nick agreed and smiled a half smile.

"Come on, Kid. Let's look at doughnuts!"

Jack and Nick exited the car and walked nonchalantly into the bakery. The man behind the counter glanced up and shot a quick nod over his shoulder. Without acknowledgment, Jack tapped Nick on the arm with the nonverbal command to follow. In rapt attention and total silence, Nick did as instructed, following Jack through a door marked 'STAFF ONLY.' Entering what looked to be the pantry area for the large commercial kitchen, Jack made his way to the far wall. Reaching down past the second shelf, Nick watched as Jack located and pushed a small, nondescript button hidden behind a fifty-pound bag of flour. Nick watched as a hidden door cracked open next to them.

"Come on, Son. And forget everything you're about to see and hear."

Three steps later, Nick found himself standing in a giant chop shop. A sinewy man in his thirties, wearing a large gold cross and red bandana, came walking up to Jack, arms stretched out wide and a broad, beaming smile on his face. "My older Brutha from another Mutha!!!" He laughed, grabbing Jack in a sincere bear hug.

Jack reciprocated equally, following up with a hearty handshake. "SYLVO! Good to see you, Pal! This is Nick. He's workin' the case with me."

Sylvesto looked at Nick with a sincere smile - and eyes that missed nothing. "Good to meet ya, Nick. Any friend of Jack's...yada, yada, yada."

Nick shook the man's hand and responded in kind. "Good to meet you, Man."

"So Brutha. WhatUp??" Sylvesto turned his full attention to Jack as Jack detailed their present plight. "Your's is the brown one outside, you say?" Sylvesto reiterated.

"Yeah." Jack confirmed. "We're gonna need the bags out of it. Couldn't walk in with them without drawing attention."

"Sure 'nuff. Dead giveaway!" Sylvesto laughed. "Tell ya what. After you make your disappearing act, we'll send Maria out to your green tail with a box of doughnuts. That'll be fun! Pick the one you want outta those over there..." Sylvesto pointed behind his left shoulder. "You want Boring and Lowkey or Sporty and Fast?"

Jack and Nick walked over to the three cars Sylvesto had designated for their consideration. "Well..." 'Manny' grinned; I've been waddling around in this fat suit for almost seventy-two hours, driving a boring old man, brown, four-door rental job. We've got ground to cover. What say you, Nick? I'm thinkin' Fast and Sporty!"

Nick raised his eyebrows and nodded in agreement.

"Dodge Challenger it is, then!" Sylvesto announced with a laugh. "That one just got its final fresh coat three days ago. She's ready to rumble. You guys go lay low in the back while I get the Partics worked out. Back in a few."

Jack placed a hand on Nick's shoulder. "I know you have questions, Nick. I'll explain everything once we're officially on our way. For now, we need to crawl in the backseat of that Dodge, lay low, and make small. Sylvo will drive us out, and someone will meet us with our bags."

"Sounds like you've done this a time or two..." Nick replied.

Jack smiled a wry smile and answered, "There are times in life when having friends in high places helps. There are also times in life when having friends in less-high places helps more. Yes, Sylvo has saved my can more than once."

A few minutes later, their plan underway, the Dodge Challenger growled its way out of the warehouse and down the street, Sylvesto at the wheel, seemingly the sole occupant of the car, Jack and Nick crouched low in the back, covered with a blanket. About ten minutes later, Jack and Nick heard the engine stop and an 'ALL CLEAR!' given by Sylvesto. Sitting up from their cramped quarters, they looked around to find themselves parked under an overpass, water in the distance.

"Leon'll be here in a sec." Sylvesto reported.

"What do I owe you, Man?" Jack asked.

"Hmmm... let me see now... Let, Me, See...Not sure you can afford me, Brutha." Sylvesto joked. "You owe me one of those big, fat, juicy, greasy Cheesesteaks and a pitcher next time I'm in Philly!"

"Done and Done, My Friend!" Jack laughed back, slapping the man on the back in a warm and appreciative way.

"Here comes Leon now."

Nick watched as a Porsche pulled up next to them. Engine still purring, Leon jumped out and placed one case and two duffles in the trunk of the Challenger. He then returned to the passenger side of the Porsche without acknowledgment.

"My Friend," Sylvesto spoke, turning to Jack. "By now, your green sedan friends have their doughnuts and know you've given The Glide. Safe travels to you both. Shoot me a text so I know where to eventually retrieve the ride.

Fake docs are in the pocket of the blue duffel. Drive Safe, 'Manny Spinoza'! Oh, and don't forget my payment now!"

Jack and Sylvesto shared a quick final embrace, and Nick watched the man slip behind the wheel of the Porsche and roar off with Leon riding shotgun.

"No time to waste, Nico!" Jack urged. "We're back in the game! Snag those papers out of your duffle, give 'em a once over, and put them in the glove box. We've gotta jet!"

Within minutes, they were headed on their way to Lake George, no one and nothing tailing them. As they cleared the outskirts of the City, after checking the rear and side mirrors several times, Jack reached up and pulled off the silver hairpiece. Nick watched as Jack then peeled off the latex prosthetic pieces he'd been wearing.

"Holy Mother, I feel like a new man!" He sighed. "Next stop, I'm ditching this damned fat suit for some normal duds. I can't wait!"

"I bet!" Nick replied with a slightly amazed tone.

"Ok, Kid, say goodbye to your 'Uncle Manny'!" Jack spoke once more, tossing the hairpiece and prosthetic pieces out the window. "Settle in. I'm about to fill you in on all you need to know. Best get ready..."

Chapter Twenty-Three

Dohr stood watch positioned at the side of the picture window, eyes watchful and keen. Gus and Jessie, having returned moments earlier from their shopping trip in town, worked together in the kitchen, putting away supplies. Suddenly stiffening and drawing his weapon, Dohr spoke in a commanding voice, "Approaching car. Everyone down!"

Immediately obeying his command, everyone in the den and kitchen dropped low and remained quiet. Dohr hit the lights and positioned himself out of sight by the front door.

First came the sound of car tires crunching gravel. Next came the sound of car doors slamming and footsteps approaching. The weather had turned bad earlier that morning, and a heavy fog and mist hung low, draping the cabin and surrounding forest in a heavy, wet, syrupy gray. Vision was obscured, and seeing difficult.

Footsteps sounded on the porch, immediately followed by a series of knocks: two loud, one soft, three loud, one soft.

"That's Jack!" Gus whispered.

Dohr nodded in silent agreement, but taking no chances, employing one quick maneuver, glanced out the side of the window to confirm.

"Yes, it's Jack - but he's not alone. Got a younger man in tow."

"He's good." Gus shot back. "Let 'em in!"

Weapon still at the ready, Dohr opened the cabin door and stood sharp while the two men gained access.

"Good Man!" Jack laughed, shaking Dohr's hand as he entered.

Nick followed in a more reserved manner, his eyes scanning the room and everyone in it. Finally, his gaze settled upon Dohr.

"Hey, Man." Dohr responded to the visual once-over. "Dohr. Dohr Moreno."

"Nick. Nick Spinoza, NYPD."

The two men shook hands as Gus walked over to greet them.

"Nick, glad to see you again. How are things with your mom?"

"She's OK, Mr. Walker - I guess. Thanks for asking. Good to see you again, too. I wasn't sure we'd make it this far."

Jack interrupted by way of providing intel: "Our bald pal, Detective Dirksen has been calling Nick's mom. Seems he's really keen on sending her flowers...."

"Guess we shouldn't be surprised." Gus replied and then added, "That confirms our suspicions."

"Oh, loads to tell!" Jack retorted.

Just then, Jessie approached. Reaching her hand out to Nick, she spoke in a warm and sincere voice. "Good to see you, Nick. I'm relieved you've joined us."

"Thank you, Ma'am." Nick replied.

She then turned to Jack. "Jack, we're glad—and thankful—to have you with us. It's good to see you again."

Jack looked at Jessie, and a look of genuine affection and respect flashed across his face. "Good to lay eyes on you again, Jessie. You're always a bright spot in otherwise dark situations!"

Jessie smiled, and the two embraced quickly.

"Hell, but we're in it good!!" Jack half chuckled.

Jessie, Gus, and Jack stood in silence for a moment. Just then, Theresa entered the room. Introductions made, she then asked, "Anyone interested in coffee? I was thinking I'd make a pot. This weather calls for something warm!"

"I always have room for a cup!" Jack answered enthusiastically and then, turning to Nick, asked, "Nick? How 'bout you?"

"No thanks." Nick answered. "I'm pretty coffeed out, but I could go for a glass of water."

"Sure thing." Theresa answered and withdrew to the kitchen.

Dohr returned to his post, and Gus, Nick, Jack, and Jessie settled on the couches in the den. Stoking the fire in the fireplace, Gus returned to his seat.

After a moment, Jessie turned to Nick. "Nick, you look a little peaked. Is there anything besides water we can get you?"

"No Ma'am. Thank you. I'm just a little off balance at this point."

Jack chimed in, casting an eye on the young detective sitting next to him, "He ought to be off balance. There'd be something really wrong with him if he wasn't. I took the trip up here to fill him in on everything. And I mean EVERYTHING. I suspect he's on overload."

Nick's eyebrows raised, and he shook his head slowly from side to side as he exhaled a long, slow breath. "You could certainly say that." He retorted. "Crap, but this is unbelievable! I just can't get my mind around it all." The young detective spoke sincerely, honestly, and with a hint of dread.

"I know, Son." Gus responded. He then looked at Jack and said flatly, "We're the ones that now need a full debrief. The sooner we get it, the better!"

"Agreed. No time like the present." Jack replied.

Theresa arrived with a tray. On it were coffee mugs, the coffee pot, spoons, a small dish of sugar, a small pitcher of milk, and a glass of water for Nick. Placing the tray on the table, she stood in thought. It was clear she had something on her mind. After a moment, she spoke. "I know I'm not qualified to be here, but could I sit in on this too?"

Jessie glanced at Gus and then Jack. Before either man could reply, she answered. "Of course you can, Theresa. You're in this just as much as everyone else."

Gus drew a breath and nodded but then glanced at his daughter with a serious look of concern and care. "Honey, you need to know that what you're about to hear will change how you view life -and this world- forever. There will be no going back."

"I know." Theresa all but whispered. There was a sound of fear in her voice - but also of determination. "Dad, I'm already past the point of no return, and any innocence I thought I had left flew out the window at Angie's farm."

Gus looked lovingly at his daughter. "I know, Sweetheart. I know. Yes - you need to come join us."

Pulling up a chair, Theresa positioned herself by the fireplace, poured a cup of coffee, and sat in silence, listening intently as the conversation began.

Leaning forward to the coffee table, Gus removed Angie's letter from an unmarked folder, handing it to Jack. Jack took the letter and sitting in silence, his eyes scanned each word, each line carefully. Without speaking, he then handed the letter to Nick. No one spoke as Nick followed suit. Gus watched closely as Jack's expression grew drawn and grim.

"What're you thinking, Jack?" Gus asked in a hushed voice.

Jack cut stern eyes Gus's direction. "I was thinking about Ted Gunderson."

"Yes. I had pretty much forgotten about him until all this started blowing up around us. Sure looks like he had it right - at least in large chunks."

Jack sat silent, nodding his head.

"Who's Ted Gunderson?" Theresa finally asked.

"Head of the LA FBI in the late seventies..." Nick answered.

"My old Chief back in my plebe FBI days..." Jack added. "He was a good guy and damn fine Agent."

"What was he right about?" Theresa again questioned.

Jack and Gus shot a look between them. It was Gus that took on the task of educating his daughter.

"Ted Gunderson," Gus spoke low, "had stumbled upon a human sex trafficking operation, and this one seemed to have a keen interest in very young children. He believed the children were being used for satanic ritual abuse - and when he testified as a Whistleblower, he claimed to have survivor witnesses to corroborate his findings."

Theresa's color faded, and a look of shock flashed across her face.

Next, Jessie spoke. Her voice was also low and serious. "Gunderson testified that the FBI not only knew about the trafficking operation but was a part of it and that young children were being supplied all the way up to the White House..."

She glanced at Theresa and then continued until her voice trailed off, and the group was left in silence. "Gunderson testified that babies and children of color were used as satanic human sacrifices and that white children were forced to watch the sacrificing ceremonies and were then sold as sex slaves."

"My God." Theresa gasped. "You mean to tell me this has been going on since the seventies?!?"

Jack shot a look at Theresa. "Truth is, a helluva lot longer than that."

A momentary look of shame crossed Jack's face. He drew a breath and spoke again. "Some of us in the Bureau consistently turned a blind eye because we either didn't want to believe the charges or were afraid to. The Curse of the Golden Handcuff... keep your head down and claim your pension at the end, no matter what. And then there's the issue of plausible deniability... who really knew or knows what? If your ops get exposed, they want you able to deny any wrongdoing and be believable. This all makes me think of the Blue Suite at the Plaza...."

"What's that?" Theresa quizzed from her seat by the fireplace.

"Oh man... a much longer story for another day, but Clif's Notes version," Nick answered, "the room where all the supposed high-powered sex orgies of the day took place, and the infamous picture of J Edgar Hoover was snapped..."

Theresa raised her eyebrows, and Jack continued, "There was a huge coverup and a hard push to label Gunderson a nutcase. The fact is, though, there's been solid talk about sexual collusion coming from the Seventh Floor for decades, and a few years back, they pretty damned near almost got caught with their pants down -literally- on the international stage. This shit's haunted me my entire career. I guess I started to believe I'd make it to my grave without having to deal with it - or know for sure."

"No such luck now." Nick fired back. "But the fact is, even though Gunderson thought the operation was limited to the halls of power and satanic occult practices - in today's world, it's grown pervasive: the music, film, sports, and fashion industries are infested, and top positions of power too: CEO's, CFO's, banking and business institutions... and government. And it's not 'just' sex trafficking. Satan worship is huge now, and people aren't even noticing it for what it is! It's like a huge, metastasized cancer. Looks like we've been tapped to dance with the devil, and this time, one way or another, it's got to be dealt with. Can't say I'm at all lookin' forward to it, but it's on us now."

"And the simple fact remains: we don't know who we can trust and who's actually in on it. I hate this position! There's even talk that all this satanism stuff is actually a spook-run psyop from the top instead of actual, organic stuff. We can only hope - but still. It's causing a shift in our culture - and not a good one by any stretch." Gus spoke candidly, and the weight of the issue hung heavy around the table.

Jack took a sip of coffee and then added, "At this point, there's precious few people or agencies we can be sure of in this mess. FBI? Most of the field agents are actually kosher, but the heads are corrupt... Center for Missing and Exploited...? VCAC? Who the hell are we going to call in? This thing's too big for just us! Normally, under any other conditions, I'd have us set with connections and materials - but crap. One misplaced moment of trust, one wrong call made to the wrong person, we're all dead."

As Theresa stood and stoked the fire, Jessie broke the silence. "So... what's the plan, Guys? Do we even have one?"

At that moment, a bloodcurdling scream poured from the back of the cabin, followed closely by the sound of furniture being overturned. Dohr was first to respond, racing down the hall toward the commotion, gun drawn. Gus, Jack, and Jessie followed closely, Theresa bringing up the rear. The screams grew louder and more intense. Piling into the bedroom, they found Lindy wide-eyed, screaming and flailing, her bruised hands tearing violently at the IV tubes and punching wildly into the air. Dr. Jackson stood trying to restrain his patient, to no avail.

"Let me! Maybe a female presence will comfort her." Jessie ordered, handing her gun to Gus and calmly stepping forward toward the writhing, thrashing woman.

"Ssshhh... Ssshhh... There, there, Lindy. Honey, it's me, Jess. You're OK... you're OK, Sweetheart..." Jessie spoke softly and lovingly as she made her way to Lindy's bedside. "Ssshhh... It's Ok, Sweetheart. You're OK."

Pale and terrified, Lindy paused her flailing for a moment as Jessie moved in to gently subdue her. Suddenly, Lindy's pounding fists began punching again, catching Jessie in the face, sending her sprawling over Lindy's bed. Dr. Jackson and Gus bolted forward. Jessie collected herself. "Stay back! Stay back!" She commanded. "Let me try again!"

Continuing to soothe, Jessie reached out and stroked Lindy's hair. "It's alright, Lindy. You're alright. You're safe, Sweetheart. You're SAFE."

The distraught woman ceased thrashing, and faint whimpers began to emanate from low in her throat. Jessie continued, "You're safe, Lindy. We're your friends. We're here to help you."

Blank eyes stared up at Jessie and Lindy's dry, chapped, bruised lips contorted, struggling to form words. Slowly, Jesse placed her arms around the terrified woman, gently rocking her and continuing to soothe.

"What can I do?" Theresa whispered from the back of the room.

"Bring us a basin of cool water and a washcloth..." Dr. Jackson whispered in response. "And no sudden movements or loud noises!"

A moment later, Theresa returned with the items. Dr. Jackson stepped slowly away from the bed and walked to meet her. Bringing the basin and cloth to the bedside, he slowly placed it within Jessie's reach. Dunking the cloth in water, Jessie gently patted Lindy's pale, sweating face. She continued whispering words of comfort. Lindy quieted and stared zombielike, oblivious to the crowd of people standing around her in the small room. Jessie looked up at Gus, tears in her eyes and a large, red welt forming on her left cheekbone. Gus looked back, a mixed expression of deep pity, concern, horror, and rage on his face. Jack tapped Nick and

Dohr, motioning for them to follow him back to the den. Dr. Jackson stood silently observing his patient. Lifting his eyes to the door, he raised his chin in acknowledgment of Dr. Paulsen, who stood standing, silently bearing witness to the scene. "Looks like it's finally time for me to get to work." She said calmly, slowly making her way to Lindy's bedside.

Just then, a strange, disembodied humming began to rise from Lindy.

Chapter Twenty-Four

As Dr. Paulsen made her way to Lindy's bedside, Gus held out his hand to Jessie. She placed her hand in his. Gus then gently raised her chin with his other hand and spoke with care, "Quite a shiner you're gonna have there..."

Reaching up and pressing the welt with her fingertips, Jessie winced and whispered, "For a frail little thing, that was one helluva wallop!"

"Terror will do that." Gus stated flatly.

Jessie looked deep into Gus's eyes. A moment passed in silence.

"Come on." He finally whispered. "Let's get back to the den and see if Jack's cooked up a plan to save us yet. Everything's under control here."

Jessie looked back toward the bed where Dr. Paulsen sat, quietly stroking Lindy's arm. Lindy swayed back and forth, eyes fixed in the distance. Her humming grew louder. Standing silent, Gus's forehead furrowed. "Don't Explain." He mumbled under his breath.

Jessie glanced up at him with a questioning look. "Come again?" She asked. "I don't follow."

Gus cut his eyes from Lindy and looked at Jessie. "'Don't Explain'... she's humming Billie Holiday's tune, 'Don't Explain'."

Jessie stood silent for a moment more; a tear formed and rolled down her cheek. "Christ, Almighty, Gus..."

"I know." Was all he answered. Shooting a weak smile at Jessie and slipping his arm around her, he then added quietly, "Let's get some ice on that eye."

Arriving back in the den, Gus led Jessie to her place on the couch and then went into the kitchen. Returning with a bag of frozen peas wrapped in a dish towel, he handed it to Jessie and sat down next to her. As she placed the bag over her swollen eye, Jack began speaking. The mood was somber.

"I fear that girl in there will never fully recover."

"Me too." Jessie agreed. "I'm sure she's experienced things we can't even fathom."

"No doubt." Jack spoke matter-of-factly. "It's going to really stink, dragging her back through it all..."

"What are you talking about??!?" Theresa aggressively challenged. "Why would you even do such a thing?!"

"Vic Debrief, Honey." Gus answered. "It's got to be done - and just as soon as she's able."

Jack spoke again, cutting a look at Theresa. "Theresa, I know it sounds cruel, and I suppose in some ways, it is, but you've got to understand, that girl has been in the belly of the beast. We've got to know what she knows."

"THAT GIRL is named LINDY!" Theresa shot back, disdain rising in her voice.

"Sweetheart," Gus calmed the situation. "Yes. We all know Lindy has a name and is a human being. But Theresa, right this moment, there are hundreds of other 'Lindies' out there being kidnapped, raped- and worse. I know it seems cold, but Jack's right. Just as soon as she gets some strength, we've got to do a Debrief."

Jack added with a caring tone, "Theresa, that's why Dr. Paulsen is here... I called her in especially to ensure no damage is done to Lindy as we extract our intel. I have no desire to hurt her in any way - but the sooner she remembers and talks, the sooner we can deploy. Lives are on the line, including our own. We can't hide out here forever. It's only a matter of time before they find us. I guarantee that bald spook fucker from Staten is putting two and two together right now, and he's not so dumb; he's gonna come up with three. Pardon my language."

Theresa sat tense, rigid with indignation, but she knew Jack spoke the truth. "It just seems cruel, that's all." She replied.

"I know." Jack reassured.

"Theresa, there's no other way..." Jessie added. "Lindy's the only witness we've got. For all we know, they've wiped her memory with all those drugs."

Gus got up and, tossing another log on the fire, stood watching the embers smolder and begin to blaze. "No matter what," he finally spoke, "we've got to get on the inside."

"Indeed so." Jack affirmed.

"But how?" Nick questioned. "We can't trust an Undercover at this point."

"I'll do it." Jessie volunteered, holding the bag of frozen peas to her throbbing temple.

"Won't work." Jack immediately shot back. "They've seen you up close and personal, Jess. We need someone they didn't get a good look at - and that can sing... no offense." Jack chuckled slightly. "I've heard you sing along with the car radio, Jess. You're immediately disqualified!"

Jessie tried to muster a faint smile at the honest insult but winced instead.

"So, what're you thinking?" Gus questioned.

"Well..." Jack responded. "At this point, there's nothing TO think about. We're dead in the water; sorry for the bad choice of words. Until we know who we can trust, we're operating with minimal assets."

"Nobody says I have to be a singer!" Jessie challenged. "It's not like this competition is even remotely legit."

"Jessie, I'm sorry to point this out, but..." Jack winced a bit as he spoke. "You've timed out of this operation anyway."

Jessie looked at Jack as his point slowly dawned on her. "Yes... I see what you mean, Jack. Tactfully stated. I'm basically a grandmother to these guys, aren't I?"

"Pretty much." Jack replied with a wink. "Not much sex work these days for grandmas...."

No one spoke for a few minutes. Finally, Theresa's voice broke the silence. It was soft but strong. "I'll do it. Let me."

Gus's eyes widened, and a shocked look crossed his face. "ABSOLUTELY NOT!!!" He spoke adamantly. "They've seen you, Theresa, and you're not trained for the risks!"

"Aside from Nurse Silvers, they never really saw me, Dad." Theresa challenged.

"That part's true, Gus." Jessie chimed in. "Back at Angie's farm, it was dark, and we stayed at least thirty seconds ahead of them at all times. Theresa had her hat on the entire time, too, when we were running for it."

Gus looked at Jessie. She could see anger in his eyes. "I'm sorry, Gus. I know you feel I'm betraying you here, but..."

"No. No. I'm sorry, Jess." Gus responded, calming himself. "I'm just furious we're even in this mess, and now it's personal!"

"Roger That," Nick threw in. "Welcome to my world..."

Gus reached over and rested his hand on the young detective's shoulder. "Sorry, Son. I know I must sound selfish after what you and your family have already endured in this mess."

"So-" Theresa took advantage of the lull, continuing to press her case. "I sing in the church choir, Dad. Put a wig on me and stick close by; what's the worst that could happen?"

"It's not that easy, Theresa - and that's a heavily loaded question! Best not to put that out there." Jessie corrected.

"No wigs!" Jack shot back loudly. "They pull a wig off your head - you're dead. Whoever does this, goes in clean!"

"True!" Jessie agreed.

"Fine then. Cut and Color, here I come!" Theresa retorted unfazed.

"Sweetheart..." Gus began.

"Dad, NO." Theresa interrupted her father, finding new determination and purpose. "All my life, I've watched you put your life on the line, doing good for others. Jessie does it... and Nick... and Jack... and Dohr. My life has pretty much been spent whining about my hardships and just marking time. What's the point? If we truly believe in our Lord and Maker, we have to believe and trust He has us safe in the palm of His hand - always. Why do I go to Mass if I'm not willing to act on faith when called? And now that I've seen what I've seen... Angie? Arlo? Nick's Uncle Pete? And Lindy? Am I just supposed to sit here and hope somebody else comes along to do the dirty work and get us out of this nightmare? There IS no one else!!!"

Jessie looked at Gus. Gus looked at Jack. Jack looked at Nick. Nick breathed a deep sigh and wiped his palms on his thighs.

"She makes a compelling argument, Augustus - much as I hate to say it." Jack finally spoke low.

"I know. DAMMIT." Gus retorted.

"We really don't have a choice." Jessie threw in her two cents.

"Good. I'm in!" Theresa spoke decisively.

Just then, another voice spoke from the hallway. Looking up, everyone watched as Dr. Paulsen entered the room.

"Just letting you know our patient is actually coming around nicely, all things considered. And... for what it's worth, I sang in a jazz trio in college. My psych training is handy in bad situations and when dealing with unstable people -like criminals- and I hold my own when the chips are down. We get Lindy coherent and stabilized; I'm in with Theresa. Two on the inside is infinitely better than one. 'Assuredly, the evil man will not go unpunished, but the descendants of the righteous will be delivered...' "

"Proverbs 11:21..." Theresa whispered in reply.

"Yes. We do this together, Theresa, or it doesn't get done."

Her piece said, Dr. Paulsen shot a stoic smile at the group, turned and retreated back to Lindy's room.

"Well, Ms. Freud has spoken..." Jessie muttered in a low voice. "I admire her pluck."

"She has a strong point there..." Jack replied. "Two on the inside... potentially safer, and a faster gathering of intel."

"The trick will be keeping them together in that environment without generating suspicion... and then making sure they're never separated, under any circumstances." Nick spoke this time, and his voice was stoic. "They get separated; we're in deep trouble. Can't risk AirTags."

"Or can we?" Gus questioned, his mind kicking into gear as he surrendered himself to the plan taking shape.

Just then, Jack's cell phone rang. Quickly pulling it out of his vest pocket, he glanced at the number and spoke hurriedly, "I've got to catch this. Just one second."

The group sat in silence as Jack conversed with the person on the other end. His eyes grew wide for a fleeting moment, and then he began peppering questions: "You absolutely sure? No doubts whatsoever? Rock Solid supporting intel on this? We can't screw around! OK. Copy. Thanks."

Ending the call, Jack drew a breath and looked at the group. "Well, Boys and Girls, highly reliable intel has Randal Dirksen as a cousin to the mayor. He's been transplanted from Staten to Nick's cage on a Temporary. No reason given, but the request came from high up. VERY high up..."

Turning to Nick, Jack continued, "Son, you've got mighty powerful enemies!"

"Hell." Nick groaned. "All this for something I barely knew anything about just a week or so ago!"

"Yeah..." Jack responded. "Quite an inheritance your partner and your uncle have left you. About as good as VD."

"Only deadlier." Nick groaned again.

Gus sat in thought for a moment and finally spoke. "Well, we best get this scheme cooking. Dirksen will find us soon enough. I'd prefer we take the fight to him instead of hiding out here like sitting ducks."

"Agreed!" Jessie replied. "Let me grab some pens and paper so we can chart our next steps."

"I'll get it!" Theresa replied. "You keep that cold pack on your eye."

Reaching the kitchen counter and locating a writing tablet and two pens, she quickly returned to the group. Handing her father a few sheets torn from the tablet and a pen, she then handed the remaining tablet and pen to Jack.

Gus then spoke again. "As I see it, our first steps involve getting Lindy to the stage where we can debrief."

"Yes." Jessie agreed and then continued. "But in the interim, we need to get Theresa and Dr. Paulsen... ANNA, polished to a believable point. That means a new look for Theresa, a believable backstory cooked up for both of them that withstands scrutiny, and some Billie Holiday coaching as to her history and style. If they supposedly love the woman enough to try to become the next HER, we need to make certain they know what they should know!"

Gus made notes while Jack sat thinking. Finally, he threw in. "This AirTag thing bothers me. We can't risk anything being found and giving them away."

"Can't risk losing contact with them either." Gus challenged forcefully.

"Without a doubt." Jack reassured. "I'm thinking our girls need 'Management.'"

Theresa's face contorted into a look of incredulous confusion. "Oh, like that's ever gonna happen!" She tossed out a forced laugh. "And besides, where in the world..? And how would we even have time for that?!"

"I see what you're saying, Jack..." Gus replied, a tone of cautious, optimistic relief in his voice. "Got anyone in mind?" He cut a look at Jack and gave a quizzical half-smile.

"I think I can dig up someone... a nice bit of a sleazy 'Manager's' just what this op needs... not too clean, not too legit... a sleazeball with just enough sleaze and desperation to be willing to make a nasty deal if and when the price is right..."

Nick sat watching Jack. It was obvious Jack's wheels were turning.

"Nick, bring me my Dopp from my case, will ya, please? I should have enough stuff still in there to come up with something."

Standing and stretching slightly, Nick grinned a faint grin and said over his shoulder as he exited the room. "Am I about to meet another long-lost 'uncle' I didn't know I had?"

"Maybe so!" Jack answered and then added with a bit of a gleam in his eye, "A nice pervy one."

Jessie sat shaking her head. "Jack - you never miss a trick!"

"Bad choice of words, considering the circumstances, Milady, but I'll take the compliment all the same!"

Jesse smiled and spoke again, "So - a disguise for Jack, a disguise for Theresa, two beaded cocktail dresses..."

"From a thrift store! Nothing too new or refined." Jack interjected. "My girls can't be too highbrow now! We've got to be believable."

"Will make note!" Jessie responded and then continued, "And some Billie Holiday education and voice rehearsal."

"Check, check, and check." Gus replied, making notes as he did so.

"Then what?" Nick chimed in.

"We need to find the entry applications for this thing and study how this outfit is set up." Jack answered. "How does the contest work? Where is it held, and when? How often do they hold this little shindig? What are the steps to gain entry?"

Nick grabbed a sheet of paper and removed his own pen from his shirt pocket. He then made notes of his own.

"Hopefully, once our vic is able to handle the debrief, we can learn most of this stuff from her." He said as he wrote. "These are steps she would've had to take to end up where she did."

Theresa squirmed in her chair and cleared her throat in agitation.

"I mean, Lindy..." Nick corrected himself.

"Once we get Lindy debriefed, I'm thinking we'll bug out and head back to the city... but not you, Nick." Jack spoke as though issuing an order.

Nick's face flushed with anger and frustration as he sputtered, "You think you're parkin' me during this operation, you've got another think coming! LIKE HELL!!!"

Jack and Gus glanced at each other. "You want to tell him, or should I, Augustus?" Jack asked calmly.

"I will." Gus responded.

Looking at Nick with determined concern, Gus spoke with care. "Nick, you've got the whole of New York City -and then some- looking for you. And they know you on sight. When they find you, you're gonna be sorry. VERY sorry. And it's safer for your family at this point to have you out of the city."

"And besides," Jack chimed in, rifling through the makeup supplies remaining in his Dopp kit, "we need an extra gun here. Company for Dohr. He gets lonely. And tired. You can spell him at watch."

Without giving Nick time to reply, and while continuing to search through the Dopp, Jack spoke over his shoulder in a raised voice, "Sound like a solid plan, Dohr?"

"Yessir! Perfect." Dohr replied without hesitation.

Nick knew not to challenge but sat silently fuming.

Chapter Twenty-Five

Two days passed in a frenzy of active preparation. Theresa and Jessie had taken the Challenger and left early that morning for Saratoga Springs to work on their assignments, obtaining a new look for Theresa and thrift store shopping for the items needed to pull off their fresh disguises. The hairstylist at the salon, thinking she was giving a freshly divorced young woman a new lease on life, took extra care turning Theresa's shoulder-length brown hair into a chin-length bob of honeyed blonde. She then tweezed Theresa's brows into a more lifted arch, dyed them to match the new hair color, and then provided a makeover. The effect was truly stunning and as the two women walked down the street, Jessie shook her head and smiled as she caught Theresa repeatedly glancing at herself in each store window. Making their way into the thrift store, they headed for the 'Evening Wear' section. Pulling a yellow sticky note from her purse, Jessie said to Theresa, "Anna is a size eight dress and a 6.5B shoe. She states, 'Something blue if possible.' "

"Okey Doke." Theresa acknowledged, looking through the racks alongside Jessie.

Eliminating Mother of the Bride dresses, Wedding and Prom dresses, they found their selection reduced to just one rounder.

"Ooooh! Still looks promising!" Jessie whispered hopefully.

"Sure does!" Theresa replied, sliding dresses by her as she whipped through the stock.

"Here's one..." she said to Jessie as she lifted a dress from the rack. "You said size eight and preferably blue, right?"

"Yes." Jessie confirmed.

"Did she say what type of blue?" Theresa queried as she carefully looked the dress over and pondered the selection.

"Memory serves me," Jessie answered, " I think she said Royal or Sapphire."

"Perfect! Voila!" Theresa chimed. "Whatcha think??"

Jessie watched as Theresa pulled the dress from the hanger and held it up for Jessie to see. Teeming with royal blue sequins, the dress was cocktail length with a plunging V-neck and three-quarter sleeves. Upon close inspection, some of the threads holding the sequins in place had broken and frayed, causing a few small bare spots and making the dress appear mildly moth-eaten.

"Doesn't get any more perfect than that." Jessie agreed.

"Now for me!" Theresa quipped, reaching for a candy apple red satin three-piece pantsuit with a wrap jacket and sequined undershell. Looking closely, this garment also harbored carefully disguised signs of wear.

"Does this color go with blonde?" Theresa positioned the jacket carefully under her chin and modeled it in front of the mirror.

"Like champagne and caviar!" Jessie chuckled and winked. "Now, if you can tear yourself away from your magnificence, we need to get to the Men's Department and then Shoes! We get this task done in a timely manner; maybe we can grab lunch out somewhere like real humans!"

"I like how you think!" Theresa chimed in reply and then grew solemn. "Jessie, do you think we'll get out of this nightmare and make it back to normal life? I get really scared sometimes, and it all just seems impossible..."

Jessie paused and leaned on the rack in front of them. She breathed a deep sigh before replying. Turning to look Theresa in the eye, she spoke in a low voice, picking her words carefully.

"Theresa, I've worked a lot of cases in my career where I wondered if I'd make it to the next minute. I always managed to, by the grace of God. We're working with your dad and Jack on this - two of the best I've ever known, and Jack has powerful resources at his disposal - but Honey, honestly, there are no guarantees. I'd be lying to you to say otherwise. There comes a point in life where you have to wrestle with the truth that there's a tipping point for most people... a point of no return, where life changes and shifts like an earthquake. Innocence is lost; dreams die... our most cherished people leave us. It's all part of the process. Up and down the street out there right now - are people having fun... going to lunch, experiencing their first kiss... achieving goals and dreams. And out there on that very same street are people on their way to the funeral home, the hospital, and divorce court. Some folks out there won't live through the night to see tomorrow. What drives me in all this is knowing that out there somewhere right this second, are young women and children... and even young men and boys, going through things so hideous we can't even begin to imagine. Who's going to help them? Who's going to come for them...? And how will they ever move on with life once they're free? So no, Theresa, I can't promise we're going to make it - or even that if we do, we'll ever be the same again. It's the price we have to pay to do what has to be done. I can only vow to make this hellish journey with you -come hell or high water- and trust the good Lord has us - like you said a couple days ago. There are people out there who will never know life from this angle. They're lucky -and cursed- all at the same time... but think of Angie... Arlo and Pete... and those young women Angie tried so hard to help. Draw your strength from them, Theresa. We don't have any other choice."

Theresa stood, absorbing Jessie's words. Reaching over, she took Jessie's hand and held it in her own for a moment. "Thank you, Jess." She replied softly. "I appreciate your honesty. And I know you're right. I passed the point of no return a long time ago. There is no going back now... no me to go back to."

Jessie wrapped her arms around Theresa and then stood looking at the younger woman. She lovingly smoothed Theresa's newly blonde hair and then said with a smile, "Come on, Goldilocks! We've got this one moment in time to be as light as possible. Let's finish our shopping and then go eat! I'm starving!"

Theresa smiled and nodded.

Continuing on to the Shoe Department, they found a pair of slightly scuffed black heels for Theresa and a pair of blue, satin pumps that had salt stains on the heels.

"Looks like somebody had a winter wedding!" Jessie noted, observing the stain damage. "These are Anna's size and almost match her dress. Even better if they don't match perfectly..."

Glancing at the yellow sticky note once more, the women made their way to the Men's Department, where, after much searching, they located a suit for Jack. Single-breasted, a dull gray, with one loose button and a coffee stain on the lapel, it was exactly what they needed. They then found a slightly dingy white shirt and a burgundy and navy striped tie. Theresa and Jessie looked at each other and grimaced.

"That color combination's just truly HIDEOUS." Theresa groaned.

"Sold!" Jessie chuckled.

Purchases made and makeover complete, they stopped for lunch at the diner down the street and then headed back to the cabin, taking care to keep an eye out for tails and arrive before darkness set in —just as promised.

In the interim, Jack had taken inventory of his makeup supplies and had spent the last couple hours perfecting his new look. He had just enough makeup and latex to stipple the effect of acne scars across his cheeks, throat, chin, and nose and enough hair lace left over for some brow work. Being sparing afforded him just enough effect to alter his features to the point of being unrecognizable to anyone who might know him while remaining believable to the near-naked eye. He'd have to be sparing with his bottle of spirit gum as he only had a half bottle left. Minus the fat suit and toupee he'd used as "Manny', no one would suspect he was the same man. Add the less-than-fresh suit, and Jack felt confident it would be a perfect disguise for the purpose.

Gus had taken the time to compile a playlist of classic, best-known and loved Billie Holiday tunes for Theresa and Dr. Paulsen to familiarize themselves with. Once Theresa returned, she and Dr. Paulsen could begin studying the tunes on Dr. Paulsen's phone. It had been a nostalgic morning for him as he listened to the songs, thinking of Mary and the times they'd listened together.

When Gus downloaded Billie's rendition of 'If You Were Mine,' he was surprised to find himself sitting and listening on repeat, his thoughts, mind, and heart focused intently on Jessie.

'Yes, even my heart
Even my life
I'd trade it all for you
And I think I was lucky, too
If you were mine...'

Taking a deep breath, Gus stood, stretched, and made his way out the back door for a much-needed smoke. Thoughts tangled and turned in his mind, and he found himself weary. The coming days were going to be fraught with danger, tension, and stress, and he had no way of knowing if any of them would even make it out the other side alive. One thing he did know for sure, in the days to come, they would encounter a degree of evil that would forever change and shape each and every one of them. He had a deep foreboding, and life stood suspended in front of him - time standing still... no past - and certainly no future he could count on. Taking a deep drag, Gus breathed a silent prayer for guidance and protection. He then snuffed his smoke and returned inside.

Nick sat cleaning his gun, still bent out of shape at their refusal to allow him to accompany them back to the city. He didn't look up as Gus entered.

The only sticking point in their preparations was Lindy. She was progressing under the watchful and skilled care of Dr. Jackson and Dr. Paulsen - but not as quickly as needed. Lindy's eyes now tracked, and she was aware of her surroundings. Her zombielike humming episodes were subsiding, and it was clear to all that she was coming back into her body, though there had been a couple more screaming and punching episodes. These happened as the light faded outside, and darkness began to set in. It was as if night held extra terror for her, and Dr. Jackson and Dr. Paulsen now utilized very small doses of sedative each late afternoon to head off the panic and to keep her soothed. It was becoming clear, too, that the presence of men around Lindy, except for Dr Jackson, sent her into full-on trauma response. Obtaining the much-needed debrief was going to be a real challenge given this issue, and Gus worried about that fact more than he let on.

Returning to the kitchen, he found Dr. Jackson pouring a cup of coffee. The doctor looked up and smiled. "Care to join me?" He asked Gus.

"Don't mind if I do." Gus answered and then added, "I've been hoping to talk with you, Doctor."

Dr. Jackson poured a cup and handed it to Gus. The two men then seated themselves at the kitchen table.

"Lindy's injuries are healing well." Dr. Jackson reassured. "Well, her physical injuries, anyway. At least as far as I can ascertain in these conditions and this environment."

He stressed the last part and looked at Gus with directness. Gus met the doctor's gaze with understanding.

"I know we can't keep her here much longer, Doctor. She needs more care than you can provide here. SOON..."

"Yes." Dr. Jackson replied. "Just from a psychological perspective, as soon as her mouth heals and swelling subsides, she will need reconstructive and dental surgery to help her move forward with her inner healing. At this point, we can't risk allowing her to see herself in a mirror. The shock might prove too much."

Gus took a sip of coffee and nodded. "As soon as we can interview her and get back to the city, we'll transport you both to the private facility Jack's got arranged. Shouldn't be but another couple days now."

Dr. Jackson nodded and replied, "Good. I'm relieved. You don't have to worry about me remaining on the case. When Jack calls, I answer -fully committed- for the duration."

Gus smiled at the loyalty. Taking another sip of his coffee, he then changed the subject. "Doctor, I need your professional opinion on something, if you don't mind."

"Of course." Came the sincere reply.

Standing and walking over to the storage closet in the hall, Gus soon returned, carrying 'Nurse Silver's' leather medical bag. Placing it on the table in front of Dr. Jackson, Gus opened it and removed the velvet pouch and its contents. Setting the unmarked vial and syringe in front of Dr. Jackson, Gus then queried, "Doc, if this is Scopolamine, what would it be used for in this amount?"

Dr. Jackson's eyebrows raised, and he looked at Gus with mounting concern. "Of course, I have no way of knowing the exact dosage of the contents of the bottle since it's unmarked, but even if it's the lowest dosage available, there's enough there to kill someone -or something- a couple times over. Is there only the one syringe accompanying the bottle?"

Gus nodded his head.

"I'd say that's most worrisome, Mr. Walker. Most worrisome. Where did you obtain this?"

Gus then relayed the saga of 'Nurse Silvers.'

Dr. Jackson sat in silence, listening with rapt attention. Finally, he spoke. "Scopolamine of this magnitude, in the hands of an unskilled person, can only be used for what amounts to murder. So are you telling me this was to be Ms. Abram's fate?"

"Seems that way." Gus answered and then added, "Not just Ms. Abrams. Whoever we're up against not only seems to have a fixation with this stuff - they have zero problem getting their hands on it. The murdered women found in the city over the last month or so had been injected to the point of overdose. It was hidden from the circulating reports."

"My God." Dr. Jackson exhaled. "Where are these people getting this in such volume? They have to have hospital connections..."

Gus shot a hard gaze at the doctor. "That's what I'm afraid of." He half whispered. "And, I'm even afraid to allow myself to..."

"Someone you know??" Dr. Jackson asked in a low voice.

"YES." Gus's one-word answer was sufficient.

Just then, Dohr's voice announced the arrival of an approaching car. After a tense moment, it was confirmed to be Jessie and Theresa.

Placing the bottle and syringe back in the velvet pouch and the pouch back in the medical bag, Gus returned both to the storage cabinet and went to greet the returning women.

Chapter Twenty-Six

Theresa's new look was met with an enthusiastic reception. Jack and Gus were relieved the change had orchestrated a drastic alteration of her appearance while remaining subtle and believable.

A couple times over dinner, Theresa had actually caught Dohr staring at her. Her new blonde persona was going to take some getting used to.

Dr. Paulen's dress and shoes fit her perfectly, and Jack was quite pleased with his suit, shirt, and tie.

"Good job, Ladies!" He said with an approving smile. "We look just motley enough while maintaining a smattering of dignity! If I was a Ukrainian mobster, I'd want us in the competition!"

Later that evening, the conversation over dinner bounced between the plans of the operation, Lindy's marked improvements, and the new pieces of intel Jack had gleaned from his vast network of sources. Finally, Dr. Paulsen spoke, looking over at Dr. Jackson as she did so.

"My sense is, Lindy should be about ready to slowly begin mild debriefing. But I emphasize MILD. Do you agree, Dr. Jackson?"

Chewing his last bite of baked chicken, Dr. Jackson set down his fork, dabbed his mouth with his napkin, and thought carefully for a moment before replying.

"Well..." he answered slowly, "all things considered, I think she might respond well to very light, generalized conversation - but I'd prefer she be a bit stronger before the difficult questions are posed. Up until now, she's had nothing but IVs and broth, and she's still quite weak physically. I'd like to get a bit more nourishment into her to pad her nervous system before the real grilling begins. If you could allow me another twenty-four to forty-eight hours, I'd like to get some of those protein drinks and heartier soups into her."

Dr. Paulsen sat nodding but didn't speak. Gus, Jack, and Jessie exchanged worried looks.

"Doctor." Jack finally spoke with concern, "I know you're aware the longer we stay here, the more dangerous things become. Time isn't on our side in this. We're hard up against it."

"Yes. Most, unfortunately." Dr. Jackson responded. "But the most pressing risk, as I see it, is pushing Lindy too strenuously, too soon. We do that before she's ready; reliving the shock and horror could cause her to shut down permanently."

Dr. Paulsen spoke again, supporting the Doctor's claim. "Dr. Jackson is correct, everyone. If we don't handle Lindy with kid gloves at this stage, we could very well cause an irreversible, total psychological collapse..."

"And then-" Jack added, "our chances of obtaining any usable intel go right out the window... permanently."

"Correct." Dr. Jackson agreed.

"SHIT!" Jack stated in frustration, tossing his napkin on his plate.

"We've got to get moving - one way or another," Gus added. "Dirksen and his goons are out there getting closer; I can feel them."

Jessie sat in silence, tapping the edge of her knife against her plate, deep in thought. Finally, she spoke.

"No two ways about it, we've got to break camp. It's pretty much a miracle they haven't already found us. Any second-tier records search would link me to this property, even though Brian and I don't have the same last name. When I suggested this as a hideout, I never thought we'd be here this long. Gus and Jack are right... each second that passes, we get closer and closer to being found."

"Any ideas?" Gus asked, focusing his attention back on Jessie.

"Yes, actually." She answered. "Jack, Anna, and Theresa need to get back to the city and start setting up their presence there. It's a given, Gus, you have to follow. That leaves me, Nick, Dohr, and Dr. Jackson to close up the cabin and transport Lindy to the private care facility Jack arranged in Boston. Lindy's treatment and progress can be accelerated there; Nick and I can debrief her incrementally and report what we learn to you and Jack by burner. After we learn all we need, I'll join you in the city..."

Just then, Nick's voice rang out across the table. His anger was palpable. "Up 'til now, I've done as ordered and instructed, but I'm through being treated like a child! I graduated the Academy, same as you, Gus - and although I may be a Newbie to you guys, I'm no fucking idiot! This op goes to the dark places it looks like it's going; we're gonna need every trained man -and every gun- we can get. I'll stick with Jessie as she's just strategized, but you can bet your sweet ass when she heads back to the city I'll be with her! And from now on, back the fuck off and let me do my job!!"

Gus and Jack sat in silence for a moment, a look passing between them. Finally, Jack responded. "You're absolutely right, Nick. I'm sure I've seemed condescending, but I assure you, I didn't mean to be. Yes, some of it is probably a bit of that deeply ingrained FBI arrogance - but mostly, I've just been trying to keep you alive. Yes, you should be with us. Gus?"

Gus took a sip of wine and a moment to answer. "Yes. Absolutely. My apologies Nick. I meant no disrespect. Your Uncle Pete was a good friend of mine for a very long time, and I've come to think of you as a godson. I need to stop letting my personal feelings interfere. So, if it's OK with Jessie, that sounds like the perfect plan."

Jessie looked at Nick as he sat at the other end of the table, face still flushed from his angry outburst. Shooting a wink his way, she replied, "Affirmative! Looks like we have our plan then."

"Good!" Nick shot back.

"Where do I officially fit in this new arrangement?" Dohr questioned Jack.

Jack took another sip from his wineglass and pondered for a moment. "I'll call for another gun to rotate watch with you, but you're taking the head position on this, Dohr. I want you on Ms. Abrams at all times. No one gains access to her or her room without going through you. Who you want working Second?"

Dohr thought a moment and then answered, "My preference is Cardoso. We know each other's patterns and work well together."

"Good. Give him a call ASAP." Jack replied.

Dinner completed, Dr. Jackson excused himself and returned to Lindy and his duties. Dr. Paulsen and Theresa retired to their room, where they began reviewing Gus's playlist. Jack, Nick, and Dohr returned to the den and continued their discussions. Gus stayed behind in the kitchen with Jessie, helping clear the table and tidy up. Jessie washed while Gus dried and stacked.

Neither spoke for a moment. Finally, Jessie cast a long look at him. "So, what do you think, Augustus?"

Gus's jaw tightened as he dried the last plate, setting it with the others on the counter. Finally, he answered, his voice just above a whisper. "Well,

Jess— every minute that goes by, the danger grows and gets closer. And every minute that goes by, somewhere back in the city, unspeakable things are being done - and to be perfectly honest, it's taking all I have to cope with that fact... I can barely stand it. We've worked some dark, hellish cases before - but nothing like this. No matter how hard I try, I can't see past the next seventy-two hours... there's just nothing there..."

Jessie placed the dishrag over the sink faucet. "I know." She whispered. "I feel the exact same... My God, Gus - this world we've been living in and thought we knew all these years... the evil that's been happening all around us - right under our noses...we're damn good at our jobs! How'd we never see it??!"

Gus turned and looked Jessie full in the face. "Maybe on some level, we did." He replied, a pained expression on his face.

Jessie's forehead furrowed. "What are you saying, Gus??" She asked incredulously.

"Well..." He replied, setting his gaze off in the distance. "Jess, the world around us... our Day to Day... it's been getting darker and darker and more and more perverse with each year. Drugs, porn, perversion, criminality... we've been like frogs in a pot of water slowly heating on the stove, oblivious to being cooked. Brainwashed and desensitized to it all... just turning a blind eye. I mean, come on - we know the corruption in our own government and three-letter agencies. We've both repeatedly had to navigate around and through it just to get our jobs done! Pardons for criminals and good people jailed just for taking a stand. We've just had the luxury of pretending this heinous shit either wasn't happening - or just wasn't as bad as it really is. Looks like those days are over..."

Jessie stood in silence, listening. Finally, she replied. "I know what you're saying is the truth - but my soul just can't bear it."

"I know." Gus answered. "God Save Us."

Jessie cut her eyes to Gus's face as he spoke. "Gus... are we gonna make it through all this?"

Another long moment passed before he replied. "We're all in God's hands now, Jess. We're in so deep, I have absolutely no read on how this is going down. We're up against a foreign mob and twisted people in our own government. We both know they're gonna fight to the death -theirs- or ours. It's gonna take every bit of our training - and then some... we're up against our own, pretty much, and they have all the same training and know all the same tricks we do. The only thing I'm hoping for at this stage, short of a full-bore miracle, is hubris on their part. Their arrogance and blatant ego might cause mistakes we can utilize. If that's not there and in play, I fear we're in awful trouble."

Jessie drew a breath, wrapped her arms across her chest, and stood slowly, nodding her head, deep in thought. Gus sighed, looking past the kitchen window into the inky, black darkness of the woods beyond the cabin. Steeling his nerve, he walked back over to Jessie and took her by the shoulders. Looking deep into her brown eyes, Gus spoke low, emotion cracking his voice and a mist of tears veiling his eyes. "One thing I do know for certain, Jessie Gifford, I've loved you since the day I first met you. I hope my telling you won't ruin our friendship - but if I die in this bad dream, that's the one thing I don't want to take to my grave with me. You need to know. I want you to know... I need you to know...."

Tears filled Jessie's eyes, and she wrapped her arms tightly around him. Gus held her against his chest, resting his cheek on top of her head. Her hair smelled faintly of vanilla, musk, and baked chicken.

They stood in the silence of the kitchen, embracing. After a long moment, one that felt like a full hour to Gus, Jessie raised her face to look him squarely in the eye.

"Augustus Walker," she whispered, tears streaming down her face, "if we die tomorrow, I'll go happy. I've loved you for years, My Friend... I've loved you for years...."

The moment was broken as Dr. Jackson entered the kitchen, clearing his throat as he observed the tender scene.

"Please pardon my intrusion." He spoke with a sense of urgency. "I thought you'd want to know Ms. Abrams is conscious and asking for water!"

Chapter Twenty-Seven

Jack, Gus, Jessie, and Theresa stood quietly in the hallway outside the bedroom as Dr. Jackson and Dr. Paulsen gently talked with Lindy, supporting her as she took small sips of water from a glass. Her voice was weak and raspy. Lindy struggled to speak in fragmented words and sentences but was insistent on what she was saying to Dr. Jackson. Glancing over to Dr. Paulsen, who was seated on the other side of the bed, the two physicians spoke low in conference. Finally, Dr. Jackson raised his voice somewhat and spoke toward the bunch gathered in the doorway.

"Ms. Gifford... Jessie, would you please come join us? And you also, Theresa."

The two women looked at each other. Jessie then looked at Gus. He nodded his head toward Lindy and whispered, "Go. Go, Jess... she obviously remembers you!"

Nodding her understanding, Jessie reached out her hand to Theresa, and the two women walked slowly toward the frail woman lying in bed.

"Ladies... ladies, please come. Lindy would like to see you..."

Dr. Jackson spoke, his voice cordial and kind but barely above a whisper. There was a look of concern and welling emotion on his face, though he hid it behind a caring smile. Jessie reached the bedside first. Theresa seated herself on the opposite side where Dr. Paulsen had been sitting. No one spoke. Without warning, Lindy handed the glass back to Dr. Jackson and with shaking hands, reached for Jessie. Jessie reached out in response, gently taking Lindy's hands in hers. They felt cold, dry, and almost skeletal.

"Y...y...you...s...sav...ed...m...me. Y...You saved...m...me..."

Lindy spoke, her voice hoarse and barely audible. Tears pooled in Jessie's eyes as she replied with a soft smile, "We ALL saved you, Lindy. Every one of us here. You're safe now, Sweetheart."

Lindy's eyes looked up at Jessie. A profound sadness filled them.

"N...n...ne...ver...safe...ag...ain... Th... they...they..."

Lindy then broke down and began to cry, her tears large and flowing without any seeming effort. Jessie cast a look of concern at Dr. Jackson.

"Doctor... may I?" She whispered.

"I don't see why not." Dr. Jackson whispered back. "Some loving, human touch might be just what she needs right now."

Jessie sat on the side of the bed next to Lindy and slowly wrapped the bereft woman in an enveloping embrace. There was total silence in the room as Jessie rocked Lindy, and Lindy continued to cry. Reaching over from her place on the bed, Theresa took hold of Lindy's hand. Gus and Jack stood silent in the hall, watching.

"Bastards!" Jack hissed under his breath. "I want 'em dead - every last one of 'em!"

Gus looked at Jack and replied in kind. "God willing, you'll get your wish - and I plan on doing everything in my power to help make it happen!"

Jessie rocked Lindy for a solid five minutes while she continued to cry. Finally, the tears subsided. Pushing herself back from Jessie's embrace, Lindy fell weakly back onto the pillows. Motioning for another sip of water and accepting the glass from Dr. Jackson, she spoke again after regaining her strength.

Y...y...you...you need..."

Lindy swallowed and drew a breath. Her bruised lips struggled to form words over her missing and broken teeth.

"I...I...things...you need...I know...things...you must..."

"Yes!" Jessie interrupted emphatically. "Yes, Lindy. We've got to know what happened to you. We've got to know what you know - and very, very soon, Sweetheart."

Lindy rested her head on the pillows and nodded.

"Pen..." She looked at Jessie and, raising her thin hand, mimicked writing.

"Pen..." Jessie repeated. "Pen! And paper - quickly!"

Jessie looked at Theresa, their eyes meeting, wide with hope and amazement at what was happening.

"I'll get them!" Theresa stated, making her way to the door. Jack and Gus followed Theresa to the kitchen counter.

"What's happening?" Gus asked his daughter as she grabbed a pad of paper and a pen.

"I'm pretty sure a miracle and an answered prayer!" She replied hurriedly. That's one strong woman in there, and she knows exactly what we need from her! God willing, she's going to tell us everything we need to know—without having to speak a word!"

Gus ran his hand across his forehead, bringing it to rest over his mouth as he fought to contain himself. Jack stood shaking his head, a large smile breaking across his face.

"Hallefuckinglujah!! Dear God, help her!" He prayed out loud, looking at Gus, eyes fixed wide in excited amazement.

Theresa ran back to Lindy's room, stopping at the door and slowing her pace. She then continued calmly back to the bedside. Once there, she handed the pen and paper to Jessie. Removing the cap from the pen, Jessie handed it to Lindy. She then slid the tablet onto Lindy's lap. Lindy looked up at Dr. Jackson with timid determination.

"Ladies," Dr. Jackson spoke low, "why don't you return to the others. This might take a bit of time, and we don't want to hurry or pressure Lindy in any way. Dr. Paulsen and I will stay here to help her as might be needed."

"Oh..." Jessie replied, a bit surprised. "Why yes, that does make sense."

Dr. Paulsen then immediately reassured, "The minute Lindy's done, I'll bring her notes to you."

Making their way back to the den, Jessie walked over to Gus, who stood stoking the fire in the fireplace. Coming beside him, she slipped her arms around him. He placed the poker back on the hearth and pulled her in close. Theresa and Jack sat on the couch, silent and thinking.

"Quite a turn of events!" Jack finally said.

"Indeed!" Jessie replied. "God bless her."

"I hope she's able to deliver..." Gus added. "We've got to get moving, and if we can leave here armed with what we need, that would be a game-changer."

"I'm almost afraid to read what she writes..." Jessie commented in a low voice, leaving Gus's side and taking a seat on the couch next to Theresa. "Once we see it in print, there's no UNseeing it."

"Very true." Gus added. "The last of the world as we thought we knew it is about to end."

Nick and Dohr returned to the den and, pulling up chairs, joined the others by the fireplace.

"Any fresh intel yet?" Nick asked.

"Soon to be forthcoming!" Jack replied and then added, "I have a feeling it's going to be a long night."

"I'll make coffee." Theresa responded. "I'm kinda queasy at the thought of it all..."

Gus and Jessie cast a look her way.

"You alright, Honey?" Gus asked with a caring tone in his voice.

"Yeah, Dad. Thanks. Just dreading 'officially' knowing what we're about to know. Up until now, I've allowed myself the luxury of not thinking about the really awful stuff. Pretty soon, we're going to know it ALL - and be meeting it face to face."

"True." Jessie chimed in. "But none of us will have to carry any of it alone."

"Except for Lindy." Theresa replied. "She'll have to carry all this evilness -all this darkness- all by herself - and for the rest of her life. How in the world..??"

Theresa began to cry. Jessie stood up and hurried to her side.

"Oh, Honey - don't go there. Don't go there..."

"Theresa," Jack spoke, his voice reassuring and filled with resolve. "This goes as I hope, Lindy will have nothing but the very best care - for as long as it takes. This goes the way it seems set to, that woman in there - and, if we can get to them, many others like her will blow the lid off this entire network. They'll be owed a giant debt!"

"But will they ever truly be repaid??" Theresa shot back. "How in the world can anything... ANYTHING - begin to make up for the abject horror these people have endured?? My God!"

"I think it's pretty safe to say," Nick said next, "that it's a given we're all going to need some heavy brain mechanics once all is said and done. I, for one, am not OK with the world we're about to enter!"

Jack looked over at Nick. "Right there with ya, Pal." Jack responded. "Sex trafficking is one thing - but satan worship, human sacrifice, baby and organ harvesting?! I missed that day's training at Quantico. We're gonna have to hang tough - and tougher than ever before. Try to view this as just another case, else we won't make it. Best advice I can give - nutty as it is."

Nick looked at Jack, eyebrows raised. "I suppose that will be the only way to get the job done - but talk about living in denial!"

The room went silent, and time stood still. Theresa returned with the coffee tray, and the long evening of waiting commenced.

Two hours later, slightly before eleven pm, Dr. Paulsen entered the den, holding several sheets of paper. Her face was pale and drawn. Walking over to the couch, she handed the papers to Jack, who cast a concerned look at her as he reached up to take them from her hand.

"You OK?"

"No. No, Jack. I'm not OK. I'll never be OK again."

With that, Dr. Paulsen excused herself. "Dr. Jackson has administered a sedative for Lindy. She'll rest well through the night, and she's earned it. The sooner we get her to Boston, the better. Now, I need a good, hot bath to cleanse the filth."

Jack nodded his understanding.

Jessie spoke, her voice solemn. "Anna, is there anything you need? Anything I can do?"

Dr. Paulsen looked at Jessie with a haunted expression. "Pray, Jessie. With all your might - just please PRAY."

With that, she turned and left the room.

Jack sat a moment longer and then, putting on his reading glasses lifted the pages from his lap. "Well, Folks... are we ready?"

"Ready as we'll ever be." Gus answered, his voice barely audible and harboring a faint hint of dread.

Taking a deep breath and clearing his throat, Jack began to read aloud from Lindy's notes.

'arrived nyc for billie holiday singing competition. paid fee, submitted entry forms. showed up first audition as instructed upon acceptance. some dive downtown. six other girls also there. four made the cut, counting me. told next phase would be following week. warehouse on sixth. showed up seven pm as instructed. waited backstage. each girl sang one tune and then told to walk thru audience and mingle, drinks with judges. mostly men-only a few women. place was cleaner than first but still off... dirty carpet, iffy sound system, most judges had heavy accents and didn't know much about music. sounded almost polish. only contestants spoke good english. twelve girls there that night. were told final competition with big prize would be following night. new place -bigger- higher quality - building off alley of west broadway. each contestant sang two tunes and told to mingle again and drink with judges and record producers. halfway thru first drink, felt faint, got sick and dizzy. passed out. came to in large room like cement warehouse. could hear water sounds, heavy equipment, loading and unloading. other girls there with me. all drugged and sick. several beaten. couldn't remember anything. no id, phone, purse or money. couldn't get out. couldn't get out! stayed one day and night, then moved to bigger room same warehouse. many more girls, young teens, children too. about fifty in all. little girls and young teens - male and female, all drugged, sick, beaten. screams and moaning from another area. something very bad. no way out. didn't eat or drink what was given. those that did more drugged and sick. took children - gone for hours. when brought back, some missing - never seen again. others bleeding. some lying on floor whimpering. some sodomized so badly they died on the floor there bleeding. young girls taken for days, raped. three older women... we tried to protect the little ones. these women dragged away one at a time. could hear beating and torture. young women and boys used for sex, young girls raped

- impregnated for baby farming...adoption ring... orphans never returned once removed... said human sacrifices...satan worship ceremonies...organs taken. bodies disposed of somewhere near. blood on floor in room with tables...rich, big men...suits and expensive clothes... gold chains and jewelry - day and night. all hours. forced to 'entertain' them. several i recognized. big people. shower, clean dress, makeup when 'entertaining'- elevator down long cement hallway. one floor like fancy club. velvet couches and beds, carpets and crystal chandeliers... tropical plants and flowers... gardenias... bar, security, men with guns. drugs. Sex - all kinds. did well, could be bought. beatings would then stop and fed better. pretty ones drugged less and fed better. some left warehouse. said five left country with heads of state of some sort... dignitaries. saw three senators, four actors, four athletes, five singers - pop and rap. big money. finally came for me. mad I tried protecting...gang raped, large room with exam tables, van...downtown somewhere, beaten. faked dying. laid in alley til found. cold... so cold... rain... taste of blood. evil. evil. evil.'

As Jack read the last, his voice trailed off. No one moved or made a sound. Reaching the back of her hand to her cheek, Theresa wiped at the tears streaming down her face as she sat quietly processing all she'd just heard. Nick looked at Gus. Gus met his gaze and held it, a pained expression on his face. Finally, Jessie spoke.

"Well. Now we know. Somewhere back in the city, dockside from the sounds of it is a warehouse full of satan."

"Certainly sounds like it," Jack responded and then added, looking at Nick, "It appears your hunch was right on the money, Nico. Some of these people have to be leaving on cargo ships and yachts... and smuggling babies on ships is a helluva lot easier than trying to smuggle them by commercial air. Hire a few heartless women to slap clean diapers on the 'merchandise' and stuff bottles in their mouths a time or two each day, and you're good to go...."

"I was really hoping to be wrong." Nick winced as he responded.

Jack spoke again, "Looks like they thought of everything in this little enterprise: sex, drugs, babies, organs, satanic sacrifice... all big, booming business in today's world. This is hardly bedtime reading - but Lindy's going to sleep through the night now. We might as well try for some shut-eye, too, although I'm sure none of us will sleep. I have some questions I need clarification on when she's able tomorrow. After that, we really need to break camp and fly the coop. Need to hit this thing full-on ASAP. Gus, Theresa, we have to get out of here tomorrow before noon if at all possible."

Gus cut his eyes to Jessie before answering. She shot him a faint half-smile. There was a loving look in her eye.

"Roger that." Gus replied. "Theresa... Honey - are you ready?"

Swallowing hard, Theresa drew a deep breath, exhaling slowly. Finally, she answered. "Yes. Yes, Dad. We need to get this done. The longer it takes, the more suffering there is."

"Alright then." Jessie threw in. "I'll go check on Anna, and we'll get plans underway."

CHAPTER TWENTY-EIGHT

Six AM found Gus, Nick, Jack, and Jessie already up, sitting around the kitchen table drinking coffee in silence. Finally, Jack spoke.

"Just as soon as she's able this morning, I'd like to ask Lindy for a bit more detail about the sounds she heard outside that warehouse. If we can pinpoint the basic vicinity, that would be incredibly helpful. Without that intel, the only way we're going to find the place is by getting the girls on the inside."

Gus shot a hard look at Jack. "That just can't - just won't - happen, Pal!! Once they're inside, we may not get them back. I refuse to allow that scenario. PERIOD."

Jack looked at Gus with understanding in his eyes and didn't balk.

"I know, Augustus. That's not my preferred scenario, either. I'll do everything within my power to make sure we don't end up working Plan B on this op, but we've got enticing bait, and there's a high probability the predators will bite. We'll need to make the most of it, if and when they do."

Gus grew fidgety, reaching for the pack of cigarettes in his shirt pocket. There were none. Looking over at Jessie, he gave a half smile and a quick wink. She reached for his hand, giving him a loving look.

Jack spoke again. "Gus, I've got the team assembled back in the city—surveillance of the highest order, and all the guys are off the grid. No NYPD or active Fed associations. Best of the best. All in all, we've got thirty highly skilled assets deploying as we speak."

Gus didn't respond. Jessie turned her attention to Jack, squeezing Gus's hand as she spoke. "That's excellent news, Jack. We truly appreciate all you're doing. Sounds like you didn't get much sleep last night!"

"None at all," Jack replied. "I can sleep after this op is done - or I'm dead... whichever comes first."

Just then, Dr. Jackson appeared in the kitchen. "Lindy is hungry this morning..." He smiled as he delivered the happy news. "A very good sign!"

"That's wonderful!" Jessie smiled back at him, genuinely thrilled at the positive turn of events.

"Dr..." Jack queried, taking a sip of coffee as he momentarily paused. "I need to press Lindy for a couple additional details pertaining to locations. How soon do you think that'll be possible?"

Dr. Jackson took a moment to consider and then answered. "She's feeling stronger today, actually. Noticeably so. I think telling her story last night helped relieve some of her internal cognitive pressure. I would think within an hour... that should be doable."

"Excellent!" Jack nodded, relief in his voice.

Looking back at Nick, Gus, and Jessie, he then added, "Well, Kids—we've got lots to do. Once Anna and Theresa are ready, we'll head out. Gus, you can follow later today once you're done here. You know where to find us. Oh! Just for the record, my card!"

With a flourish, Jack slid across the table a white business card printed in gray, burgundy, and blue ink: one for Gus and one for Jessie. Gus picked up the card and studied it—a faint chuckle emitted from him.

"MILTON COHEN??!"

"Sure thing!" Jack answered with obvious satisfaction. "Cohens have a long and storied record of serious contribution to the entertainment industry! I thought the little Comedy-Drama masks were a nice touch..."

Gus shook his head and cut a look at Jack, appreciative humor registering on his face. "You think of everything, Pal." He replied.

Jessie chuckled as she looked at the card. "I see you went with the color scheme of that spiffy tie we bought you the other day."

"Ah, yes." Jack retorted. "Brand continuity is everything!" He then added with a change in tone, "Jessie, the ambulance will be arriving tonight at seven. One driver. Dohr knows the code. It would be safer if you and Nick rode with Dr. Jackson in the back with Lindy. Dohr will ride shotgun -literally- upfront. I'll send people for the two rental cars that will be left behind."

"Sounds good." She responded. "Would've been nice to have an extra day to get the house buttoned down, but I'll get started and make hay."

"One more day here might end up being one too many." Gus said and then added, "I'll help, Jess. Just tell me what to do."

Looking at his watch, Jack stood and stretched. "I have just enough time to shave and slip into something more 'Milton.' Jessie, when Dr. Jackson says it's time, here are the details I need from Lindy. Mind talking with her? She's bonded with you, and right now, a strange man's not the thing to spring on her."

"Not at all! Happy to do it." Jessie answered, picking up the piece of paper Jack had placed on the table.

A couple minutes after Jack left, Nick finished his coffee. Taking his cup to the sink, he turned and asked, "What can I do to help close up shop?"

"Well..." Jessie thought for a moment. "How are you with a vacuum?"

"An old pro!" Nick answered with a grin.

"Great!" Jessie acknowledged. "If you could vacuum the den and hallway, that would be a huge help. You'll find it in the hall closet - but we should avoid Lindy's room."

Nick nodded and quickly headed down the hall to begin his assigned task.

Seizing the moment, Gus walked over to Jessie, wrapping her in a hug.

"Mmmmm... good..." she sighed, hugging him back.

"I'd like to think, maybe one day, we can actually be alone, Ms. Gifford..." Gus whispered in her ear.

"At this point," Jessie whispered back, "I'd settle for five minutes together on the porch swing!"

Reaching down, Gus gently tilted Jessie's chin up toward him. Holding her close, he placed one slow kiss on her mouth. His lips were enticing and still warm from coffee.

Drawing back, Gus winked. "Consider us 'pinned'!" He said with a loving smile.

Just then, Dr. Jackson reappeared in the kitchen doorway. Clearing his throat, he looked genuinely sorry and embarrassed to have intruded on the tender moment.

"My sincerest apologies." He said quietly. "I seem to have absolutely terrible timing! Just wanted you to know Lindy is ready to talk with you."

"I'll be right there." Jessie smiled and sighed.

Reaching for Gus, she placed a quick peck on his cheek and whispered, "Don't sit under the apple tree..."

Gus laughed a soft laugh. "Not on your life!" He said as Jessie turned and walked down the hall, Jack's paper in hand.

Chapter Twenty-Nine

By noon, Jack, Anna, and Theresa were in the Challenger, heading back to NYC. Jack's disguise, though subtle, had completely transformed him, to the point Anna and Theresa couldn't quit staring at him. The women sat in silence, only speaking occasionally, as every moment brought them closer to their rendezvous with Evil.

After taking the garbage to the local dump, Gus returned, helping Jessie and Nick complete the tasks necessary for shuttering the cabin. Embers from the fireplace were doused, sheets and towels were laundered and put away, dishes washed and returned to cabinets. Finally, Gus loaded the sedan, said his goodbyes to Nick, Dr. Jackson and Dohr, and embraced Jessie one last time. He then drove down the long, wooded driveway, disappearing in the midafternoon mist. Jessie stood on the porch, waving until she could no longer hear the car. Sighing heavily, she returned inside. Nick was collecting his papers, guns, and ammo, preparing for their looming departure.

"Another four hours, and we'll be on the way!" He said matter-of-factly.

"Hmmm? What?" Jessie asked, her thoughts obviously elsewhere.

"Ambulance will be here in four hours." Nick repeated.

"Yes. Oh yes." Jessie responded. "I'd better get a move on then!"

Walking into the den, she found Dohr on his phone. Ending the call, he looked up from the couch and reported, "All is on schedule, Ma'am. Cordoso will meet us at the Admitting Entrance there in Boston and will provide cover for unloading of cargo. Driver is on time. Probably best we sit tight, shut off any extra lights and pull the curtains and blinds. Don't need any visitors now we're down a couple skilled guns."

Jessie looked at Dohr and nodded. She suddenly felt extremely alone and vulnerable. Not a feeling familiar to her. Wanting to remain busy, she did as Dohr instructed and then made her way to Lindy's room. There, she found Lindy napping. Catching her eye from the doorway, Dr. Jackson rose quietly and joined her in the hall.

"Yes?" He asked in a whisper.

"Dohr suggests we turn out all extra lights, draw curtains and blinds, and wait quietly. The ambulance will arrive at seven and is on schedule. Nick and I will ride with you in the back with Lindy. Will be a tight fit, but we'll stay out of your way."

Dr. Jackson nodded his understanding and then said with a reassuring smile, "We'll make it work. I'm just relieved that soon she'll be getting more thorough care."

"Yes," Jessie whispered in reply. "But you've been wonderful, Doctor. You've worked miracles."

Dr. Jackson looked appreciative of the praise, but then concern clouded his face.

"We're not out of the woods yet." He replied and, casting a sympathetic glance at Lindy, added, "She's got a long, long road to recovery - and to be perfectly honest I'm not even sure what recovery looks like for someone that's been through so much horror..."

"I know..." Jessie whispered, shuddering - and then added as an afterthought, "You'll find a fresh pot of coffee and the last of our rations, some cookies and sandwiches, on paper plates in the kitchen, Doctor. Dohr, Nick, and I will be in the den if you need us."

Dr. Jackson nodded, smiled, and quietly made his way back to Lindy's bedside.

Returning to the den, Jessie carried a small duffle and placed it by the front door. She then went to the storage closet, removed 'Nurse Silver's' medical bag, and placed it by the front door as well. The remaining hours passed in almost total silence. Finally, at six forty-five, Dohr arose from the couch and stood rigid, listening intently. Jessie and Nick observed him closely but didn't speak.

"Tires on the gravel!" He whispered and motioned for Nick to accompany him to the front door.

Weapons drawn, Nick took position as Dohr peered carefully from the edge of the window. Headlights pierced the darkness; the crunching of gravel grew louder, and the low rumble of an emergency vehicle came to a halt directly outside the house. Jessie sat perfectly still on the couch, gun at the ready. Footsteps on the porch stairs and then three loud knocks. Then three more. Dohr leaned toward the door and knocked once -hard and loud- from the inside. One more knock issued forth from outside.

"CHAMPAGNE." Dohr spoke through the closed door in a commanding tone.

"JELLY." A man's voice answered cautiously.

Motioning for Nick to cover him, Dohr unlocked the door and cracked it open - just enough to view the man standing on the other side.

"Credentials - quick."

"Here ya go." The man responded, shoving two cards into Dohr's waiting hand.

"Enter." Dohr commanded and then quickly closed and locked the door behind him once he was inside.

"Pringle! Good to see ya! Glad you're on the job! Come meet the rest of the team!"

Dohr shook hands with the man as Nick strained in the darkness to make out features.

Without fanfare, Lindy, now placed on a gurney, was loaded into the back of the ambulance by Pringle and Dohr; Nick and Jessie providing cover. Dr. Jackson took his place in the back, and once Jessie had locked the door to the cabin, Dohr accompanied her to the back of the vehicle, slammed the doors tight, and quickly took his place in the passenger seat alongside Pringle, pistol in hand and shotgun at the ready by his right leg. The ambulance lumbered down the dark drive, accelerating quickly as it reached the main road, heading toward their final destination in Boston.

***

Meanwhile, back in the city, Jack, Anna, and Theresa were settling into their new digs. The motel was somewhat seedy but just enough to lend credibility to their cover while not putting the women in additional danger. Once checked in and their few belongings unpacked, the trio made their way to the all-night diner down the block. Following Jack closely, Theresa and Anna walked to the back of the establishment, seating themselves in a booth containing a man they'd never seen. Once everyone was seated, Jack made the introductions.

"Dr. Anna Paulsen, Theresa Walker, meet Alan. Alan is one of our close 'friends.' If you keep your eyes peeled, you'll see him hovering about in the background everywhere you go."

"Ladies." Alan greeted without registering any readable emotion.

Theresa and Anna greeted him with reserved but nervous 'Hellos.' The group ordered food, although Anna and Theresa merely picked at theirs. Alan and Jack took notice. Leaning in, Jack whispered to Theresa, "It would really be best if you Ladies could eat something... I know you've got nerves, but you'll need your strength, and from here out, it's going to be catch as catch can."

Theresa looked at Jack and nodded. Taking her fork, she picked at the omelet on the plate in front of her. Anna followed suit.

Speaking low, Alan did his best to reassure. "Ladies, most of Jack's inner network is on this op. All carefully handpicked. You'll have eyes, ears -and weapons- trained on you at every turn. We need you to stay true to character and do not - repeat, Do Not be looking for us. Your job is to trust. Think of us as guardian angels - but you slip up and tip us to the targets, this will not end well for any of us. Do you understand?"

Theresa looked at Anna, and Anna looked back, a solemn and uneasy look on her face.

"Yes. Yes, Alan. We understand." She answered for them both. Theresa nodded her agreement.

Alan then continued, "Eat when it's time to eat, rest when it's time to rest... and sing and socialize, like you were made for it when they tell you to. Got it?"

The two women nodded again. Jack then leaned in and whispered, "We have eyes in the motel parking lot and the rooms on either side of ours. There will be eyes on us -both inside and outside the building- when you audition, which, by the way, will be tomorrow afternoon at three."

Anna's expression became one of shocked surprise. "But..." she stammered. "We haven't even sent in our entry forms! How - and why so fast?!?"

Jack smiled slyly. "Ladies, might I remind you, you're represented by one of the best agents in town! 'Milton' sent in your stuff. I made the follow-up call yesterday and greased Anton's palm with a bit of promised green. Red carpet treatment, all the way straight into Hell! You can thank me later."

Theresa immediately began to hyperventilate. "I think I'm gonna be sick!" She whispered, her breath coming in rapid, shallow sputterings.

"Steady, Theresa. Steady..." Anna whispered from across the table as she reached for Theresa's sweating hand. "Theresa, look at me... breathe with me now..." Anna coached, and slowly, Theresa's panic subsided. Alan and Jack looked at each other, and Alan raised an eyebrow.

"She'll be fine." Jack assured. "She'll be just fine."

Alan shook his head, doubtful at Jack's assurance.

After a few sips of ice water, Theresa regained her composure.

"I'm sorry, guys. It's just all so fast! I was hoping for a bit of time to get my bearings."

"That, Milady, is a luxury we don't have," Jack spoke low. "This will be a surgical op -God willing- in and out as fast as possible once we learn what we need to know."

"This won't happen again, Jack. You have my word." Theresa apologized.

She looked at Jack as she spoke, and he could see her determination and sincerity. He winked and nodded.

"That's my good little Trooper!"

The meeting with Alan completed, and back in their motel room, Anna set to work preparing for the events of the next day. Laying out her blue dress and shoes, she then retreated to the bathroom for a hot shower. The water pipes hissed, clanked, and banged. Jack sat on his bed, staring straight ahead, formulating the next moves. Suddenly, his cell rang. Answering, Theresa noted his expression lighten somewhat.

"Hey, Friend. You make it OK? Good. Good. You in the dive down the block? Excellent. There's someone here who could use a little convo... you know, Daddy-Daughter stuff. Just a sec."

With that, he handed the phone to Theresa.

"Dad?" Theresa spoke with relief. "Are you here? It's all starting so fast, Dad! I'm not ready!"

Gus reassured his daughter in a conversation that lasted all of ten minutes. It was both loving and all business in tone. Completing the conversation and feeling bolstered, she handed the phone back to Jack.

"Thank you, Jack. I needed that. Dad wants to speak to you again."

Five minutes later, Jack disconnected and resumed his planning. Anna came out of the bathroom and sat next to Theresa on their bed. The mattress was lumpy and somewhat concave. Looking at Theresa, Anna grimaced.

"I don't even want to think about what's taken place on this thing!"

Theresa shivered at the thought. "Oh Man..." she replied. "Now I need a shower! Hope you saved enough hot water!"

Anna cast a dubious look at Theresa, and half laughed. "Girl, at this stage, there's not enough hot water in the world!"

Turning to Jack, Theresa asked if he needed the bathroom first.

"No thanks! I'm good." He answered. "Knock yourself out!"

They passed the rest of the night in fitful sleep. Jack snored lightly off and on, and Anna and Theresa tossed and turned. Everyone's dreams fitful, disturbed, and filled with a sense of foreboding.

Chapter Thirty

The next morning dawned all too soon. Theresa and Anna both felt hungover, despite not having had alcohol.

"Welcome to the world of high stress and minimal sleep!" Jack commented. "You Ladies are getting a crash course in what this line of work feels like."

"No offense, but I think I'd prefer to take a pass!" Anna commented dryly. "I look like a raccoon... these circles under my eyes!"

Jack turned and cast a discerning look over the two women. Finally, he spoke with a wry half-smile. "Ladies, we're not entering the Miss America Pageant. Those circles you're complaining about will actually work in our favor. Remember, we're shooting for 'motley enough to be bribable -and somewhat desperate- but with enough remaining dignity to hold out a bit before we cave.' Dark circles work!"

Theresa returned her gaze to the mirror and just shook her head. "My God, I want today to be over with! My stomach is tied up in knots."

Anna stopped what she was doing and replied, a pained tone in her voice. "Don't wish today away so quickly, Theresa. This afternoon just kicks off the horror show... there will be heavy doses of fresh hell from here on."

Theresa winced at the realization. "Thanks. That really helped..." She sighed heavily.

"Now, Ladies, let's get our game faces on. First things first. We hit Anton's office at two forty-five, and you girls sing like songbirds. Wouldn't hurt anything if you found a way to show some leg... and other miscellaneous girlie bits. Not too much now, mind you, but the mousetrap will snap shut faster if we put some real cheese in it!"

Anna shot Jack a look but chose to keep her reply to herself.

At two fifteen PM, Jack, Theresa, and Anna, all dressed in their Thrift Store finery, made their way to the curb outside the motel. With a shrill whistle and forceful wave, Jack secured a cab. Piling in, he then gave the driver the address to Anton's office. He noted the driver's momentary grimace as the address was given, and several times enroute, Jack caught the man watching them by way of the rearview mirror. As instructed, once inside the cab, conversation was kept to a minimum. After a quick fifteen-minute ride, despite the beginnings of rush hour, the cab pulled up to a rather gloomy, old, brick building. Casting a gaze out the car window, Jack noted it stood seven stories and had a strip club adjacent two doors down. Reaching in his pocket, he forked over the fare and a tip.

"Thanks, Pal." He said in his best 'Milton Cohen' voice, and then exited the back seat, holding the door open for Anna and Theresa.

"Disembark, My Lovelies!" He instructed with flair. "Your bright future awaits!"

Glancing at the cab driver as the girls exited, Jack shot him a lecherous grin. The cabbie nodded knowingly and then sped away, leaving the trio standing on the sidewalk. A wino sat next to a garbage can taking slugs from a bottle of Boone's Farm.

"Hardly Château D'yquem..." Jack grimaced as they made their way to the entrance. "Deep breath, Girls. Let's get this done and get outta here."

"None too soon!" Anna replied under her breath.

Squeezing into the graffiti-splattered elevator, the trio rode in silence to the fourth floor, where they bounced to an unceremonious stop. The moment the doors opened, Jack completely transformed.

"Come My Lovelies! Come! Must be on time and not keep these fine folks waiting!"

Anna and Theresa fell in line, following Jack down the dingy corridor; their shoes sticking slightly to the floor as they walked.

"Ah— here we are, Suite Four Twelve."

Reaching down, Jack turned the knob, opening the frosted glass partitioned door with a creak. Once inside, they were greeted by a less-than-welcoming waiting room. The carpet was a dirty beige, and folding chairs were lined up against the walls - minus cushions. Two plastic plants, greatly in need of dusting, sat on a water-stained coffee table in the middle of the room. Two young women sat waiting nervously for their 'turn' and made no bones about sizing up the newly arrived competition. The clock ticked, and the two younger women were finally summoned to the back 'studio.'

As Jack, Theresa, and Anna sat awaiting their turn, the office door opened, and a man walked in. Stopping in his tracks, he cast a hard once-over at Theresa and Anna. They recoiled instinctively as he stared. Starting through the door to the studio, he turned again, this time looking squarely at Jack, who sat calmly reading a heavily thumbed issue of 'People Magazine,' obviously pilfered from a more prosperous office down the hall.

"Don't I know you?" The man bluntly asked.

Jack cut his eyes past the top of the magazine to find Detective Randal Dirksen glaring at him. Totally unruffled and fully in character, Jack responded.

"Certainly possible, My Good Man. Certainly possible! Milton Cohen. You've probably heard of me... I handle only the finest talent in the world of 'Blue'!"

Dirksen stood unflinching, rubbing the stubble on his chin. His gaze shot from Jack back to Anna and Theresa.

"You must be the three o'clocks I was told to come see... uh - hear." He spoke without emotion or warmth.

"Absolutely and Undoubtedly!" Jack blathered enthusiastically. "Here, Friend." He added formally, standing to present Dirksen with his card.

Dirksen stared him in the eye before taking it. "Milton Cohen." Dirksen read aloud.

"And you might be...?" Jack queried with mock friendliness and interest.

Detective Dirksen stood firm and peered into Jack's face without taking the bait.

"I MIGHT be your ticket to the Grand Prize; that's who I MIGHT be."

Cutting his eyes back to Theresa and Anna, Dirksen's gaze pored across their breasts and down Anna's legs.

"They have such... talents, don't they?" Jack teased.

"They know you're here?" Dirksen asked, nodding his head toward the door to the studio. His eyes remained fixed on Anna.

"That, I couldn't say," Jack replied. "There are two others being 'seen' now... Anton is expecting us, and I brought his... Greens...."

Dirksen nodded, eyeing Jack hard one final time.

"I could swear we've met somewhere before..." He mumbled, taking another look at 'Milton's' card.

Just then, a swarthy man of about thirty-five opened the door to the studio, escorting the two younger women out of the office. The girls were ecstatic to have made the cut. Giggling as they left, the room fell silent upon their exit. Anton cast a look at Theresa and Anna and then caught Dirksen's gaze, eyebrow raised.

"You're both a bit older than we usually take." Anton stated bluntly.

"Now, now, Big A." Dirksen chided by way of challenge. "All women have useful talents... let's not limit ourselves - or them!"

Anton cut an angry glance at Dirksen but hid it under a stiff, forced smile. "This way." He half hissed in a heavy accent, motioning for the women to follow. Turning, he forcefully pointed at Jack and commanded, "You - stay here."

With that, Anton waved Dirksen in behind the girls, and the group made their way toward the 'studio,' leaving Jack alone in the waiting room.

Tense moments passed as Jack carefully calculated the time. He knew each Billie Holiday song the girls were going to sing for their audition, and the tempos. Factor in some basic conversation, and he could calculate, with reasonable accuracy, just when they should return. Much past that time allotment would indicate trouble. He also knew the only way out of that office was past him. Finally, twenty-five minutes later, Theresa, Anna, and Anton returned.

"Your girls made it to the next round," Anton spoke without enthusiasm. "You have something for me, No?"

"Ah, Yes! Yes!" Jack bubbled in an overly agreeable manner.

Slyly, as though not wanting Anna or Theresa to see the exchange, he slipped Anton a folded, dogeared envelope with a coffee stain on it.

"As discussed and agreed upon." Jack leaned in and whispered.

Anton snatched the envelope from Jack's hand with a faint look of disdain.

"Your girls know next place for to compete. Two days from now. Be on time. They have info."

With that, Anton stuffed the envelope into his pants pocket, turned, and strode back through the door from whence he came.

"Bravo! Bravo, My Lovelies!" Jack gushed and applauded, escorting Anna and Theresa out of the office and back to the elevator. "Oh, My Sweet Songbirds!" He praised as they made their way back to the street in front of the building.

As Jack worked to secure a cab, Theresa grew restless. "Oh, let's hurry and get out of here! This neighborhood... it's all giving me the creeps!"

"That bald pit viper back there doesn't help my mood much either!" Anna agreed, a look of revulsion flashing across her face. "Another second of his staring, and I was afraid my clothes were going to vaporize! Damn, predatory psychopath!"

As a cab responded and began to pull toward them, Jack smiled a faint smile. "Patience, My Lovelies..." He chuckled and winked. "Not all is as it seems!"

With that, he tilted his head slightly toward the wino, dozing on the sidewalk by the trash can. Following his gaze, Theresa's eyes fell upon the filthy figure. It was none other than Alan himself.

Registering a brief look of shock that quickly turned to embarrassment, she stooped and followed Anna into the cab, Jack taking up the rear.

Back at the motel, Anna and Theresa changed out of their outfits and back into their 'civilian' clothes. As they did, Jack read over the printed information Anton had supplied.

"Anything stand out in that stuff, Jack?" Anna asked, pulling her hair into a ponytail and wiping at the excess makeup piled on her face.

"Well..." Jack answered slowly, "Just like Lindy indicated, it appears this operation starts in the dumps and slowly works its way 'uptown,' so to speak. The next venue appears bigger and better."

"That just seems really odd to me." Theresa chimed in. "I mean, why start in such a nasty environment if you claim to be a big-time singing competition? That just seems so backward!"

Anna agreed.

"Actually, it makes perfect sense," Jack replied, "IF you think like a perverted criminal. Start too fancy and 'uptown'; your prey isn't as vulnerable or as needy as you want them to be. Start in the pits; you're guaranteed to get a full-on harvest of desperate souls— people one step away from living on the streets, runaways looking for their big break..., and people in need of cash to keep the monkey fed... see what I mean?"

Anna thought for a moment and nodded. "Yes, that does make perfect sense. The desperate person is more willing to ignore red flags - and their gut instincts. Starting in a squalid office pretty much assures you're dealing with the most vulnerable. It's all just so very repulsive and cruel."

"I fear, Anna, you ain't seen nuthin' yet," Jack said, looking at her with a knowing yet pained expression. "You know as well as I do most of what takes place out there."

She nodded in hesitant agreement.

"My best advice, Ladies - do your best to 'enjoy' the next shindig two days from now. It won't be much, but it will be the best they can present. After that, we collectively slide down the razor blade. That said, though, you know the drill: never leave the other alone - not even for a second. Pee together if you have to. They want to 'meet' one of you, you sell yourselves as a package deal only - two for the price of one. And for godsakes, don't eat or drink anything they give you! If that gets dicey, keep your eyes peeled for our team on the inside. They'll be watching out for you. But only use that as a fallback. These asshats get tipped; we're in deep shit."

Theresa took a deep breath, sat on the bed, and changed the subject. "Have you heard anything from Dad today?"

"Nope." Jack answered. "He's chasing leads and coordinating with the team. You want I should call?"

Theresa nodded a timid 'Yes' and felt like a little girl on her first day in kindergarten.

Burner in hand, Jack called the motel down the street where Gus was staying. Four rings in, Gus answered.

"Hey, Pal!" Jack spoke. "Just checking in. Anything thrilling?"

"Spent the day snooping around the next venue," Gus replied. "The alley entrance and exit bother me, but Jones will be in attendance on the inside that night and Romano and Peters will be serving as waitstaff. Surely, since you're 'management,' they'll let you in."

"I feel good about the prospects," Jack replied. "I gave the mark a good dose of 'salad' in that envelope. Need be, I'll force the issue. Oh, and by the way, our high-ranking, bald friend was on hand this afternoon. Damn near jacked when he caught sight of Anna. I think it's love!"

"Not surprised he showed - but keep him at bay. These assholes can look, but they can't touch!"

"True." Jack agreed and then added, "He sure hangs it out there for the world to see. I think he's rather confident he's Untouchable."

"Excellent." Gus chimed in, enthused. "That's exactly what I've been praying for!"

"Yeah, he's in it deep, to the point they called him in to peruse the merch personally this afternoon."

Gus grunted. Jack then added, "Just by way of convo, and at the risk of trying to pull another Capone... what are the odds this next venue doesn't have their liquor license in order?"

"No such luck." Gus responded with a light laugh. "Academy, Day Five, for chrissakes, Jack! I checked that first!"

"I know, My Friend. Just poking for any break we can get. Any update on our little patient and the roadshow?" Jack questioned.

"No. Nothing yet," Gus answered flatly. I know from tracking they arrived safe and sound, but that's all I got."

"Say, G, before you go, there's someone here that would like to hear your voice. She's had a big day! After that, we're gonna hit an early dinner. Next stop, fame and fortune. Stay frosty - and don't be a stranger!"

Chapter Thirty-One

T he afternoon of the big competition was spent in a flurry of activity. Anna and Theresa, well-fed and hydrated, now sat doing their hair and makeup. An hour had been spent with Jack carefully reviewing their instructions and having them memorize the faces of Jones, Peters, and Romano from photos he provided. They had then spent the remaining time warming up with vocal exercises and reviewing the songs they'd be singing that night, not that it actually mattered. For his part, Jack reapplied his 'Milton' disguise and spent ample time on the phone, coordinating with Gus and the other team members active in this portion of the operation.

The time inched closer, bringing heightened anxiety and concern along with it. Jack sat thinking. Finally, he spoke. "Our biggest concern at this stage, Ladies, is whether or not I'm allowed in with you tonight."

Theresa paused, applying her lipstick, and looked at him.

"Don't get me wrong now." He reassured. "I'm prepared to force the issue -and will- but me getting popped right out of the gate isn't what we need. You girls stick close to 'Uncle Milt' at the door now. DO NOT get separated from me!"

Theresa nodded and returned to her lipstick, hands trembling slightly. Anna glanced at Jack in the reflection of the mirror.

"What's that you guys say... 'Roger That?'"

Jack smiled and nodded.

Finally, the hour arrived. Escorting the two women to the street outside the motel, Jack hailed a cab, checking his breast pocket for the necessary paperwork they were to present in order to gain entry to the venue. As the cab approached, Jack made eye contact with Theresa and Anna. Speaking low, he said quickly but with sincerity, "You both are very brave. You Ladies look beautiful... far too beautiful for the depraved animals we're about to parade you in front of. Anything happens to me, I want you to know I think you are both stellar, and it's been a true honor."

Just then, the cab arrived, as Theresa's eyes welled with tears.

"Now, now, My Lovelies!" Jack admonished with a wink, "Don't muss the makeup!"

The cab made its way through the illuminated city streets. With every block that passed, Jack mentally noted the pertinent landmarks. The cabbie attempted conversation, but Jack shot him down. "Sorry, my good man. My ladies have a big night tonight and have to prepare mentally. No time for happy talk."

"Well, pardon the hell outta me!" The driver retorted, rolling his eyes.

After thirty minutes, the cab pulled curbside.

"You're here, your Highnesses!" The cabbie said, voice dripping with sarcasm. "Right down that alley, you'll find the entrance."

"Thank you kindly!" Jack replied.

Checking the fare on the meter, he tossed in a hefty tip.

"Hopefully, your next fare will be better company, Friend."

The driver, accepting the cash, looked sheepish. "You folks have good luck tonight..." He responded in embarrassment.

Opening the door, Jack stepped onto the sidewalk and extended a hand to both Anna and Theresa. His eyes scanned the surroundings, registering every detail.

"So - here we go. Remember, Ladies, everything we've discussed - and I mean EVERYTHING."

With that, he reached up and straightened his tie, removing the papers from his jacket pocket. Walking down the alleyway to the club entrance, Theresa caught sight of a bum passed out in a darkened corner. She caught Jack's eye quizzically, but he didn't respond. Approaching the entrance, they were met by a large African American man in an expensive, double-breasted suit.

"And you are?" He asked in a haughty, aloof tone.

"Milton Cohen and his two clients for the festivities tonight."

Handing the forms to the man, Jack braced himself and waited.

"Yes, numbers twelve and thirteen..." the man replied, casting his eyes over Anna and Theresa. "Right this way, Ladies. Good Luck!" He directed, opening the door for them.

As Jack neared, the bouncer blocked entry. "You've delivered them. We'll take it from here."

Jack stood his ground as Anna and Theresa stopped in their tracks and turned to watch the scene play out.

"My good man," Jack rebuffed, "these two are the biggest talents in my stable right now. If you think I'm dropping off my best merchandise at the curb, you can guess again. Milton Cohen doesn't offer a 'try before you buy' policy and Anton's been paid a premium for our admittance. I'm sure he'd hate to miss out on such prime, tender filet... and besides, there's lots more where they came from. I can supply Grade A regularly - depending, of course, on how things shake out tonight!"

The man stood a moment, pondering Jack's words. Just then, several others arrived behind them, awaiting entry and drawing attention to the alleyway.

"Fine. Go in."

Decision made, and not wasting a moment, Jack shoved Theresa and Anna through the open door, following very close behind.

Once inside, the trio surveyed the dimly lit venue. A small stage stood at one end of the large room, where a jazz trio was already playing. From a large, mirrored bar situated off to the side, three bartenders worked in tandem, keeping the alcohol flowing. Several waiters dressed in formal attire circulated through the venue, carrying silver trays. On top of each tray, sat a silver bowl filled with fine, white powder. Already, the room was packed. Making their way to a booth, Jack handed the women their numbers.

"How fitting." Anna commented dryly. "Do away with names and just refer to us by numbers! Goodbye, humanity."

Theresa took the lanyard with her number on it, grumbling as she placed it over her head. "Oh great. My number would be THIRTEEN! God, I hope this isn't an omen..."

As the threesome sat surveying the surroundings, Anna's eyebrows raised, and a shocked look flashed across her face. Jack followed her gaze.

"Christ." He muttered in disgust.

There, racing through the throng, were five little children, heavily made up and wearing skimpy costumes.

"Oh my God!" Theresa exclaimed with horror. "What is THAT about??! Those poor babies! They shouldn't be in a place like this..."

"Let alone dressed like that! I'm afraid to even think about it..." Anna whispered, cutting a horrified and disgusted look at Jack. He looked back and winced.

After a few moments, a man walked over to the booth, speaking in what had become a familiar accent.

"You-women-come. Outfits in dressing room. Change."

Jack cut a look at Theresa and Anna. "What outfits?" He asked. "My ladies have their own."

The man cast a disapproving eye and spoke bluntly. "No. These rags will never do. Outfits in dressing room. Have your numbers on them. Go, Change. Quickly."

Anna and Theresa looked at Jack with fear and concern.

"Alright, Ladies - I'm sure they have lovely things for you. Sir, I know how very busy you must be... so much to do! How about this waiter show them to the dressing room so you don't have to waste any more of your valuable time on us?"

As Jack spoke, he reached out and caught the arm of a white-jacketed waiter serving cocktails at the booth next to them. The waiter turned in response, and Theresa immediately recognized him. It was Romano. The man stood a moment and then nodded his agreement. Snapping impatiently at Romano, he ordered, "Go. Hurry. Back in ten!"

Jack watched as Theresa and Anna disappeared from view, Romano escorting them to the back of the venue and through a black curtain. As he sat, Jack nonchalantly observed the goings on taking place around him. Drinks were being served by a flurry of waiters, and the silver bowls atop the silver trays were garnering much attention and eager use. It appeared most of the inhabitants of the venue were men, many of them foreign and extremely well-to-do. A few faces, Jack clearly recognized, though he tried not to stare or register recognition.

Ten minutes later, Theresa and Anna returned to the table. Jack's eyes bulged at the sight. Wearing skimpy outfits that looked somewhat Grecian and left nothing to the imagination, both women looked extremely embarrassed and uncomfortable.

"Good Lord, but I don't think I've ever been this self-conscious!" Theresa muttered. "This outfit barely covers my backside! I've never felt more like a piece of meat!"

Anna looked at her and then brought her gaze to rest on Jack. "One deep breath, and I'll blow this outfit wide open... and Theresa, I hate to be the one to tell you, but at this stage now, that's pretty much all we are!"

Jack raised his eyebrow at Anna's comment but didn't speak.

"They made us leave our bras, clothes, and purses in the dressing room, Jack!" Theresa spoke again, her voice incredulous.

"And just what the hell does this have to do with Billie Holiday??" Anna insisted, looking down at her ridiculous costume.

"I'm sorry, Girls." Jack answered. "But now you know why I insisted you carry nothing in your bags but makeup. I suspected they'd confiscate your purses. They're probably going through them right now. And as for your question, Anna, aside from Billie's early start in a brothel, I'd have to say not much!"

"I guess if this is the worst thing that happens to us tonight, we'll be lucky..." Theresa groaned.

Finally, at ten PM, a man they'd not seen before took the stage, and the 'competition' commenced. One by one, number called, women would take the stage and sing a Billie Holiday tune. Some were asked to sing two or three songs. Jack observed the workings closely and began picking up the patterns. Younger, prettier girls were asked to be on stage longer, and the more they played up the skimpy outfits, the more they were encouraged to 'meet and greet' with members of the audience. Less pretty girls were only asked to sing one song, and their time on stage was kept to a minimum. They were then escorted to another room in the back of the venue, and Jack never saw them return. As the competition wore on and more competitors were sorted through and brought to the floor for 'mingling,' Jack began to overhear conversations. There were promises of 'fame and fortune,' 'riches beyond your wildest dreams', and 'the big life.' A few of the younger women left with men after papers and briefcases were handed over to Anton. He was present at every transaction and never left the side of an unidentified, armed man.

Finally, number twelve was called. A fleeting look of horror crossed Anna's face. Shooting a pleading look at Jack, he merely nodded at her, holding her gaze with silent encouragement and reassurance. Taking a careful, deep breath, she stood, making her way to the stage. The trio behind her rifled through their sheet music, locating her selections. Soon, the strains of 'Fine and Mellow' filled the air. Anna began to sing, perfect pitch and impeccable delivery, speaking each word as though she herself had lived it. She couldn't have picked a better tune for the environment. As she sang, Jack looked around the room. Men -and a few women- sat captivated as the spotlight played off Anna's hair and revealing costume. Continuing, his eyes came to rest on Randal Dirksen leaning on the bar, scotch in hand. His eyes devoured Anna in a way that made Jack sick to his stomach. As Jack observed from the booth, Dirksen motioned for Anton to join him. A conversation ensued, piquing Jack's curiosity. Anton seemed agitated and protesting, with Dirksen overriding him at every turn. Finally, the song concluded. As Anna began to leave the stage, Anton raised his chin at the bass player. He then held up one finger. Motioning for Anna to return, the musician then asked her what she'd like to sing next. Glancing at the audience surrounding her, she whispered to the man, "Might as well go for broke. Let's do 'I'm A Fool To Want You'. The man nodded and reported her selection to his bandmates. As Anna's voice filled the room, the lyrics:

'To seek a kiss, not mine alone-

To share a kiss the devil has known...'

reverberated.

Jack looked at Theresa, and they shared a knowing half-smile. Suddenly, Theresa's eyes grew wide, and she gasped. "Good Lord! That's FRANCESCA!"

Jack followed her gaze, trying to appear nonchalant. Theresa continued, "I wonder what she's doing here?? Do you think this is really legit, after all? Why in the world would she waste her time or even want to be in the middle of this awfulness??"

Jack positioned himself in the booth so he could get a better look. Attractive and oozing wealth, the creamy-skinned, fortyish woman wore hair extensions, heavy makeup, and false eyelashes and was draped on the arm of a man about the same age. Both wore designer evening attire, and Francesca fairly dripped with gold and diamonds. As Jack watched, she caught the eye of a waiter carrying a silver tray. Slowly and carefully, she laid out two perfectly straight lines of white powder on the tray's surface, snorted them through a small, gold straw, and then washed them down with a fresh glass of champagne.

"I'm not gettin' 'legit' vibes," Jack replied.

Anna's second song came to a close, and as she made her way toward the booth to rejoin Theresa and Jack, she was quickly intercepted by Randal Dirksen. Just then, Theresa's number was called. Jack sat torn as Dirksen steered Anna out of his line of sight just as Theresa made her way to the stage and began to sing. Clamoring for one of the team members in waiter attire, Jack couldn't readily locate any of them. Theresa continued singing as Jack scanned the room with growing urgency. Anna was nowhere to be seen - neither was Dirksen. As Theresa's song continued, Jack exited the booth, pushing his way through the crowd, eyes darting from table to table.

His heart rate began to increase, and a sick feeling overtook him. Finally, near the kitchen area, he caught sight of Romano. Catching Jack's eye, the man approached, attempting to look like nothing was amiss.

"We're down one." Jack whispered. "Down One."

"Copy." Romano responded, snapping to immediately.

"She's with that bald rat." Jack spoke low, urgency growing in his voice.

Romano shot a fast look around. "Not present." He responded.

Just then, Theresa's song came to its climax.

"I have to get back to the booth." Jack spoke in Romano's ear.

"Find her. FIND HER!"

Returning to the table, Jack forced a smile and applauded as though all was well. Leaving the stage, Theresa returned to the booth.

"Man, I'm glad that's over! Guess I didn't rate. No encore, do you believe it??!" She laughed with relief. "I've never been so happy to be rejected!"

She chuckled and then caught sight of Jack's face. "Jack... what's wrong?!"

Jack shot a stern and angry look at her. "MILTON, Theresa. MILTON. Don't blow it. Listen to me now - Anna's missing. Taken by Dirksen. Scouring for her now."

The color drained from Theresa's face, and she sputtered, "WHAT?? How??!"

"Grabbed her while you were singing. Our friends are on it now - but I have to get you out ASAP. They've split you up, and now there's high probability I lose you while searching for her."

"What are you saying?" Theresa gasped in shock and disbelief. You're leaving her?!"

"Snap to, Theresa! We don't have time." Jack hissed, agitation boiling over. "This is one of the oldest tactics in the book - lure one, end up with two. If I play along, we'll lose you both. Get up and follow me -quick!"

With that, Jack grabbed Theresa by the wrist, pulling her to her feet. Throwing his suit jacket over her shoulders and covering her as best he could, he pushed through the crowd toward the exit.

As they neared the door, a shot rang out behind them, coming from the kitchen area. The young woman on stage screamed and dropped to the floor. People mingling in the audience followed suit and the sounds of screams and tables being overturned filled the air around them. Jack turned just long enough to see Romano lurch forward and fall to the floor, blood seeping through his white jacket.

"Filthy spy!' Anton hissed and fired again. "Get Dirksen in here NOW!" Anton shouted in rage.

Jack shoved Theresa through the exit door, dragging her as fast as he could through the alleyway toward the street. Rounding the corner, the heel of Theresa's shoe snapped, causing her to stumble and violently twist her ankle. Jack heard an audible 'snap'. Without hesitating, he yanked her to her feet.

"RUN!" He growled. "One block! Just one block!"

Reaching for his burner, Jack dialed with one hand as he dragged Theresa with the other.

"ABORT! ABORT!" He yelled into the phone. "Corner of Murray and West Broadway. We've lost Romano. Anna is AWOL. OUT."

Disconnecting, Jack continued dragging Theresa along behind him. Each step was agony for her, and Jack's mind raced.

Finally arriving in front of the corner liquor store, Jack cast a fast look around them.

Out of nowhere, a blue sedan appeared, tires screeching. As it came to a hard stop in front of them, the back door flew open. Shoving Theresa inside, Jack piled in on top of her.

The car sped on.

"SHIT. SHIT. SHIT. SHIT. SHIT!!! Divide and Conquer! The oldest fucking trick in the book!" Jack hissed and pounded at the seat in front of him.

Calming somewhat, he cut his eyes to find Jessie staring at him from the front seat. She was sitting next to Gus, who was driving.

Chapter Thirty-Two

Gus skillfully guided the sedan through the streets as Jack kept watch out the back window. Finally, coming to a stop in the parking lot of a convenience store, he slammed the car into 'Park' and killed the engine. Glancing at his watch, he then turned in the driver's seat to face Jack.

"We've got five minutes." Gus spoke in a flat tone. "Debrief."

Jack banged his fist against the inside of the car door and then ran his hands through his hair in an attempt to collect his thoughts. Finally, somewhat composed, he began to speak.

"Dirksen snatched Anna right out from under my nose when they called Theresa to the stage, and she began to sing. The second I realized she was gone, I knew the game. Theresa became my sole focus. I tried to scramble the guys, but the only one I could find was Romano. Is he...?"

Gus grimaced at the question. "We don't know for sure yet, but it doesn't look good. Peters and Jones are on foot. Should be here to rendezvous in just a few."

Gus's face softened, as did his voice. "Thank you for saving Theresa, Jack. I'm terribly worried for Anna, but without your quick thinking, we'd be in a doubly bad bind right now."

Casting a look at his daughter, Gus turned further in his seat, wanting to look her straight on. "Sweetheart, are you OK?"

Theresa sat rigid with shock and pain, hair disheveled, mascara streaked down her face, Jack's suit jacket still draped over her shoulders. Arms wrapped tight around her, she shook from adrenaline. Jessie reached out from the passenger side front seat and rested her hand on Theresa's knee.

"How's that ankle, Honey? We should get you to the hospital pretty soon."

Shaking her head, 'No,' Theresa turned her body toward the car window and didn't reply.

"Theresa—" Gus spoke low. It's not over, and Jack isn't to blame."

In a wild outburst of tears and rage, Theresa turned toward Gus and shrieked, "He LEFT her! He left her back there, Dad!!! With those filthy, perverted animals!!!"

Her sobs came in hard, unforgiving waves.

Jack cut pain-filled eyes at Gus and Jessie.

"Listen to me, Theresa." Gus chided, insistence growing in his voice. "Jack did what he had to do to save your life. He did exactly what he should've."

Gus then stopped speaking for a moment and, with a strange look on his face, glanced back at Jack. "They must've been on to us, Pal. It's the only way to explain this mess."

Jack returned Gus's gaze, his eyes now steely and determined. "That's what I've been thinking. I got past that bouncer way too easy - and how'd they know about Romano? Why couldn't I find Jones or Peters anywhere when the shit went down? They're top men...I've worked with 'em for years! I know they aren't on the take. Where the fuck were they?!?"

Gus glanced at Jessie and then back down at his watch again. "We'll find out in another couple minutes - God willing, they make it to us."

Jack reached over to console Theresa. She shook his hand off her shoulder and turned her back to him, continuing to cry.

"We'll need to get her looked over soon." Jack said in a low, caring voice. "She's in shock, and I'm pretty sure she's torn tendons, ligaments, or both. I heard one helluva snap when she twisted her ankle..."

Before anyone could respond, Jessie spotted two men running toward the car. Weapons were drawn and held at the ready as the figures neared. Squinting his eyes, Gus announced with relief, "It's them!"

Quickly opening the car doors, Jessie and Jack slid over, allowing the men to gain fast access to the vehicle. Breathing hard and rapidly, it took Peters and Jones a few seconds before they could speak coherently. Then, the debriefing began. Peters spoke first.

"Romano's gone. Shot twice in the chest. Salazar is notifying next of kin and accompanying the body."

This news hit Jack especially hard. Lighting into Peters, he hissed, "Just where the fuck were you two?! You were nowhere to be found when the shit hit! Why is that?? What gives, Man?"

Jones shook his head in shame and grief and was next to speak. "They had us squirreled away down in the pit. They tried to keep all three of us down there, but we recognized what was happening. Romano stayed on deck while we created a rouse to justify his not staying there with us. It was the only way to keep at least one pair of eyes on deck for you, Boss. There was no way to get word to you without tipping them."

Jack's eyes narrowed. "What are you talking about 'the pit'??

Peters looked at Gus, then Jack, and then Jessie.

"There's a tunnel in that place none of us knew anything about... under a trap door in the kitchen. Underground is a bunch of orgy rooms and an escape tunnel that dumps out one or two blocks over. It's not mentioned or documented anywhere on our maps or diagrams. Intel had a huge hole."

"DAMMIT TO HELL!" Gus yelled, banging his hand on the steering wheel.

"How in the fuck did we not know that?!" Jack questioned in controlled rage. "How in the hell do you recon a place and miss an entire fucking level? Someone's going to pay holy hell, if we make it out of this shitshow alive!"

Jessie's voice spoke low and calm, breaking the wave of tension rising in the car. "What tipped them to Romano? Do we have any idea?"

Peters and Jones looked at each other.

"That's the big question." Jones answered. "And I wish we knew the answer. The only thing we can figure is, as the panic to locate Dr. Paulsen grew, he became overzealous trying to find her."

Peters added, "Best we can determine is our mark caught on, thinking Romano was either a private dick, a low-rent bodyguard, or boyfriend there to keep his eye on her."

"What makes you think that?" Jessie asked, pushing for detail.

Before either of the men could answer, Jack interjected, "That would explain the words Anton yelled as he shot—'filthy spy'... not 'filthy COP.' 'Filthy SPY. Maybe Anton fears competition, perhaps?"

"All that's up for grabs..." Jones threw in. "But one thing's for sure, in the chaos that ensued, nobody we were around mentioned anything about cops or a bust."

"Well, that's hopeful..." Jessie muttered, continuing to think.

"I guess you could say that - but it ain't hopeful for Romano. Poor bastard's wife just had a baby six months ago."

Just then, Gus's burner rang. Glancing at the number, placing the call on speaker, he then asked in a tense voice, "Did you get it?"

The voice on the other end began speaking, and both Jack and Theresa immediately recognized it as Alan's.

"Affirmative. Tracker successfully installed in target's duffle."

"You sure he's got it with him and won't dump it somewhere?" Gus questioned, seeking much-needed assurance.

"Target's bag was secured while he was at bar. Contents inventoried prior to tagging. Duffle contains target's weapon, supplemental ammo, large wad of cash - mostly fifties and hundreds, and a single serve portion of smack, at the very least. He'd be an idiot to let it out of his sight. Target now moving fast toward I-478 S. We're in pursuit. Four car cat and mouse."

Gus and Jessie locked eyes. Jessie's forehead furrowed, and she strained to think. Finally, speaking in a hoarse whisper, she stated, "They have to be heading to Red Hook... got to be the docks! That would match up with Lindy's report about the sounds she heard outside the warehouse!"

Alan's voice spoke again. "Affirmative. Appears that way. Pursuing now. Switch to Plan B rendezvous point?"

"Copy." Jack shot from the back of the car and then added, "We've got a patient to get to the ER. Transporting now. Call us ASAP with an update. Will be on our way forthwith. OUT."

Disconnecting, Gus cast a glance at their surroundings. "Let's move. Too many unknown variables on the streets tonight, and we're wearing out our welcome in this parking lot."

As Gus started the engine, he spoke in the direction of Jones and Peters. "I need you to stay with Theresa at the hospital fellas, while we do this mission to completion. Please push to get her admitted but you two stay on her!"

"Understood." Peters confirmed.

Theresa opened her mouth to protest, but the look from Gus and the searing pain in her ankle kept her silent.

Dropping Theresa at the local ER entrance, Jessie and Gus exited the car and helped her walk toward the door, Peters and Jones standing watch. Jack stayed behind in the car. Hugging Theresa close, Gus cut a look at the two men, pointed a finger at them, and raised his eyebrow. "Anything happens to her, you'll answer to me!"

With that, they joined Jack in the car and sped off into the night. As Gus drove, Jack removed his phone from his pocket and dialed. Placing the call on speaker, they could hear Alan answer quickly.

"We're leaving the hospital now." Jack reported. "What's your 10-20?"

Alan replied in a low voice. "Parking lot five blocks from the docks. Suspects traveled here in unmarked brown van. Two men in front, one Caucasian, bald, the other unknown origin. Van looks to be carrying human cargo in back - can't make out number. Hoping our 'missing package' is on board. No sign of her yet, though."

Jessie looked at Gus. He looked back with a worried expression.

"Which lot? Approaching rapidly."

"AmeriChem Corporation - lot C. In far enough to not attract attention. You'll have to look to find."

"Copy." Jack ended the call.

The trio rode in silence the rest of the way. Finally, nearing their rendezvous point, Gus spoke. "This is looking bad." He said without emotion. Once we get on scene, it's likely to go down fast. We've already had one unexpected oversight and plot twist. I just pray to God there aren't any more headed our way."

"I know." Jessie replied. "All I can do is think about Anna..."

"This was my worst fear..." Jack said matter-of-factly. "Having one or both of the girls on the inside, for even a minute... now, here we are!"

"Not your fault, Jack. Don't let Theresa get in your head, Friend. She's naive and doesn't understand." Gus attempted to reassure his old friend.

"That's right, Jack." Jessie said softly, turning and reaching her hand out for his. "To someone not in the game, it all seems so simple, cut and dried. We all know it's anything but. No one blames you."

Jack nodded and turned his gaze out the window, swallowing hard in an attempt to keep his emotions in check. Gus cast a worried look in the rearview mirror.

"Head in the game, Pal."

Jack caught Gus's eye, smiled faintly, and nodded. He then added,

"Once we get the final intel from Alan, I'll spring the rest of the team. The agonizing part will be the time it'll take getting them in position. Every minute that passes is another minute in the bowels of hell for Anna... made me want to puke watching Dirksen look at her. That's one evil, sick SOB, and I'd truly love to be the one to punch his ticket."

"We've done all the prep, Pal." Gus responded. "It should come together quick enough."

"We do need to bear in mind," Jessie all but whispered. "Depending on where we are in their 'merchandise' collecting process, if Lindy's accountings are right, there may be alot of poor souls in that building we're about to meet."

"True." Jack answered. "I hope because tonight was a 'collecting' event for them, the number of vics in the warehouse may be minimal at this point. I'll arrange for extra medical all the same."

Finally, coming alongside Alan and his partner, Silvestre, Gus brought the car to a stop, surveying their surroundings. Alan rolled down his window, and Jessie did the same. Leaning toward Jessie, Alan spoke clearly but quietly. "The van in question has come to a stop outside a warehouse on the south lot of the terminal." He reported. "We have a good, strong signal transmitting from what we believe to be Port Building Ten. Abuts the water, and all necessary equipment for loading/unloading is immediately adjacent. Heavy container activity, which would account for your vics report of hearing sounds while inside the warehouse. This has to be the location."

Jack's jaw tightened. "No offense Al, but it's been a real crappy night. I need you to qualify 'HAS TO BE.' On a scale of one to ten, how sure are you we have this right? God knows we can't afford any more fuck ups."

"Nine point seven five." Alan responded. "I have eyes on the van, and there's been recent in and out activity. Up until that point, I was at a seven."

Jack raised an eyebrow. "What do you think, Guys? Shall we pull the trigger and call in the troops?"

Jessie sat a moment and then lifted her gaze past the windshield into the fluorescent lighting that bathed the parking lot. The group sat surrounded by concrete and then nothing but inky blackness beyond. Drawing a heavy breath, she replied simply, "I vote 'Yes'."

Looking over at Gus, she gave a soft smile and touched his hand with hers. Sharing a momentary glance, he answered, "I vote 'Yes'."

Jack looked over at Alan sitting in the car next to him. "I vote 'Yes'." Alan answered.

"I vote 'Yes'." Silvestre added.

"Alright then." Jack said decisively. "Here we go."

Dialing, Jack waited for Nick to answer on the other end. After three rings, he heard "Spinoza."

"Nico- it's a Go. We're in place down the hill from Warehouse Ten. Signal reads clear. Rendezvous point as planned. First team rolls exactly as planned. Before dispatching, call Wilcox for extra med transpo- just to be safe. Might be more vics in there than we know to expect. Ping when in place. ROLL."

"Copy. Out." Nick replied and then quickly disconnected.

Chapter Thirty-Three

The twenty-minute wait felt like an eternity. Time ticked by in total silence as Gus, Jessie, Jack, Alan, and Silvestre sat awaiting Nick's notification to roll. The plan being utilized was, indeed, Plan B, as things had been somewhat altered upon Anna's disappearance. Half the team would now approach from the water side, three buildings down from Warehouse Ten, and would proceed on foot to the near side of the building. Once there, they'd wait while the remaining team members approached on foot from vehicles queued in a parking lot four warehouses down in the opposite direction. This arrangement posed a sizable risk, as all vehicular means of escape now required a lengthy scramble in order to access. But, all things considered, it was the only safe way. Given the darkness of the late hour and the relative quiet of the surrounding facilities, any approach would have to be made in complete silence: no car engines, no lights, no boat motors. Any tip-off could potentially lead to a rapid extermination of the victims held inside the building. It was this scenario that most worried Jack.

As the minutes continued to pass, tensions mounted. Jack felt the burden the heaviest. Finally, he spoke. "This 'vigilante justice' is mighty lonely work..."

Gus chewed on the corner of his lip and nodded. "Roger That." He muttered in response.

Jack continued. "Henderson has been alerted and is on Standby. If this goes bad, he'll call it in and raise a 10-35. Hopefully, they'll forgive us our transgressions and move on it."

"Here's hoping." Jessie half-laughed and then added, "That was good of you, Jack. I hate to tip the enemy, but at this stage, we don't know who is and who isn't. Help would be nice. And yeah, I agree with you. This vigilante stuff can make a person feel pretty damn isolated. I've never been good with liminal spaces... this waiting to find out if you're going to live or die brings the entire world to a stop. I envy folks whose biggest concern is whether to take an umbrella to work that day! Sometimes, I think I'd like Boring, but I'm just not cut out for it, I guess..."

Gus looked over at Jessie. There was great love and tenderness in his eyes. Reaching over, he intertwined his fingers with hers and, lifting her hand to his lips, held it there for a moment. As his eyes swept across the rearview mirror, he caught Jack watching. Upon discovery, Jack looked momentarily embarrassed.

"I envy you both." He whispered and then added, "If I bite it, please at least come to my planting. More than likely, you'll be the only two there."

Jessie smiled. "You might be surprised!"

Just then, a text came through on Jack's burner. The message was from Nick and contained one word: 'PING'.

"We're on! Roll! ROLL!!" Jack ordered as all hint of softness or emotion immediately faded from his voice.

Guiding the cars to the rendezvous point, Gus and Alan cut the lights well before reaching it, bringing the cars to a stop in the pitch blackness. Everyone quickly exited and began the silent trek to the warehouse, splitting up and taking their designated positions upon arrival. Finally, the command was given.

In the moments that ensued, controlled chaos played out from every direction. Warehouse Ten breached; the team flooded into the facility. Soon, a cacophony of screams, crying, shouting, and gunfire permeated the space, echoing off the concrete walls. Breaking from the pack, Gus, Jessie, and Jack made their way quickly down a long corridor, which then turned a sharp corner. Following, another hallway appeared, this one with several closed doors on each side. Weapons drawn, the trio made their way down the hallway, throwing each door open wide as they went. The rooms were mostly empty except for very basic pieces of furniture: broken chairs, small tables, and bits of trash and debris scattered on the floors.

Turning a corner, Jessie reached yet another closed door. Reaching down and turning the knob, it slowly opened. Gasping in shock, she instinctively backed away toward the wall behind her. Gus observed as she raised a hand to her mouth, eyes transfixed. The color drained from her face. Racing to her side, he looked in. There, lying on threadbare blankets, were three small, naked children: two girls and one boy, all pale, malnourished, and filthy. They met Jessie's and Gus's gaze with haunted looks. Choking back sobs, Jessie whispered reassurance in a hushed voice.

"It's OK, little ones. It's OK... we're here to help you..."

Just then, Jack joined them. The find hit him like a punch to the gut.

"Good God in Heaven." He groaned and then proceeded forward. There was no time for emotion.

Entering the cramped room, they began the difficult -if not impossible- task of comforting the children trapped inside. The room reeked of urine and small piles of feces stacked in the corners.

Wrapping the two youngest children in their blankets, Jack picked them up in his arms. Looking down at the eldest girl, he smiled a kind but very sad smile. "Can you walk, Sweetheart?"

The girl didn't speak but nodded her head 'Yes.'

"Will you walk with us downstairs so we can get you out of here?"

Again, the child nodded, 'Yes.'

Gently wrapping her in the remaining blanket, Jack instructed,

"Take hold of my arm, Sweetheart, and don't let go. No matter what, don't let go!"

With that, he looked at Gus and Jessie, horror and anger in his eyes.

"Pray the next person I meet is one of ours!" He then added, "You both keep going! KEEP GOING! God only knows what's on the next level. Be careful, and I'll meet up with you as soon as I can!"

With that, Jack turned and began making his way down the hall they'd just traversed, his precious cargo in tow. The sounds of shouting and gunfire continued but with less rapidity.

As Jack disappeared around the corner at the end of the hallway, Gus and Jessie collected themselves. Continuing to the stairwell, they cautiously proceeded to the next floor.

Inching down another long, cement corridor, Gus in the lead and Jessie following close behind, they were careful not to make a sound. Communicating by hand signals, they made their way past more locked doors. Stopping to listen at each, they detected no sounds coming from inside. Finally, reaching the end of the hallway, Gus cautiously approached a sizable room. No lights were on in this space, and it appeared almost cavernous from the hallway. Stopping at the side of the doorway, Gus reached around each side of the wall, feeling for a light switch. Finally, fingers brushing the familiar toggle, he flipped on the overhead fluorescents. They clicked and buzzed, struggling to activate. Incrementally, the blinding blue lights kicked on. Jessie felt the room spin slightly as she took in the view sprawling in front of them. Sizable and devoid of anything remotely symbolizing comfort, the room housed two rows of six exam tables each, complete with wrist straps and stirrups. There were no privacy screens or curtains separating the tables. A dirty, plastic bucket sat at the foot of each table.

As they inched their way toward the center of the room, Jessie looked down, catching sight of blood stains that had spattered and discolored the floor beneath her feet. She could feel herself growing nauseous and lightheaded. Taking a few deep breaths, she continued behind Gus as he led them deeper. Walking over to a cabinet, Gus placed his gun in the waistband of his pants and reached for a pair of latex gloves stuffed in his back pocket. Putting them on, he then opened the cabinet door and peered inside. There, tossed randomly on the shelves, were open boxes of gauze, several unwashed surgical implements, and used syringes and needles. Three suction machines sat unceremoniously nearby, none of them clean.

As he continued to peer inside the cabinet, Jessie cleared her throat several times. Finally, she spoke, her voice low and hoarse. "Gus, I'm gonna be sick..."

Staggering to one of the buckets, Jessie proceeded to heave, cough, and gag.

"You need help, Jess?" Gus asked over his shoulder, distracted as something caught his eye deep inside the cabinet.

Her retching subsided; Jessie wiped her mouth on her sleeve and replied. "No. No... better now."

"Good." Gus replied. "We'll get outta here in just a minute... Stand watch, OK? You able?"

"Yeah." Jessie muttered and turned her back to Gus in order to face the open door behind them.

Reaching carefully into the cabinet, doing his best to avoid the used, bacteria-ridden implements, he brought his hand down upon what appeared to be a small notebook.

Retrieving it, he rifled through the pages. There, scribbled in pencil, were several names and phone numbers, notations made by each name, all with numerous misspellings.

"Whatcha find?" Jessie whispered, her voice still rough from vomiting.

"A notebook..." Gus answered. "Looks to be names of medical suppliers... doctors... nurses... midwives..."

"Want to bet none of them are licensed?" Jessie shot back.

"Hmmmph... probably." Gus replied, still focused on his find.

Turning the last page, a name immediately caught Gus's eye, sending shockwaves through his system. "Son of a bitch!!!" He hissed.

Jessie raced to his side, looking over his shoulder. There in pencil scrawl was: 'M. Anderson/ Mad Gen Hosp/ Scop'

Looking at Gus with questioning eyes, Jessie asked, "Isn't that...?"

"Certainly seems to be." Gus answered in disgust. "None other than my boss and longtime friend. Guess now we know who tipped them to our hideout at Angie's."

"Rotten SOB!" Jessie exclaimed, her voice barely above a whisper.

Continuing to look over Gus's shoulder, she pointed to the final word of the listing. "I assume 'scop' means Scopolamine? You think Mark's their supplier?"

"More than likely." Gus answered. "For the amount of stuff this group has blasted through, it had to be top-grade and untraceable. What better way to get supplied than by a hospital Administrator? He'd know how to cook the books and override supply requisitions without raising suspicion."

Looking back at Jessie, Gus then asked, "Did Dr. Jackson ever get the contents of that pouch in Silver's bag analyzed?"

"Working on it." Jessie answered. "He wanted to focus on getting Lindy settled first. We should hear from him soon."

Gus nodded. Taking the small notebook, he stashed it in his shirt pocket.

"Come on, Jess." He whispered. "Let's get out of here while we still can."

Heading back the way they came, the pair stealthily made their way toward the first floor. Sounds of shouting could be heard, growing louder as they approached, but for the most part, the screaming and gunfire had subsided. Taking no chances, they rounded the corner and descended the stairs, weapons drawn. Jack stood in the middle of the large room, orchestrating various team members as they scurried around him. Gus and Jessie watched as several women, young girls, and small children were escorted past them out of the building. Security was tight.

Catching sight of Gus and Jessie, Jack motioned for them to approach.

"So far," he began as they reached his side, "we've removed twenty vics. The extra aid cars are on the way. We've got everyone huddled together, taking cover by one of the large containers in the next lot. We're missing our two main perps, though, so eyes are peeled."

"Any sign of Anna?" Jessie asked, voice hopeful.

Her question was met with a steely reply. "Not yet." Jack's voice monotone as he answered.

"How about Anton and Dirksen? You say they're awol?" Gus asked for clarification.

Again, Jack bristled. "So far, no sign of either, but they're still lurking around here somewhere. Of that, I'm sure."

"What makes you say that?" Jessie inquired with surprise. "You sound so certain."

"Well.... one thing," Jack responded, "Dirksen ran off and left his little bag of party favors - but the real reason they'll be back - and probably much sooner than we think - is... well... follow me."

Motioning over his shoulder as he walked, Jack turned and headed toward a large, closed door on the far side of the room. Once there, he pushed it open. Jessie's eyes grew wide.

"Come in! Come in!" Jack said in a jokingly formal tone. His demeanor began to brighten. "Welcome to what was the inner sanctum. I can only assume this was Anton's office, but he doesn't seem sharp enough to warrant such trappings. I'm thinking a bigger fish called this 'Home Away From Home'."

Gus entered behind Jessie and whistled in amazement.

"Quite a setup!" He then followed up with, "Do you have anyone specific in mind?"

Jack cut a look at Gus but didn't answer. Instead, he waved them deeper into the office.

Unlike the other rooms in the facility, this one had been professionally decorated. Plush purple carpet, expensive, Italian white leather chairs and sofa, crystal chandeliers, modern art sculptures, a full bar and a large mahogany Executive's desk created a highly luxurious ambiance. Walking over to the desk, Jack reached into what had been a locked drawer. Holding up a leather-bound notebook, a large smile flashed across his face.

"Looky what we found!"

Gus and Jessie glanced at each other and then back at Jack.

"You've got to be kidding me!" Gus finally whispered. "Please tell me that's what I think it is!"

"Well..." Jack answered with a laugh, "If you're thinking 'THE SMOKING GUN,' I'd say consider it Christmas morning! This little gem is none other than the list of names, numbers, and deviant preferences. The 'Who's Who' of perverse appetites - and who gets bribed for doing what. I've only scanned a couple pages, but man, oh man, this thing's smokin' hot."

Jack looked at his friends and then spoke again. "Oh, but it gets better if you can call it that. Here's another treasure trove from satan's playpen..."

Walking over to a large floor-to-ceiling bookcase, Jack pushed a tiny button positioned on one of the shelves. A panel slid into the wall, revealing a large hidden compartment.

"NO WAY!!!" Jessie gasped incredulously.

"WAY." Jack answered. "Videos of the rich and famous gettin' their funk on with all manner of things... animal, vegetable, mineral, child, woman, boy... That nightclub-type arrangement Lindy discussed in her notes...? That's the beehive to this Honey Trap! We've got guys up there now doing a sweep. It's on the top floor. Private elevator access to get there."

"You didn't waste any time! This is a Blackmailer's paradise..." Gus whispered.

"Yes indeedy!" Jack retorted. "Anything and everything a deviant could want - all under one roof. Screw, maim, or snuff; one-stop shopping - no questions asked. But you'll be owned for life once you partake. Too bad they weren't more creative in how they set up this little storehouse of intel! One locked desk drawer and one sliding bookcase panel... the first things any good dick looks for!"

"So, we have the book of names and numbers and the vids to match up to them. Talk about the motherlode..." Jessie said with a smile.

Jack's expression grew serious. "I'm sure you realize, Kids, a lot of folks we're counting on to help us clean up this mess are actually in this book...."

Gus raised his eyebrows and nodded. "I've already encountered one..." He said quietly.

Reaching for the notebook in his shirt pocket, he handed it to Jack. Jack studied it for a moment before responding.

"Well, well. That certainly explains a lot, doesn't it?"

"Yes." Gus answered. "The books and files at the hospital are going to have to be audited and examined, but at this point, how many are involved there? Has Anderson been acting alone in this, or are there other Madison hospital personnel involved?"

"We're in deep shit, no two ways..." Jack quipped. "Many folks are gonna want -and need- us gone. We have to act fast."

"What do you suggest?" Jessie asked, continuing to look around the room in amazement.

"Well..." Jack all but whispered, "We've got to find Anna, Dirksen, and Anton ASAP. My guess is, even if they suspect we've found all this -and I'm pretty sure they already do- Anna's going to end up as collateral."

Jessie winced.

"So, for now," Jack continued, "I advise we hand the book over to Nick for safekeeping until this op is concluded. At this stage, we don't dare trust anyone else."

"Agreed." Gus replied and then added, "Levels two and three need to be swept. Jess and I encountered several locked doors, and even though we listened for signs of life, just to be safe..."

"Already on it." Jack reassured. "Anderson and Pulletti are up there now."

Taking his cell out of his pocket, Jack texted Nick. In a matter of minutes, the young detective entered the room.

"Shut the door behind you, Nico," Jack said in a low voice, and then, using hand signals, motioned for Nick to hide the book on his person. Nodding his understanding, Nick unbuttoned the middle buttons of his shirt and stuffed the notebook firmly into the waistband of his pants. He then buttoned his shirt over it, concealing the bulge.

Just then, Jack's burner rang. It was Alan.

"Jack - exit through south entrance. Get out here now. We're pinned down by the container, and we've got trouble!"

Making their way quickly to the exit, Jack, Jessie, and Gus skirted along the wall of the warehouse, hugging it close; Nick bringing up the rear.

The early morning light was just beginning to break. Coming alongside the container, Gus's eye caught movement on the rooftop behind them. It was Alan. His eyes were fixed on the warehouse roof directly across from him, and he was attempting to sight through the scope of his rifle. Gus followed Alan's gaze. Straining to see clearly in the predawn shadows, Gus detected something fluttering on the roof of Warehouse Ten. Jessie stood slightly behind Gus, not daring to move. Just as Gus was about to signal Jack and Jessie, Anton's heavily accented voice rang out. It was filled with arrogance and disdain.

"Stupid fucking cops!" Anton yelled, his voice echoing through the parking lot, leering and laughing like a cornered hyena.

"So big! So bad!" Anton continued taunting, gun in one hand, he staggered toward the edge of the rooftop, holding something bulky in his arms.

"Idiots! You want?? You get!!"

With that, he took one final, lurching step, and just as he flung the load into the air, a shot rang out. Anton staggered backward and dropped, a gaping hole blown through his forehead. Alan had taken his best shot - but not in time.

The group watched in horror as the body of a woman began its twisting descent, plummeting toward the ground, blonde hair billowing, pale morning light glinting off her blue sequined dress as she fell. Jessie gasped in horror.

"Oh, Gus! MY GOD! It's Anna! That's Anna!!"

Gus stood transfixed, watching the body hurtle silently toward him. Even though it was all happening quickly, his eyes trained on the falling figure, following its every sickening contortion without flinching. Something was off. Just as the woman hit the pavement, Jessie turned her back and covered her ears.

"Anna! Anna!!!" She began to retch and sob.

Approaching the dead woman, Gus knelt, casting a studied eye over the mangled heap of flesh. Reaching down, he gently turned the woman over onto her back and smoothed her blood-splattered hair from her face. Just as he'd suspected, it was not Anna. And just as he'd suspected, the body was already cold. Blood spatter was minimal upon impact. Whoever the woman was, in probably what was her only 'lucky' break, she'd been killed before being thrown off the roof and, from the looks of it, hours earlier. Taking Jessie in his arms, Gus held her tight until she calmed a bit. He then said firmly and with conviction,

"Jess - listen to me. That's not Anna! It's NOT Anna!"

It took several seconds for his words to break through the shock and panic. Eyes wide, Jessie whirled around and looked at him incredulously. "What?! Gus... what??"

Gus repeated, "It's not Anna, Jess. I don't know who the poor girl is, but she was dead before he tossed her. She's ice cold."

Jessie grabbed Gus, held tight, and began to sob, her face pressed into his chest.

Jack and Nick arrived from their vantage point several yards away and walked over to the body.

"No screams." Jack stated flatly. "Just what I thought—we still have a womanhunt on our hands! This isn't our girl. Thank the Good Lord."

Just then, Alan arrived from his perch on the adjoining rooftop.

"Nice shot, Al." Jack said, slapping the man on the shoulder.

"Thanks. Believe me when I tell you, I enjoyed that." Alan spoke, his voice flinty. "Almost too much."

Jack nodded and then replied, "No time for chit-chat...We've got a search to conduct, and time isn't on our side. Dirksen is nearby. I can smell him."

Nick and Silvestre soon returned, carrying a blanket, which they carefully placed over the dead woman's remains.

Gus stood, holding Jessie tight against him, waiting for her to calm.

As he did so, he took the moment to draw a deep breath and whisper a silent prayer. The night and its events had taken a heavy toll. Upon his 'Amen,' Gus opened his eyes. They fixed upon the warehouse in front of him - but on nothing in particular. Glancing over at his friend, Jack noted Gus's expression begin to change. He watched without interruption as Gus's lips began to move as he counted to himself. Following Gus's line of sight, Jack scanned the facade of Warehouse Ten, searching for whatever it was that had piqued Gus's interest.

Eyes suddenly opened wide; in a hushed voice, Gus asked, "Do you see what I see, Jack?!"

Jack's eyes tracked back and forth over the building for a few seconds, and then - there it was.

"Holy Shit!" He exclaimed. "Augustus, you're a freaking genius!"

Composing herself, Jessie pulled away from Gus's embrace and turned her attention to the building herself. Jack winked and looked back at Gus. "How many you count?" He asked.

"Only nine on the top floor. Ten on every other level. You?"

Jessie looked at the two men and then back at the building. It took her a few moments, but she soon caught on. There, on the top floor, the very floor that housed the 'nightclub' Lindy had referenced in her notes, was a row of only nine windows. All the other floors beneath had ten. To make matters more intriguing, the missing window was on the left corner of the building.

"You thinkin' what I'm thinkin'?" Jack asked.

Gus nodded. "Hidden room."

"Yep," Jack replied. "That's got to be where Dirksen is holed up... and God willing, Anna's there too!"

Leaning toward Nick, Jack whispered to the young detective. "Dispatch a couple men up to the roof to retrieve that fucker's remains - and then give this poor young woman a more private and dignified place to rest while she waits for her limo ride to the morgue..."

Stopping in mid-sentence, he then looked back at Nick and added, anger in his voice, "This one gets her own private ride. Do NOT, repeat, DO NOT transport her in the same vehicle with that satanic piece of shit on the roof!"

"Roger That." Nick whispered, casting a solemn look at Jack. His eyes were sad and tired.

"Gus, Jessie, and I are going back up to the top floor..." Jack continued. "We think there's something there that's been overlooked. Join us when you can - but for godsakes, announce yourself before you do! We're all tired and jumpy and the last thing we need is another shock to the system. Would hate to shoot you after you've come this far!"

Nick raised his eyebrows at the thought and then nodded his agreement. Looking over at Jessie, Jack smiled a soft, sympathetic smile. "How you holding up, Jess? It's been a helluva night, huh?"

A faint blush of color flooded Jessie's face, and she answered, determination in her voice, "I'm good now. Thanks, Jack. Let's get this show on the road. If Anna's trapped up there with that monster, every second counts!"

Gus looked down at Jessie, nodded his head in agreement, and gave her a loving look. "The last few hours have been rough on us all." He said in a low voice. "Don't know about either of you, but I've seen things tonight that are going to haunt me forever."

Jessie drew a breath and then spoke, sounding strong. "I just want to see Anna's smile again. Finding her safe would help alot."

Gus pulled his 9MM from its holster and gave it a quick once-over. Jack did the same, with Jessie following suit.

"Locked and loaded." Jack proclaimed.

"Let's go get this bastard." Jessie replied.

Piling into the express elevator on the ground floor, Jack reached into his pocket, retrieving a coded keycard. Inserting it into the slot on the control panel, the doors closed, and the trio began their ascent to the seventh floor.

"We have no way of knowing what to expect once these doors open," Jack said as they continued the ride. "Our guys spent a couple hours up here earlier sweeping the place, so best case scenario, Dirksen will still be holed up and not circulating out in the open."

"He's bound to be desperate by now." Gus said. "Desperate psychos aren't at their chummiest in that state. Eyes and ears on swivel!"

The elevator eased to a stop, and the white, tufted leather doors opened silently. The club stood empty, with only the increasing morning light playing off the mirrored walls. Just as Lindy had recalled, this floor was quite something; more purple carpet graced the floors and halfway up the walls. The vast floorplan held numerous couches, chairs, and round beds. Glass coffee tables scattered strategically around the room, and crystal chandeliers hung from the ceiling. Off toward the very back of the room, another sizable, mirrored bar stood waiting to serve. It was well stocked.

Walking quietly through the space, the trio again communicated using only hand signals. Approaching the far wall, they fanned out, Jack on one side, Gus on the other, and Jessie in between.

Feeling over every inch of the paneling and the flooring, several minutes went by with no obvious point of entry found. Jack began looking more closely around the bar.

"It has to be here..." He muttered under his breath. "HAS to be!"

Nothing appeared out of the ordinary. The bar was neat, tidy -with everything in its place- except for one bar rag. This lone item sat crumpled atop the bar, oddly positioned.

Walking over to it, Jack reached for a bar knife. Sliding the knife under the rag, he lifted it just a quarter of an inch. Peering underneath, Jack smiled.

Removing the rag the rest of the way, he exposed a small button built into the wooden bar top.

Catching Gus's and Jessie's eye, he pointed. They nodded their understanding. Holding up one finger, Jack paused one second. He then held up a second finger and waited another second. Then, he raised the third. With that, he reached over and pushed the button. Instantly, a panel behind the bar slid open, revealing a room beyond. Training their weapons on the interior, Gus and Jessie peered inside. It took a second for their eyes to adjust to the darkness of the room. There, in the corner, stood Randal Dirksen, his arm wrapped firmly around Anna's throat. With his other hand, he held tight aim with his Glock 23. Anna wavered, unsteady on her feet. Pale and battered, she had a large bruise forming over her left eye, and congealed blood crusted on her lower lip. She still wore the skimpy, white outfit from the night before.

"Well, well." Dirksen hissed. "You guys are smarter than you look. Took you long enough, though. You damn near didn't make it in time."

Gus leveled a hard look at the bald man and spoke. "What do you mean, Dirksen? What are you implying?"

A cold, evil smile curled Randal Dirksen's lips. "My lady and I started the party without you... your prize here is just now beginning to enjoy her little trip! One Way only, of course!"

From the back, a guttural growl filled the room as Jack shoved his way past Gus and Jessie.

"You fucking asshole!" Jack roared, charging in two large strides over to where Dirksen stood. Tearing at Dirksen's head and face, Jack gouged at the man's eyes. Gus ran forward, grabbing the hand holding Dirksen's gun. As the men wrestled, Jessie ran to Anna's aid, prying the woman from Dirksen's grip. As the two women tumbled to the floor, a shot rang out. Gus lurched forward, fell against the wall, and then slumped to the floor, his legs giving way beneath him.

"GUS!!!! AUGUSTUS!!" Jessie yelled, crawling toward him.

Dirksen and Jack continued to brawl, tumbling and stumbling through the room, Jack repeatedly banging Dirksen's wrist against the door jam and floor in an effort to disarm the man. Finally, nothing left to lose, Jack bit into Dirksen's forearm, tearing at the man's flesh like an animal.

Dirksen howled in agony and fell to the floor as Jack continued to rip and shred with his teeth, his mouth filling with the metallic taste of Dirksen's blood. Regaining his footing as Dirksen fell, Jack trained his gun squarely between the man's eyes. Breath coming in gasps from the exertion, Jack yelled at Jessie, never once moving his eyes from his prey. "Jess...? Jess, how's our boy?"

Shaking with emotion, Jessie answered, her voice flat from shock, "Shoulder wound, Jack - but it's bad. May have artery involvement! He's bleeding heavily!"

As she spoke, Jessie ran out of the room, quickly returning with an armful of bar rags. Lying Gus flat on the floor, she then began applying pressure. Gus's blood pooled through his shirt and poured onto the floor.

"We've got to hurry!!" Jessie yelled in urgency.

Jack cut his attention back to Dirksen as he spat on the floor several times, clearing his mouth of Dirksen's blood. Racking the slide, Jack again took aim between Dirksen's eyes.

"You minion of satan - one breath more from you is one too many!"

Just as Jack was about to fire, Gus's voice shocked him to his senses. It was weak and barely above a whisper, but it was insistent.

"Jack - Pal... don't ...do it. DON'T. We... need... him."

Jack's breath still coming fast and shallow, he stood pondering Gus's words. Dropping his gun to his side, he stared Dirksen in the eye. Dirksen scoffed and smirked.

"Awww... not your lucky day, is it?" Dirksen hissed.

"More mine than yours, you son of a bitch."

With that, Jack leaned over and spat one more time. Once finished, he stood and shot Dirksen in the leg.

"Oops. Look what just happened! I'll kill you a piece at a time if I have to, you Bastard."

Chapter Thirty-Four

In the three weeks that followed, it seemed the entire world turned upside down. They'd gotten Anna to the hospital just in time, and she had been pulled back from the brink by a dose of Naloxone administered by the EMT in transit and then charcoal therapy once stabilized and admitted. Fortunately, things at the warehouse had proven too chaotic at the time, so Dirksen's darker and more base plans for Anna hadn't been consummated. All in all, she seemed relatively recovered but deeply and fundamentally changed, made more subdued by the experience.

Jack and Nick had indeed phoned in a 10-35, after the fact, as Gus was being loaded into the ambulance. It seemed the thing to do, despite their concerns and misgivings. Prior to surrendering the leather-bound notebook, Nick had made several digitized copies, and he and Jack let it be widely known that said copies had been circulated among key contacts and sources, to be opened and utilized only if something were to happen to them. Their self-styled dead man switch.

Gus had only gotten through the first fifteen pages of the notebook himself, but the names listed there were staggering, and he struggled to get his mind around it all.

The scandal enveloped several police precincts, the mayor's office, three city hospitals, CEOs and CFOs of numerous large, well-established corporations, several film, recording, and sports stars, and also touched heavily on field divisions of both the FBI and CIA, as well as numerous leaders within the nation's government.

Randal Dirksen had been grilled for hours at a time and, true to his pathetic nature, sang like a canary. Jack made a point to be present for each interrogation. Just as Jack had suspected, Dirksen had indeed killed Brad Bandeshaw, Sam that morning in the alley, and also Pete Spinoza, but at the behest of higher-ups in the organization, not of his own accord—a useful idiot.

The three dead women whose remains had been found scattered throughout the city, now dubbed 'The Gardenia Girls' by the press, had been murdered and dumped by Anton and his goons for the very reason Lindy cited in her notes; trying to help defend the young children and girls trapped in the warehouse holding facilities.

And also, as Jack had suspected, Anton had only, a few months earlier, risen to head the syndicate, having recently won a protracted turf war. Fancying himself a Ukranian hybrid of Jack the Ripper and George 'Baby Face' Nelson, Anton had cooked up the idea of leaving a gardenia stuffed down the throat of each of his victims, his personal signature. A stupid and flamboyant move on his part - but a lucky and helpful break for Gus, Jack, Jessie, and the team.

From Dirksen, it had been learned that Mark Anderson had indeed taken it upon himself to provide the racket with their drugs and medical equipment. Happy to do it and of his own volition, Anderson received vast sums of cash for his procurement skills and participation. Without his help, more than likely, the scheme would've collapsed inward on itself much earlier, despite the mayor and other higher-ups running cover.

Lending credence to this was the lab report that had finally been provided by Dr. Jackson. According to his findings, the syringe found in 'Nurse Silver's' medical bag was indeed hospital-grade Scopolamine, extremely pure and extremely potent. The syringe in question had contained enough doses to kill four people slowly or one person extremely fast. It was that eventuality that had been slated for Lindy when the time conveniently presented itself. Fortunately for everyone, it had not.

Following the money trail, it was discovered that the racket had been international in scope and reach, operated with impunity by the extensive help of several people in governmental positions, all extremely well paid for their time and trouble.

The ring had worked with full autonomy for five years. Numerous children had been sold for black market adoptions. Other young children -mostly orphans- had been lifted from foster homes, orphanages, and off the streets, falling to a worse fate: medical experimentation and satanic ritual abuse.

This well-oiled machine began to break down under Anton's inexpedient leadership. Lazy, full of himself, and rather unrefined, it had been Anton's brainchild to create the recording contract/singing competition ruse. The idea was developed to make it easier to procure high-quality 'merchandise' without the need to physically comb the streets. It had been Anton's hope to attract young, twenty-something women in a steady stream for use in sex trade and baby farming enterprises, all while sitting comfortably on his ass. Being less than jazz-savvy, his first error had been deciding to search for the 'next Billie Holiday.' This ruse ended up attracting an older woman - older than he preferred, as - with age comes wisdom. As these older women got unwittingly scooped up in the net, they, more often than not, fought back, leading to death by scopolamine and gardenia. This was becoming highly inconvenient, not to mention messy. It was this little niggle in his grand plan that started the organizational threads unraveling, much to the dismay and dread of those smarter syndicate members.

Billie Holiday may have started her life in a brothel, but in a weird and twisted way; in this case, in particular, she was bringing the entire system crashing down around her decades after her untimely death. Such is the way of karma.

Gus sat in his bathrobe, looking out the window of his room at the rehab facility. His shoulder had been severely injured by Dirksen's bullet, and there had been artery involvement. For the first couple days after surgery, it was feared he may actually lose his arm. Now, that prospect behind him, he faced many months of recovery, but what pained him the worst was the ache in his heart.

Jessie had saved his life, accompanying him to the hospital in the ambulance, drenched in his blood. As he had faded in and out of consciousness, he was aware of her hand squeezing his the entire ride. According to Theresa's accounting, Jessie had stayed for the duration of Gus's surgery and had then sat watch by his bedside, waiting for him to come out of anesthesia. Several hours into their vigil, as Theresa later reported, Jessie's cell had rung. Excusing herself and taking the call in the hallway, she'd disappeared and never returned. It made no sense to either Gus or Theresa but in conversations with Jack on the phone, he assured them that Jessie was OK and that both her cell and credit cards were pinging regular use. Beyond that, Jack said nothing.

The days felt hard and heavy to Gus: endless rounds of mediocre meals, happy talk with nurses who came and went, physical therapy sessions and meds, followed by hours of staring out the window, thinking about Jessie and all that had transpired. Theresa came daily and stayed to visit with

Gus for hours at a time. Together, they made quite a pair: Theresa, still on crutches, and Gus, heavily bandaged and mostly wheelchair-bound.

As Gus sat staring out the window, early spring buds popping forth in the courtyard garden, Theresa entered his room. Sighing as she watched him, she forced a smile and proceeded.

"Hi, Dad! Today's the big day! Are you ready to watch Jack and Nick testify before Congress? It should be starting in just a few minutes."

Gus turned an unshaved face toward her and smiled softly at his daughter's attempt to brighten his mood. "Sure." He replied, picking up the remote and wheeling over to the television.

"Should be interesting, that's for sure!" Theresa continued, eyebrow raised.

"Yep." Gus responded. "They're in the belly of the beast, those two, no doubt about it."

"Are you sorry you're not there, Dad?" Theresa asked, reaching over and holding her father's hand.

Gus raised empty eyes and looked at her. "Not on your life!" He exclaimed, forcing a sarcastic chuckle.

The Investigative hearing started right on time, and as Jack and Nick took the oath, the camera panned in for a tight closeup. Nick wore his best suit. He looked sharp, and Gus noted how much more confident and seasoned Nick looked now than when they'd first met. Jack looked thinner, weary, and somewhat gaunt. Wearing beige slacks, a black cashmere turtleneck, and matching sport coat, there was an air of anger, indignation, and hardness to him. It had been over two weeks since he'd returned to his life in Pennsylvania, and his presence was missed. Sitting down at his place at the large table, Jack opened the bottle of water sitting in front of him and drew a swig.

The hearing commenced with lengthy opening statements by the Chair, followed closely by a statement from the ranking Minority leader. It was already sounding like a fixed sham.

When it was his turn to speak, Jack spoke clearly, concisely, his voice low, monotone, and direct.

"With all due respect," he began, "It's long been my personal and professional experience that when officials lie, their narratives become more and more complicated and convoluted over time. As a career FBI Agent, now retired, I've trained in the doctrine of Narrative Simplicity, an adjunct, if you will, to Occam's Razor. Clearly stated, this law says that if and when officials tell the truth in an investigative scenario, the narrative simplifies with time and becomes easier to understand and believe. But when officials lie, their narrative tends to become pendulous, complicated, harder to understand or believe..." Locking steely eyes at the Committee, Jack went all in.

"So far, my team and I have been fed a steady diet of nothing but word salad, and none of it makes sense. We've recently busted open a huge and hideous sex trafficking ring that's been conducting business in NYC right under our noses for five years. Countless human beings missing, lives destroyed, millions of dollars exchanging hands for human flesh - and no one seems to really care or be bothered by it! Just yesterday, 145 of your members voted AGAINST a bill that called for the deportation of illegal immigrants convicted of sex crimes. And as of this morning, the UK is awash in a scandal involving rape houses, grooming gangs, and the organized and systematic raping of literally thousands of young girls over the last many years. Add to that, at our own southern border, we've managed to 'misplace' almost half a million children. Just what the hell is actually happening here??! Sex trafficking and pedophilia is everyone's problem! Everyone's issue! It takes all of us to stop it! I don't see anyone here actually caring or doing a damn thing about it!"

Jack banged his open hand on the table, causing the Chair to gavel him down. The man then replied in arrogant disdain, "And do you think the way you and your 'team' went about it is at all acceptable??! We don't do Vigilante Justice in this country! We're a DEMOCRACY!" The man hissed and then added, "We're a nation of LAWS - and you've pretty much summarily broken every last one of them!"

Gus fidgeted in his wheelchair and rubbed his forehead with his hand. Theresa felt herself growing angry, her breath coming in shallow gasps.

"Come on, Jack-" she all but whispered. "Hit him back!"

Jack's face was flinty with barely controlled disgust and rage. Drawing a breath and maintaining his composure, he replied, not holding back or mincing words.

"With all due respect, Congressman, #1) we are NOT a Democracy. We are a Constitutional Republic. Big difference and you really should know that. #2) My team and I assisted in this matter because, quite frankly, there was no one else we could trust to help, and lives were on the line. We did what had to be done. And for the record: five of you here today are in that notebook."

At that moment, the chamber lost all decorum, and it took several minutes to restore order. The Chair, looking deeply shaken, decided to fight shame and humiliation with same. Lowering his voice for dramatic effect, the Congressman leaned in close to his microphone. "Sir - does the name Brian Michaels mean anything to you?"

Jack paused before answering. Gus sat upright in his wheelchair as he exchanged a glance with Theresa. Jack lifted his voice to answer.

"Yes, Sir."

"Tell us who Brian Michaels is, please." The Congressman continued.

"The brother of a friend," Jack answered.

"The brother of a friend -a member of your team of vigilantes- was he not?"

"Yes, Sir," Jack answered again, lips drawn tight.

"Do tell us more, please!" The Congressman enticed, fighting a grin, obviously pleased with his line of questioning.

Jack drew a breath. Holding his demeanor steady, he answered. "Brian Michaels was the brother of Ms. Jessie Gifford."

"A member of your very own team, this Ms. Gifford?" The man's grilling continued.

"Yes." Jack replied.

"I notice you say 'was'... 'was' the brother of Ms. Gifford. Tell us about how he became a 'WAS'..."

Jack's jaw tightened, and his eyes went cold. Drawing a breath, he spoke low, his voice raw. "Brian Michaels committed suicide approximately three weeks ago."

"Oh my, such a waste." The Congressman sarcastically and theatrically feigned sympathy.

"Why did Mr. Brian Michaels commit suicide approximately three weeks ago?"

"Because..." Jack began, paused, and then pushed through to completion, "Brian Michaels was a highly successful and respected commercial banker, very well-known, trusted, and liked in powerful circles here on the East Coast. It's also been recently discovered that unbeknownst to any of us, including his beloved family, he was a pedophile."

"And as luck would have it," the Committee member went in for the kill, "his name is listed on page fifty-six of this mysterious leatherbound notebook of yours, is it not?"

"Indeed, it is." Jack hissed in reply. "Fifteen pages after YOURS."

Having seen and heard enough, Gus reached for the remote, turning off the television before anything more was said. He looked over at Theresa. She sat, a bewildered look on her face.

"Did you know anything about this, Dad?" She asked, an incredulous tone in her voice. Gus looked back at her, eyebrows raised in shocked surprise.

"I was just going to ask you the very same thing!" He replied.

"Well one thing's for certain." Theresa spoke again. "Jack knew! Why do you think he didn't tell us?"

"Must be because Jessie asked him not to..." Gus answered, sadness in his voice.

Theresa stopped for a moment and stared into space, counting on her fingers subconsciously.

"Dad, that phone call Jessie got that night at the hospital... that had to have been when she found out. She took that call in the hall while I stayed with you in your room. I never saw her again after her phone rang!"

"You must be right," Gus responded in a half-whisper. "I just don't know why, after everything we've been through, she'd think this would make a difference."

Theresa hobbled over to Gus and rested her cheek on top of his head. "I don't know, Dad - but I'm just so very sorry. Jessie's a wonderful woman, and I know you two share deep feelings. I hate to see you hurting. Let's not give up hope, OK? She obviously needs our prayers now. We can keep her close to our hearts that way."

With that, she kissed Gus on his cheek. "I'll be back tomorrow morning at ten thirty. Don't forget you're gettin' sprung from this place tomorrow!"

Gus smiled. "I had forgotten!" He replied. "Thanks, Honey. I can't wait to get home. It's been way too long."

Casting a look out the window, Theresa breathed a sigh. "Spring's coming, Dad. Soon the sun will be shining and flowers blooming. Better days ahead! See you tomorrow morning. I love you."

***

July Fourth dawned hot, steamy, and bright. Gus's shoulder had continued to heal nicely, and in the course of physical therapy, he'd managed to quit smoking and drop twelve pounds. In another month, he'd resume his job at Madison General, having been awarded a substantial pay raise for his heroism in defending Lindy and exposing Mark Anderson.

Theresa had also recovered well. Her ankle only ached occasionally, and the nightmares she'd initially suffered after the ordeal had subsided for the most part.

In the backyard, Gus refilled the birdfeeders, basking in the mid-afternoon sun and enjoying a cold beer. His favorite jazz show played on the radio. In between the strains of Glenn Miller's 'String of Pearls,' he heard the squeak of the screen door behind him. Knowing it was Theresa bringing the steaks out for grilling, he continued on with his work. After a moment, he was startled by a familiar voice behind him.

"Hi, Augustus. Remember me? How's the shoulder?"

Drawing a breath to steady himself, Gus turned to find Jessie standing behind him.

She looked timid, and her eyes were somewhat uneasy. Beyond her left shoulder, Gus could see Theresa watching from the kitchen window.

"Hello, Jess." Gus said with a soft smile. "This is quite a surprise."

"A good one, I hope." Jessie answered in a whisper and then added, "You look wonderful. How are things? How's Theresa? How are Lindy and Anna doing?"

Gus just nodded. For a moment, no one spoke. Only the raucous, angry caws of the blue jays fighting at the feeders filled the air. Finally, Gus answered. "All is as good as can be, I guess. Theresa is doing well. Lindy is recovering nicely; making good strides, considering how far she's had to come. Anna is in Boston with her. We've gone to see them a couple times. Lindy's wanting to stay in Boston once she's well enough to leave the care facility, and she's thinking of becoming a trauma counselor. I think she's hungry for a new start somewhere nobody will know her." Gus paused and then cut to the chase. "I was very sorry to hear about Brian, Jessie. That must've been truly awful. My condolences."

Cutting her eyes to the ground, Jessie responded. "I don't know what hit me the hardest, Augustus... finding out he'd killed himself - or that he was a pedophile. Both nightmare scenarios."

"I'm sure." Gus spoke low. "Can I get you a beer, Jess- or anything?" He asked, sympathy in his voice.

"Nah. I'm good. Thanks all the same, though..." Jessie whispered. Raising her eyes to look squarely at Gus, she then added, "There's something I need you to know, Gus."

"Ok. Shoot, " he replied. Let's go sit at the picnic table and get out of this heat."

Following Gus to the table in the shade, Jessie sat opposite him. Gus cut his eyes to her. She had difficulty holding his gaze. This was not the Jessie he knew.

"We've been friends a mighty long time, Jess. You know there's nothing you can't tell me." He reassured.

Tears filled her eyes as Gus reached out, taking her hand in his.

Drawing a deep breath, and with tears streaming down her face, Jessie finally brought herself to speak. "Gus, when Brian and I were little ones, our home life wasn't good... my dad was a drinker, and it brought out all his demons. He did... he did bad things to me and Brian. Really bad things - and often.

He sexually abused us both for years, and our mom turned a blind eye most times. She'd always try to make it up to us in some way- like there's any way to do that..."

Gus sat listening in total silence. Jessie continued.

"We both left home just as soon as we were able, and we never went back. Brian and I never talked about the things we'd endured. I guess we just hoped to put them behind us and carve out decent, normal lives for ourselves... That's why I ended up in this line of work... my attempt to set it all right and do whatever I could to get the bad people off the streets. And I guess Brian did what he could to make himself feel clean and upstanding too. Not enough money or fancy things can ever cover up the festering wounds inside, though..."

Gus nodded his agreement. "Augustus, I had no idea Brian was a pedophile—and I had no idea he was an active part of the hellscape we found ourselves in while working the op. I would've told you, Gus, and turned him in!"

Jessie started to cry.

"This is why you disappeared on me, Jess?" He asked in a whisper.

"Mostly." Came her honest answer. "But Gus, I needed to get my head screwed on straight. I'd run from this ugliness my whole life, never looking back - terrified to look back. I needed to finally stop running and let it all overtake me. I went to Florida to stay with my cousin and got myself some counseling.

"Wise move." Gus reassured. "How does the world look now?"

Jessie wiped the streaming tears from her face. "I'm starting to see light again," she replied simply. "But I'm still afraid."

"Afraid of what?" Gus asked gently.

"YOU." Came Jessie's shocking answer. "Augustus Walker, I love you with every fiber of my being, but we were in that sinful, awful hell together, and that world is in me! I'm no different than those little children we found in that room! They were ME! I can't bring that filth into your world - or Theresa's!"

Gus stared across the picnic table, a look of incredulity on his face. Tears in his eyes, he finally spoke. "Jessie Gifford, those little ones we rescued had no part to play in what happened to them. NO PART! They were victims. Victims of the worst, most heinous type of predator on the planet. Same as you and Brian. We all have demons and wounds, Jess but love sees us through. Love sees us all through. These months without you have been misery. You took my light when you went away. All I've done is miss you, think about you, worry about you. Jess, you are far from broken—far-far-far from broken. You are a treasure to me. Please don't make me live without you because I just can't do it."

Jessie looked across at Gus, a very faint, very small smile shining through her tears.

Just then, the strains of 'Moonlight Serenade' begin to play on the radio.

Gus smiled. "I love that song." He sighed wistfully. "I've always believed in my heart that no matter what's happening out there in the world, as long as somewhere, this tune is playing, it will all be OK."

Reaching out, Gus pulled Jessie to her feet. Wrapping his arms around her, they began to sway to the music.

Theresa watched from the kitchen window, a broad, approving smile curving her lips.

***

At that very same moment, approximately two thousand seven-hundred-some-odd miles across the country, somewhere in an amusement park on the West Coast, a little girl was sitting on a park bench waiting patiently for her young parents to bring her promised ice cream cone. They stood only a few feet away, backs turned, in line at the concession stand. As the little girl patiently waited, her favorite cartoon character skipped up to her, waving and flirting with his big, floppy ears. She smiled shyly and laughed. The character reached down with his giant, velvety soft, fabric paw and drew the little girl's hand into his. Laughing and skipping, they all too quickly disappeared around a corner. A few seconds later, only the frantic screams of her mother could be heard, as an ice cream cone hit the pavement and started to quickly melt in the blazing sun.

In Memoriam

Laurie Allyn

Laurie Allyn was an American jazz singer and former model, best known for her sole album entitled 'Paradise', which was recorded in 1957 and amassed critical acclaim after a much-belated release in 2004.

Born into a musical family and raised in Waco, Texas, she began her career as a singer in the mid-1950's. While performing at events near Scott Air Force Base, Laurie auditioned for songwriter Tommy Wolf and began performing as house singer at the nightclub 'The Crystal Palace, owned by

Fran Landesman, with Wolf accompanying Laurie on piano. They became good friends, and she was the first singer to perform Landesman's and Wolf's song 'Spring Can Really Hang You Up the Most'. This iconic song would later become a standard recorded by many artists.

In 1954, Laurie was hired to work as house singer at the nightclub 'The Cloister Inn', in Chicago. While working at the Cloister, she met singer Tony Bennett for a breakfast date, and discussed her then-accompanist, Ralph Sharon, with him. The conversation led Bennett to hire the pianist away from her. Ralph Sharon would go on to perform with Bennett for over forty years.

In 1957, Laurie was performing again at the nightclub 'The Nocturne', where the Chicago Tribune reported on the popularity of her 'throaty, seated-on-a-piano, moody Julie London-ish' live performances.

Red Clyde, founder of Mode Records, heard Laurie sing at 'The Nocturne' in 1957 and invited her to Los Angeles to record an album with the label. She was flown to LA, all expenses paid, to record the album 'Paradise'. The recording engineer was Bones Howe, and the players included conductor Marty Paich, guitarist Al Viola, bassist Red Mitchell, drummer Mel Lewis, trumpeter Don Fagerquist, and the members of the Hollywood String Quartet. Mode Records planned to bring Laurie back to Los Angeles after the album's release, when she was scheduled to perform on 'The Steve Allen Show' and audition for a television pilot at NBC. She also appeared on Hugh Hefner's television show of that time.

However, a short time after the recording of the album, Mode Records went into bankruptcy. Subsequently, the album was not released. This was a devastating blow. Laurie returned to Texas to care for her ailing mother and then went back to Chicago to work as a model. But she didn't pursue singing further. She loved it too much- and it had become too painful.

In 2004, Laurie and her family began researching the whereabouts of the master tracks of her album, which were then owned by the archive label VSOP Records and were being considered for release. Half the master recordings survived, but the remaining tracks were salvaged from a dub of the masters. Bones Howe, the engineer of Laurie's original session, remembered her and her album project and graciously agreed to master the album for release, almost fifty years after the project had originally been recorded. The album was released as 'Paradise' by VSOP Records that year and received worldwide critical acclaim. This was a great joy to Laurie and revived her singing spirit.

At AllMusic, Scott Yanow gave the album four and a half out of five stars, stating, 'her choice of notes is excellent, and she draws listeners into the music.' Paul Clatworthy described the album as 'captivating' in the Robert Farnon Society's Journal Into Melody, adding, 'Laurie's bell-like diction fits the songs so well they could have all been written just for her.' The album was submitted for consideration for a Grammy Award but didn't win. It can be found for purchase and also streaming listening online.

Laurie began singing again and sang up until a year before she passed away, two weeks shy of her ninetieth birthday. Her older voice was rich with life experience and was hauntingly compelling. She also went on to co-host with her daughter (Carrie) a syndicated jazz radio show called 'Tea For Two' which was very well received.

In between reviving her singing career, Laurie remained a devoted wife, mother and friend. She loved- and lived- life passionately, and she cherished the written word. Quality writing and literature were important to her.

Laurie carefully crafted the original concept and storyline of 'Becoming Billie' several years ago, and it was originally published in a softened version as a serialized story in a women's magazine. Because of the readership, there was no raw language in the original version - nor was the topic of sex trafficking and ritual satanic abuse discussed so candidly. It always troubled her that the topic was not being addressed as it deserved. The day before Laurie passed away, she asked her daughter Carrie to complete the manuscript as she'd originally intended. Carrie agreed. Now, three years to the day that promise was made, it has been fulfilled. The book you hold in your hand is Laurie's literary magnum opus - a testament to a worthy and worrisome issue, and a brave, strong woman and spirit.

Laurie passed away in Carrie's arms February 11th, 2022, at 7 AM PT, leaving a legacy of love, and a huge hole in the hearts of those who knew and loved her.

If you enjoyed her book, please consider raising a toast to her and a life well lived. She was partial to dirty martinis (vodka - not gin), icy cold champagne, genmaicha green tea, and tall-double Caffe Americanos with a zest of lemon.

RESOURCE

For immediate assistance or to get help for someone who may be a victim of human trafficking, please contact the National Human Trafficking Hotline. Available 24/7, they provide support and crucial resources. You can reach them by calling 888-373-7888 or by emailing Help@HumanTraffickingHotline.org. Don't hesitate to make a call that could potentially save a life or offer a lifeline to someone in need.

About the Author

Carrie E. Pierce has written professionally, across many genres, for more than 20 years. During the course of her career, she discovered there was a real need for quality children's literature that could be enjoyed by parents and grandparents, too, as they read aloud to the youngsters in their lives. Eager to fill this niche, Carrie began crafting quality stories that contain important life lessons, written in a style that doesn't talk 'down' to children but, instead, encourages them to learn new words and ask deep questions as they gain important tools for overcoming fear, pushing past loss and accepting themselves just as they are. It is her children's books that Carrie is most known for.

During the course of her life, Carrie has known great highs – and very deep lows. She's attained her dream of working in the Film and TV industry. She's been published numerous times and has also co-hosted two acclaimed, internationally syndicated radio shows. She's seen dreams come true – and has also walked through very dark times of tragedy and heartbreak. She walked with her dad as he bravely fought Lewy Body dementia – and lost. And just recently, her beloved Mom -and very best friend- succumbed to cancer, dying in Carrie's arms.

Awful as these events were, they've provided her with an even richer insight into the human heart and spirit, providing a wisdom and gentleness often lacking in today's world. These qualities are found throughout her books and articles- and are also evident in personal interactions with her. Carrie always speaks from experience, with an honest voice that holds nothing back.

Carrie lives in Idaho, surrounded by good friends, gorgeous scenery, and amazing people. When not writing, she enjoys snowshoeing, gardening, good food and wine – and dancing. When writing, Carrington, her cat, is almost always found snoring on the cat tree next to Carrie's desk.

Dive into the imaginative realms crafted by the acclaimed author Carrie E. Pierce!

'The Tale of Tommy Tomlinson's Tennis Shoes'

'Abby Apple Tree'